SARAH BARKOFF

Evernight Teen ®

www.evernightteen.com

Copyright© 2019

Sarah Barkoff

ISBN: 978-1-77339-997-3

Cover Artist: Jay Aheer

Editor: Melissa Hosack

SARAH BARKOFF

For Matt.
Because if it weren't for you, I never would've
discovered this dream at all.

SARAH BARKOFF

#

Sarah Barkoff

Copyright © 2019

Chapter One

If I go to school two days a week out of five it's a lot.

Today is one of those rare occasions. I slink down in the last seat at the back of AP English Lit, trying my best to be invisible. All I've wanted these last four months since the accident is to shrivel up and disappear.

Mr. Russo starts class with a discussion about how literature is going down the toilet because of so many novels being adapted into big budget films that rely too much on special effects. I stare out the foggy window, barely listening and watching the steady flow of traffic in the distance until the sound of my name snaps me back to reality.

"Sosie?" Mr. Russo asks. "Sosie?" My head turns before my eyes make the trek over to where he stands at the front of class. He adjusts his black-framed glasses on the bridge of his nose while he waits for my attention.

"We need a volunteer to read Tuesday's assignment. Would you be so kind to share your work with us?"

"I actually don't have my assignment," I say, wrapping my chunky knit cardigan around me.

"Again?" Mr. Russo asks, his eyes narrowing above his glasses. I twist a strand of my stringy hair around my finger, and pull it across my mouth like a mustache. He sighs and scratches his temple. "Anyone else want to be our guinea pig?" No one volunteers, so he sifts through a manila envelope until he finds what he's looking for. "Here we are." He walks down the aisle, single sheet of paper in hand, and stops two seats over from where I sit. "Nolan, can you read your poem for the class?"

My eyes, along with the rest of the class, fix on Nolan Sawyer, waiting. I don't know much about him, other than the fact he moved here a couple of months ago and is maybe the only other person in this school as anti-social as me. He stares at the floor, his long, shaggy bangs falling into his eyes like well-positioned curtains, aiding his concealment.

He swallows hard, his Adam's apple moving up and down, and then begins to read through a shaky voice. *"I swim out to sea. I let the water carry me. I feel so small in this symphony of eclectic characters. The water hits my skin, it makes me feel alive, like I'm one with something bigger than right now, bigger than me, and bigger than life. But the water is cold. Autumn is here."*

He has a southern accent, thick and slow like a dense milkshake that has to be eaten with a spoon instead of sipped from a straw. My jaw drops. Who is this boy? The sound of his voice, the slow warmth of his words, makes me want to leap into the moment with him, and feel the water on my skin, too. His words touch me in an unexplainable way that leaves me enchanted, mesmerized. My heart skips. There's an aching in my soul to know him. I'm holding my breath, but don't realize it until my head starts to feel light.

"Thoughts anyone?" Mr. Russo asks, and then waits. "What? No one's ever felt the ocean water hit his or her skin? It didn't conjure up any memory or emotion from any one of you?" The class is dead, no sounds or whispers. Not even a breath.

Nolan shudders, stares at his hands.

The words are on my lips. They want to break out, and shout a million things about Nolan's poem and how it made me feel, but my stomach churns with nerves, afraid to steer everyone's attention to me. "I have," I pipe in, my voice catapulting without my brain's permission. The sounds of bodies and desks rustle, shifting, and coming to a screeching stop on me. I bite my lip, and nervously look around. "I've swam in the ocean," I murmur.

"Ms. Friedman, thank you for your participation," he says, eyebrows raised, surprised as much as I am that I've spoken up. "For future references, it's actually 'swum' in the ocean, but thank you for your contribution nonetheless. Did this piece by Mr. Sawyer make you feel something?"

"Yeah." I glance over at Nolan. "It did. Especially the part about how the ocean feels so big but makes you feel like you're one with it. Like you're part of something bigger than life. Yeah. I've felt that." Nolan's eyes lock with mine for a second before quickly breaking away. "I thought this piece was really beautiful."

Garret Simmons turns around in the seat in front of me and clears his throat while he grunts, "No one cares." Everyone around us snickers, and all I want to do is die.

Mr. Russo doesn't hear. "What prompted you to write this piece, Mr. Sawyer?" he continues. Nolan blinks, but says nothing. "What I mean to ask is, was this written from a personal experience?"

"Yeah, it was," Nolan finally says. "I like to surf, so I wrote it after spending the day out in the water."

Their conversation is still going back and forth when I get up, grab my books, and push my way down an aisle of desks. "I need to use the bathroom," I mumble to Mr. Russo and grab the hall pass from the basket by the door as I dart out.

Third lunch is getting out so I hurry down A Hall toward the girls' bathroom, books clutched to my chest like a shield.

"Sosie!" A familiar voice shouts out to me. "Hey, wait!" Johnny, my on-again-off- again best friend, ambles toward me.

"Not now," I grumble and escape into the bathroom just before he reaches me. The bathroom is crowded, swarms of girls gossiping and touching up their make-up before the next class starts. I wait in line for a stall, and as soon as one becomes free, I dart inside, shutting the door behind me. Methodically, I place a paper liner on the seat, and then sit down, knees clutched to my chest, feet off the floor. When the bell rings, everyone rushes out, and I finally exhale. This is the place I come for peace, where the whoosh of the hand dryer hums me back to a state of calm in a few moments to myself.

But today is different.

Today that's not happening.

There's no peace, and nothing drowns out the way they were all laughing at me. I'm rocking back and forth, their snickers echoing in my ears.

A toilet flushes with a swish, and footsteps click

across the tile.

"You skipping, too?" a girl's voice asks, over running water at the sink.

"You know it. I'm failing anyway," another voice answers.

Stragglers. Great.

"Did you see Sosie Friedman a minute ago? Dude. What happened to her? She literally looks like she hasn't showered in a month. She's starting to look homeless."

"Have you gone anywhere near her? She smells like B.O." I peek through the crack in the bathroom stall, careful to not make any noise. It's Shira Simon and Mandy Jenks. Figures. They've been talking shit about me since last summer after they ousted me from their click for hanging out with Johnny when Shira set her sights on him. Never mind Johnny and I have known each other since we were five. But Shira can be lethal when you disobey her, and Mandy is her compliant pet.

"She sits two rows over in my first hour, and I can smell her from across the room. Seriously, like, everybody talks about it," Shira says.

They snicker. I lift my arm and sniff my pit. Maybe a little stale, but not too awful.

"It's actually kind of sad, to be honest," Mandy says. "She looks like she should be locked up in a mental hospital or something. She doesn't talk to anyone, and just, like, mumbles to herself constantly. Seriously, she talks to herself! I heard her today."

"I guess it's to be expected. Her mom was a legit psychopath. Remember that time she showed up at the school without a bra on and her hair all crazy-town, screaming for Sosie to come out of class?" Shira laughs, recalling one of the most embarrassing moments of my life. It wasn't my mother's finest hour, but she also wasn't well at the time. "My dad said that car accident was no accident. She totally killed herself. Check this out." Shira pulls out her phone and plays a video for Mandy. There's a lot of interference in the background, like the sound of feet crunching through thick leaves, before a man can be heard saying, "Wowza, that must've hurt. She's not so pretty anymore." The video comes to a scratchy end, and Mandy is left staring wide-eyed with a hand over her mouth in a gasp.

"Put that away. Seriously, don't ever show that to me again," Mandy tells her. "I'm literally going to throw up my lunch right now. Where did you get that?"

"C'mon, my dad's a cop. He's got access to everything. I found it on his computer," Shira boasts. "If you can't handle that, I definitely won't show you the video of the little boy. Poor kid is laying there with his legs all broken and stuff."

"Stop," Mandy says, slapping her arm. "Don't tell me anything else."

"What? At least he's alive. For now," Shira points out, but Mandy is plugging her ears, not listening. "Honestly, I wouldn't be surprised if Sosie kills herself before senior year is over." Shira applies gooey lip-gloss while she talks.

"C'mon, lets get out of here," Mandy hurries her.

Shira smacks her lips together a couple times and admires her reflection. After a few moments, they finish up and leave, and everything is quiet again.

I sit back down on the toilet seat, numb and vacant. I want to scream that my mother didn't kill herself. I want to know what they were looking at, run after them and demand they show me, but I'm trembling with fear for what I might see. I have to make them and everyone else understand that it was an accident, but all I can do is sit here paralyzed.

When I get the courage, I leave the bathroom and finish the rest of the day in a haze, failing an Algebra quiz because my brain is scrambled with the sounds of crunching leaves and the mystery man's gruff voice. *Wowza. She's not so pretty anymore.* What the hell did that mean?

I somehow make it to U.S. History and Economics, but gaze out the window the entire time, trying not to cry. When the last bell rings, I bolt toward the double doors of freedom, anxious to get home and curl into a dark abyss. Alone.

I've almost made my escape when Mr. Mitchell, the principal, starts down the corridor in my direction. I pretend not to see him as he pushes past loads of students, making his way to me from across the hall.

"Sosie," he says, once he reaches me. "How are things?"

I shouldn't hate the guy, but I can't help it. I do. He's nice enough. It's not that. It's probably because he's so careful with me, always choosing and gathering his words like I might break. Like now, as he stands before me, doing that thing he does with his lips, kind of licking, kind of biting. I wait, car keys digging hard into my palm, ready to dart out the door when given the first opportunity.

"Things are fine," I manage.

"Classes are good?"

"Yep."

He ushers me over to a more private corner, and I swallow down a groan. Here we go.

"I wanted to give you a heads up," he says. "Your dad and I spoke this afternoon, because I'm concerned about your absences. I know he's always traveling, but I wanted to keep him in the loop." He smiles at me, nodding over and over like he hasn't dropped a shit bomb on my entire existence. The last thing I need right now is my father popping in and acting like father of the year when he's the furthest thing from it. All I can do is stare through Mr. Mitchell. "I know you've been having a hard time since—"

"Did my dad actually pick up the phone?"

"Yes, and we had a very nice chat. He said he's going to be back from London in a few days and that the three of us should sit down and come up with a plan to get you back on track." I cross my arms over my chest, and blink hard. "Sosie, we just want you to be successful."

"We? So now you guys are BFF's or something?" I retort.

He sighs, his shoulders slumping, and starts with the lip licking again. "This isn't meant to make you feel defensive."

I repress my urge to scream, and instead take a deep breath, steadying my skipping heart. "Look, I'll be better about going to class. I know I need to do better." I barely get the words out. Anger boils in my chest. If I don't leave now, I might do something I'll regret. Without another word, I push by him and out the door, the cool October air rushing through my sweater as I beeline toward the senior parking lot.

That's when I see him. Nolan crouches down next to a bike rack, fiddling with the combination on his lock, an unlit cigarette dangling out of the side of his mouth. He pulls a rag out of his back pocket and buffs a scratch off the royal blue paint, and then cleans mud off the custom yellow rims. A car pulls up next to him. A guy hops out, and then a girl from the driver's seat, the engine idling. Nolan greets each of them with a limp side hug, and they converse for a few moments. I stand half-hidden behind the school mascot statue, staring. I don't mean to, but I can't help myself.

The girl is pretty with long red hair falling down her back in loose waves, and the guy, tall and gangly, sports a broad, white smile. Nolan spots me. We exchange glances. I raise my hand in a wave, but he quickly looks away, says something to his friends, and gathers up the chain and lock from his bike, stuffing it into his backpack. I wait to be noticed again, but he never looks back. Instead, he hops on his bike and rides away, trailed by the guy and girl in their car.

The words from Nolan's poem replay in my head on the drive home, keeping me from thinking of my mother and the weird video from the bathroom. Somehow, his words steady my thoughts, and every time the man's voice echoes in my brain again, I recite the verses, lips barely moving and the words coming out like a whisper. "The water hits my skin, it makes me feel alive, like I'm one with something bigger than right now, bigger than me, and bigger than life."

I'm connected to Nolan, somehow, even if I don't know him. Maybe it's because he's the only other person in school as lonely as me, always sitting by himself at lunch, never talking to anyone as he sips on his can of Coca-Cola. We have an unspoken solidarity, like he understands me without knowing it yet.

I find myself stopped at a railroad crossing, my old car idling as the gates for the Long Island Railroad come down and a train whizzes by. The horn shrieks as it passes, snapping me out of my thoughts. Across the tracks, the artesian market where my mother and I used to pick up groceries, and next door to it, the handmade soap shop we both used to love so much taunt me.

I refuse to see it. It hurts. I shut my eyes, willing the poem to fill my thoughts once again. Make me feel less alone.

I stop for dinner—a supersized cherry Slurpee from 7-Eleven—on my way home. I round the last corner and turn down the street that leads to my house. A news van sits on the roadside, a reporter standing in front holding a microphone. Mrs. Filipio, my neighbor and Long Beach's resident gossip whore, leans against the van, sticking out her ballooned up fake boobs while she animatedly talks to the journalist.

What's going on? I pull in my driveway and slowly get out.

A blonde woman in a skirt suit approaches me with a microphone, cameraman trailing close behind, slow and steady like they're ready to pounce.

"Sosie," she begins, the microphone in one hand, while she attempts to place her other hand on my shoulder in a showy way for the camera. I jerk away, but it doesn't deter her. "How do you feel about the news that the last victim from your mother's deadly suicide crash has died? Bradley Markle was only five years old when your mother put him into a coma. His family wants answers. Can you tell us if your mother left a note before she purposely drove into oncoming traffic to end her life?"

"No comment." I make my way up half the driveway before changing my mind and whirling around. "No. Wait. Actually, I do have something to say." I look into the camera, the bright lights blinding me through billowing tears. "It wasn't my mother's intention to hurt anyone. She would never do that … especially to a kid. It was nothing more than a horrible accident."

"Sosie, we feel for you and know how hard this must be, but what do you have to say to the people who don't believe that?" the reporter goes on. "There's plenty of evidence that suggests the contrary."

The world around me starts spinning, spinning,

spinning, and the ground threatens to open up and swallow me whole. Fire consumes my belly and throat as I open my mouth to speak. "I'd say they're wrong," I tell the reporter, through gritted teeth. "Everyone thinks they know, but they have no idea. You think you can just show up here with your stupid camera and stupid microphone and tell me shit about my life, but you don't know anything. It's all gossip and crap theories, but I'm going to prove it was an accident. Somehow, I'll prove it to everyone."

My attention shifts to Mrs. Filipio who's still chattering away, her voice ringing through the air. "She's clearly having a hard time. She used to be such a nice girl before all this. Now she's depressed, and she's made herself sick over it, just sick. I wish there was something I could do. Her mother was unstable, though, I can go on the record and tell you that much."

The blackness shades my periphery, and I'm sweating—the clammy sort that happens when you're about to vomit, or as I imagine, murder someone in cold blood.

Mrs. Filipio flips her blue-black hair over to her other shoulder as her mouth continues to run.

I march toward her, coming up from behind, and for a split second, a twinge of guilt for what I'm about to do ricochets through me.

But only for a second.

She doesn't see me coming. I step in front of her and dump my cherry Slurpee on top of her head.

Mrs. Filipio screams, the red iciness washing over her perfectly applied make-up while the cameramen rushes to capture the moment.

In the midst of all the confusion, I slip away, into the safety of my home, before anyone can get another decent shot of me or ask me any more questions.

Chapter Two

The TV purrs its way into one of my dreams, the faint sounds of a laugh track resonating in the background of an old sitcom, stirring up my brainwaves. I lift my head off the pillow, a puddle of sticky spit where my cheek had been resting. The room spins. How long have I been sleeping?

I don't bother looking for the remote and force myself out of bed, my body crackling like an old person as I stretch. Memories from last night creep in. Hearing the news about Bradley Markle dying. Dumping the Slurpee on Mrs. Filipio's head on the live local news. The false accusations made about my mother. It all makes my head pound like someone dropped a bag of bricks on top of my face.

I throw my favorite sweatshirt on, the one two sizes too big with the chocolate ice-cream stain on the right elbow, and wobble my way to the bathroom down the hall. The toilet seat is cold against my skin, and my urine burns as it leaves my body, hot and angry from the toxins it's been holding onto. It smells of booze, the hard kind, and the kind that gives you a very bad hangover. Vodka seemed like a good idea, but that was before I woke up with a piercing migraine that's making my eyes blurry, and the same problems I had yesterday.

I pull up my sweatpants and shuffle over to the bathroom cupboard. Four pills jangle around the bottom of the Advil bottle. One, two, three, four, I shake them into my palm. A sharp pain pulses between my brows. I pop the pills into my mouth and gulp them down with sink water from a cup I've made out of my hands.

The doorbell downstairs chimes. There's a pause, followed by aggressive knocking. I'm not in the mood for visitors. I trudge down the staircase and fling the front door open.

It's the first time I've opened the door since the fiasco with the news reporter, and it looks like the day after a carnival shuts down and moves onto the next town. Trash scatters the driveway, the grass on my front lawn smushed from people trampling along it. A young police officer, no more than a few years older than me, stands on my doorstep, the backdrop of a grey sky and violent wind behind him. He opens his mouth to speak, and a gust takes his breath away.

"Police, ma'am," he finally manages. He smiles, friendly-like, his plump baby face and stubble free cheeks making him less intimidating. "I'm Officer Reinhart." Before he says any more, his radio begins spouting off information, interrupting. His hand brushes across a knob, hushing it to a murmur. "Are you Sosie Friedman?"

"That's me."

"How are ya, ma'am?"

"I'm fine. Please, just call me Sosie. What's up?"

"Your father hasn't been able to get in touch with you for a couple of days, so he asked us to take a ride over here. Are you aware people have been trying to reach you?"

"No," I say, still groggy, my voice trailing off. "Wait, a couple of days? What day is it?"

"It's Saturday." He looks at his watch. "At about 1:00 PM."

"No shit!" I say, half amused, half impressed. "Wow, I was out longer than I thought. Two days might be a record for me."

"Is that, uh, an empty bottle of alcohol on your floor over there?" he asks, craning his neck to see into the house.

I shut the door a little to block his view. "Look,

things got really crazy the other night. Like, really crazy, and I had a couple of drinks. I just needed to blow off some steam and sleep it off. You know how that is, right?" I say, trying to relate, but he remains unmoved and serious. "C'mon, it's not like I got wasted and went out joy riding."

"I'm gonna pretend I didn't hear that, considering the fact that I have knowledge you're underage," he says. "I'm here because your father called us to check on you, because he believed that you might've hurt yourself, or that you could be in serious danger."

I can't help laughing. "I'm sorry, I'm sorry, I don't mean to laugh." I apologize in between cracking up. "It's just that my father doesn't give a shit about me, that's all. Look. If you talk to my father, you can tell him I'm fine, and he can relax, okay?" I start to close the door, but the officer shoves his fingers in the doorjamb.

"Have you turned on the news at all?" he asks.

"If this is about my mother, I've already heard the news about…" I trail off as he squints at me, bewildered. "You're talking about my mother's accident, right, that little boy?"

"No," he says slowly. "I'm talking about the really bad storm that's coming this way. It could be a hurricane. The town of Long Beach will be issued an evacuation zone at any moment. We're expecting some serious flooding and damage." The faint storm sirens blare in the distance, and the sky churns in eerie shades of green and grey. It's raining, not hard, just the misty kind, but the wind is lashing about so furiously that one of the street lamps could easily unhinge from the ground and go for a ride. The whole neighborhood is quiet, too, and my next-door neighbor is packing up his minivan. His wife and children sit anxiously in their seats, while he neatly loads suitcases and a large cooler into the open trunk. The officer snaps his fingers in front of my nose. "Most people have already packed up and left. What are your plans?"

"I'm staying with a friend," I lie, automatically.

"You're staying with a friend?" he asks, raising his eyebrow. "Does your father know? Because it's part of the reason he wanted us to come and do a welfare check."

I study the officer, trying to place him, and then it hits me. "Your name is Will Reinhart, right? You graduated two years ago from Bolton Academy, no?" He shifts a little on his feet. "Yeah, I know you, and you know me, so why are you rolling up here, busting my balls, and acting like we're strangers? Weren't you the one who used to smoke pot in the back stairwell with Johnny every day before sixth hour when you were a senior? Now that I think of it, I'm pretty sure you were the one who sold him his first dime bag sophomore year."

"I did go to Bolton Academy, but I never smoked pot in any stairwell, and I definitely didn't sell any dime bags," he says, clearing his throat.

"Alrighty, Mr. Officer, whatever you say." I wink. "I get it, you're just trying to do your job, but I've got everything under control, okay? I'm fine. Everything's fine. I'm going to call my dad, and I'm going to get out of here ASAP." My cell phone rings on the coffee table where I left it a couple nights earlier when I helped myself to my mother's old liquor cabinet and drank until I passed out cold. There are benefits to having a mother who used to be an alcoholic, among other things. "See, that's my dad calling now."

"Why don't you go and answer it?" he suggests.

I roll my eyes and retrieve my phone while the officer waits in the doorway. I hit the ignore button as I pretend to answer it. "Hi, dad," I say. "Yeah, I'm good. The officer is actually here right now. Yeah. I'm okay. I was sleeping, don't worry." I pause. "Yes, I've got plans. Hold on a minute, dad." I take the phone away from my ear for a moment, and mouth to the officer, "Are we good?" He nods, still hesitant to leave. "I'm going to Jen's. She's on her way to pick me up, actually." Will, *aka* Johnny's-pot-smoking-kingpin-dealer from Bolton Academy, slowly backs off the porch and into the misty rain. I wave goodbye, give him an enthusiastic thumbs up, and close the door before he can change his mind. I watch through one of the carved, diamond shaped windows that border the front door as he lingers for a minute. I take the phone away from my ear, and put it into my sweatpants pocket.

"I'm at 558 Francis Avenue. Welfare Check on Sosie Friedman," he says, into his radio. Something indecipherable comes through in response. "Yeah, she's here. She's fine," he says, and then waits. Another garbled message sounds back. "She's made contact with her father, and she's aware about this being an evacuation zone."

"Just leave, asshole," I whisper, as I watch him.

After a minute, he walks back to his car and drives away.

I go into the living room and turn the television on. A flashing red banner runs along the bottom of the screen with storm warnings as a journalist, reporting live from the shore on Long Beach, stands within feet of the violent ocean, sand whipping across her face. People who aren't heeding the storm warnings stand in the distance from her but within camera shot, taking pictures of the waves and sky, and getting dangerously close to the rough water.

"The city of Long Beach is now under a coastal

flooding watch, and no one knows how bad this storm is going to get. The Governor has declared a statewide state of emergency, and has asked the President to sign a pre-disaster declaration, which he's expected to do later today," the journalist shouts over the wind.

The camera cuts back to a pretty reporter sitting in the safety of a quiet news studio. "It's looking bad so far, Cassandra. Is the wind as violent as it seems?" she asks, her face crinkled in worry.

There's a slight delay as the camera returns to Cassandra on the beach. "It sure is, and that water is rough," she says, managing a smile. "But from what I've been told, this is only the beginning. As you can see behind me, the shops and restaurants along the boardwalk have already shut down, and preemptively boarded up their windows. Right now, it seems like your typical windstorm, but the rain and wind are expected to gain much more momentum by the end of the day, as well as overnight. Just because it doesn't seem that bad yet doesn't mean the evacuation notices shouldn't be taken seriously."

Suddenly, a group of teenagers in wet suits with surfboards come up from behind her, screaming at the top of their lungs in party mode. One of the boys pumps his hips back and forth near Cassandra's back end as she turns to see what's going on. The camera flips, and a male voice shouts through the laughter, echoing in the background. After a moment, the camera refocuses, up close on a face—a face I know. It's Nolan, and the guy and girl I saw him with a couple of days earlier at school.

"Party at 185 Park Place!" Nolan's friend yells into the camera, just before it cuts back to the reporter in the studio.

Speechless, I can't suppress a small giggle at their antics, and wish I were there with them, a part of their circle, acting all careless and free. I've never seen that side of Nolan, grinning and wild, and it makes me even more curious about him, and about these friends of his. I wonder if they were with him on the day that inspired his poem. A yearning rushes through me to know him on that level, and to be a part of his world.

I shut the television off and go upstairs for a long, hot shower. I'm halfway up the steps when my cell phone rings in my pocket. I peek at it. Dad again. I hit ignore and continue on my way to the bathroom. It starts buzzing again, and then again and again. He's not going to get off my back until I answer, I know this much. His burning need to validate himself as not being a shitty father motivates him and probably helps him sleep at night. I groan as I answer the call, knowing I must play the game in order to get what I want in the end, which is to be left alone to sleep off this hangover.

"Sosie. Jesus Christ," my father says, on the other end. "Where the hell have you been? I've been trying to reach you for two days. I thought something happened to you." I take a seat on the carpeted steps and don't say anything at first. "Sosie, say something."

"I was sleeping."

He exhales, in one of his signature Sosie's-being-a-pain-in-the-ass-again ways. "Do you have any idea how worried I've been? I'm on the other side of the world, there's a hurricane about to hit New York—a hurricane for Christ sakes—and you decide it's a good time to go MIA." I rotate my head around in a stretch, but there's still no relief from the hangover headache pounding against my eardrums. "This isn't a joke. I had to call the cops … and I had to skip work today."

"God forbid you skip work." My father misses work for almost nothing. Work is his baby, the love of his life. He didn't even take the day off when my mother gave birth to me. I perk up a bit and bask in his displeasure, knowing it must've killed him to call out today because his daughter is such a screw up.

"Look, it wasn't fair how those reporters bombarded you with the news about that little boy dying or the things they were saying about your mom. Sosie, I'm sorry. You shouldn't have found out that way, but you can't just go off the grid." He takes a long pause before continuing. "I should've been there. It's just horrible timing. This movie is about to wrap, and I have big stakes in it. It kills me to be so far away when so much is happening."

"Yeah, well, so what else is new?" I say, bitterly. "It's always horrible timing, isn't it?"

My father's been using the same, tired excuse for the last five years since he left us. Funny thing is, he never officially divorced us or moved out. He's not that virtuous. He just stays away, travels constantly, and takes on new movies and projects to produce so he doesn't have to be here. Some of his stuff is still here, a pair of his old dress shoes still sit on a mat by the front door, and his toothbrush is still on the bathroom counter where he left it on the last night he ever spent here. Leaving his belongings behind makes him feel less guilty, like he's not officially gone, but it doesn't matter. He's still a ghost.

He's as much of a ghost in this house as my mother is.

"I know you're upset, but your mother wouldn't want you to do this."

"Do what?" My voice catapults from my throat, coming out in a shriek. His mention of her punches me in the stomach, robbing my breath. "Have a drink to deal with all the shit that's been happening? You're wrong. She'd tell me live my life."

"Live your life? That's what you call it?" He chuckles.

"Don't laugh at me. It makes me crazy when you laugh at me like that."

"It used to make your mother crazy, too."

"So, now you're calling me crazy?"

"I didn't say that." He grunts, and I imagine him wiping the sweat from his brow, the way he does when he's exasperated with me.

"You didn't have to," I retort.

"I'm worried about you. I talked to Mary and she told me what you did the other night. Pouring a Slurpee on top of her head? Why would you do that, Sosie?"

"Do you really need to ask?" I challenge. He backs down, doesn't answer. Of course he doesn't. He knows I know the truth about what I saw that day, even if he'd like to pretend he's forgotten. That vision is etched in my brain with such permanence that it feels like a tattoo. "I'm not doing this right now. I'm going to take a shower. I've got to go." I take the phone away from my ear, about to hang up.

"Sosie, don't go yet." His voice is tiny and far away. I put my cell back to my ear and listen. "Please. Look, I know you like to have space to do things your way, and I've tried to let you do that, but this isn't working. You're not going to school. You're drinking and doing God knows what else. You're unraveling, Sosie."

"I'm fine." My jaw clenches, the words barely coming out.

"I know you're hurting." He's silent, except for a few heavy breaths on the other end. "What I mean to say is, what happened with your mother wasn't your fault, okay? It has nothing to do with you, and it doesn't say anything about you. Okay, Sosie? It wasn't your fault."

In my life, he's never been so emotionally open. There's always been a barricade between us that's impenetrable, like a concrete wall I keep pounding on where no one answers, and all I'm left with are bloodied fists. Even at my mother's funeral his shield was up. On that day, he gave me a pat on the top of my head and mumbled, "I'm sorry, Sos," and then left for L.A. that evening. His change in demeanor takes me aback. It's touching even. A sudden sobbing breaks free, noiselessly. Not a sniffle, not a breath, a private unraveling. He's got no idea I'm breaking down.

"It wasn't your fault," he assures me. "It wasn't even her fault. She didn't know what she was doing."

And then as easily as I'm in the moment, I'm out, his words sobering me, silencing my tears. "You're wrong." My backbone straightens, and I wipe the tears with the back of my hand. "You don't know shit. It didn't happen the way you think it did, the way everyone thinks it did. She didn't kill herself. It was an accident. I'm going to prove it, you'll see. I'm hanging up now. Goodbye."

I take the battery out of my cell and go back upstairs to the bathroom for a long, hot shower. When I finish, I change into my pajamas, brush out my wet hair, and go to lie down in my mother's bed.

I used to crawl into bed with my mother sometimes when I couldn't sleep. Not only when I was little, but also when I was old enough for some people to think it's weird. My mother never minded, not even when I woke her up at two in the morning and started talking to her like we were in the middle of having turkey sandwiches and raspberry iced tea for lunch, as we did sometimes. She was wonderful like that. It didn't matter how tired she was or how trivial the topic; she'd start talking back without any sign of a sleep fog.

"Am I defective or something?" I asked her, one night last summer.

"Darling, what are you talking about?" She rolled over to face me as I lay on my back, looking at the ceiling. "Is this about that boy again?"

"No." I lied at first. "Well, yes, kind of."

"Darling, what have I told you? You're perfect. There was never a more perfect girl on this planet. If he doesn't love you, he doesn't know what perfection is."

"That's not a lot to live up to or anything," I said, and we both busted out laughing. "But seriously, I'm basically the only sixteen-year-old on earth who's never had a boyfriend."

"It's different once you get older, my love, easier to meet people."

"But you'd already had two serious boyfriends by the time you were my age," I pointed out.

"People don't get so serious so young anymore. They date around."

"Johnny will never love me," I said, with a sigh.

"Why are you so hell-bent on Johnny? Plenty of fish in the sea, my love."

If my mother were still living, I would tell her about Nolan from my writing class. I'd probably recite his poem back to her. I have it memorized word for word after all. She'd have loved it as much as I do, and she'd like the fact he's different from all the other boys I've had crushes on in the past. Nolan's deep. He appreciates the beauty in nature.

Then again, for all I know, he might be exactly like Johnny.

****

"Oh c'mon, Sosie, it's not like I set your house on fire and killed your whole family," Johnny said, over burgers and chicken fingers at the diner last May.

"No, it's worse. You do realize that, right? Liz Greenberg," I said, rattling the ice around in my Diet Coke, as I stewed about the two of them hooking up.

"Quit being dramatic," he told me.

"I'm not being dramatic. Way to sabotage our entire friendship, though."

"Are you serious?" he asked, and I nodded. "Relax. You and I have been friends since we were five, and we'll be probably be friends for the rest of our lives."

"Probably?" I asked, overanalyzing his words as I so often did.

"We will be," he groaned, correcting himself. "God. Your attention to detail is so aggravating sometimes."

"Liz Greenberg? Seriously, her of all people," I said, pushing my food away.

"Now you're not hungry anymore?" he asked.

"No."

I sat quiet, sulking.

"It's not like I'm with her. I slept with her once. And I've barely said anything to her since."

"Do you know how asshole-ish that sounds?" I asked, suddenly defensive on Liz's behalf.

Johnny chewed his burger with a smile, his mouth wide-open, and the food smacking back and forth between his cheeks. He was proud of himself, proud to be an alpha male.

"Why do you care so much if I got with Liz anyway?" he asked, as he wiped his mouth with a napkin.

"Because," I said, standing up. "Because I hate her! You literally couldn't have boned a worse human being."

I slipped my jacket on and got up to leave.

"Boned?" He laughed. "Who even says that?"

"I do," I said, and started walking away, leaving him to pay for my chicken fingers and soda.

"You just hate her because she won that writing scholarship," he called out after me. "You hate anyone who gets what you want."

"You have no idea what I want," I muttered, my back to him as I threw my middle finger into the air and walked off.

Chapter Three

I need to see my mother's face. I sit down at her writing desk with two thick photo albums, one of my parents' wedding and one from when I was a toddler. I open it up to the first page, my favorite page, and run my fingertips along the tattered binding. There's that photograph of my mother on the beach.

My mother was so beautiful when she was young. She was beautiful just before she died, too, but there was something easier about her face when she was in her twenties. She smiled with her eyes more, happiness radiated from the tops of her cheekbones. She wasn't wearing make-up, none at all, and she was brighter and more alive than I'd ever remembered her.

When I was younger, I used to look at these same albums and say things to her like, *"Ma, it doesn't even look like you! Are you sure that's you? You look so young, you look so different,"* not understanding how saying such things might be hurtful, but she'd just laugh and shake her head.

Now, however, I notice something different, something I've never paid much attention to before. They were in love, my mother and father. It's obvious in the pictures they had been madly and passionately in love at the beginning. In every wedding and honeymoon photograph, my mother's hand is resting on my father's chest, while my father looks at my mother instead of the camera, his nose always nuzzling her cheek. He loved her. She loved him.

It shocks me—I don't know why—but maybe because I have no memory of my parents this way. To me, they'd only ever been the contentious duo, full of spite and passive aggressive slights when the other wasn't around. I barely even remember my father being there. He's stayed away for so long now.

Then there are the pictures of me once I joined them, dozens of pictures of us visiting my grandmother's house in Pennsylvania. My father pushing me on the hanging tire in her front yard, while my mother stands in front of us, waiting to catch me when I swung her way. And there I was all the while, always smiling, beaming with the gummiest of grins, mugging for the camera, and thrilled to be with the two of them. They loved me, and I loved them.

But did they still love each other once I came along? Something went wrong somewhere along the way, and I was the only difference between those first snapshots and these. Maybe if it had remained the two of them, they'd still be in love now, traveling the world, living together in peace. At the very least, living. My mother might still be alive if I'd never existed.

I toss the albums onto the floor and out of my sight, chilled by the thoughts. I slip underneath the covers, pulling them up to my neck, and close my eyes, but all I can see are images of my mother replaying in my head.

****

"Mom, can you hear me? Are you going to get out of bed today?" I asked my mother this same question countless times throughout my childhood and adolescence. This past winter she'd gotten the worst she'd ever been, staying in bed for days at a time, not showering, not brushing her teeth, and not looking after the dog. I remember peering into her room, easing the door open to see the curtains drawn and only the top of her curly brown hair peeking out from between two fluffy pillows. The stale smell of sleep lingered in the room, like the air hadn't circulated, and like there hadn't been any signs of life or movement in hours or maybe days.

"Hi, Sosie girl," she said, trying to sound upbeat. "Why do you have your backpack on? Is it time for school already?"

I pulled the curtains apart, the afternoon sun rushing the room in a sudden fit. "It's three-thirty, Mom. I've already been to school."

"No kidding," she said, trying to smooth out her ratted hair. "Why do you look irritated with me? Are you mad at me? Don't be mad at me, Sosie. I'm just so tired. I really need to catch up on sleep."

"Has Tippy even been out today?" My childhood dog—the one we had to put to sleep three weeks before she died—tugged at my heels. Tippy crossing over the rainbow bridge had been a major blow for her. After he died, she carried around a little trinket of his ashes in her pocket so he'd always be close to her. When she died, it went with her. It's what she would've wanted.

She was quiet, thinking.

"You can't even remember if you let the goddamn dog out today or not?"

"Let me think for a second!"

"It's a pretty straight forward question. You either did or you didn't," I snapped. I started to walk out of the room. "C'mon, Tippy. Poor dog."

"You don't know how hard this is," she shrieked after me. "I can see you judging me. Stop judging me! I'm trying to get well, okay? You know how I've tried, and I'm still trying. I haven't given up, so stop acting like I have."

In all the years watching my mother fight depression, I'd never seen her so low. Her eyes were empty pools of black, and her mouth was wrinkled into a scowl, old and tight, like she was wearing the rubbery mask of a woman twice her age.

"You have given up," I said, but she didn't hear me. She had already laid her head back down on the pillow and was fast asleep.

****

I need fresh air, away from the linens in my mother's bed that still smells like her, the unmistakable mixture of her favorite lavender shampoo and stale Jack Daniels, and away from the haunting images. I trudge downstairs and over to the front door, pressing my face against the cold surface on one of the large glass panels. Outside, the sky is dark even though it isn't yet four o'clock in the afternoon.

I open the door and walk out onto the porch, the wind rushing over me and stealing my breath. It's raining, harder now, fat raindrops splattering across my face as I step onto the front lawn in my thin pajamas and look up at the sky. I stand there, the powerful wind threatening and pushing me back and forth like a ragdoll.

Soaked through to my skin and shivering, I go back inside and sit down on the couch, still wet, not bothering to dry off or undress. The grandfather clock's tick-tock, tick-tock lulls me into a trance.

****

"Sosie, you're home." I can almost hear my mother's melodic voice echoing in the foyer, standing in front of me just as she had that day, freshly scrubbed and wearing that crisp oxford shirt. "My sweet darling, I'm making matzo ball soup for dinner."

The week before my mother died, she had without any warning at all, snapped out of her depression and escaped the beast that had taken hold of her for so long.

I'd approached her, as I walked through the front door, unbelieving that she was really okay, afraid that I might spook her back into a black hole.

"Somebody's feeling better," I said, dropping my backpack by the front door.

"Oh honey-bunny, so much better. I'm sorry I've been so out of it lately."

I followed her into the kitchen, her gait like a sashay rather than the usual slog as she glanced behind to make sure I was still following, grinning when she saw I was there. Eagerly, I sat on a kitchen chair, hesitant and skeptical, while I observed her.

"That smells delicious, by the way," I said.

She sat down next to me, took my hand, and kissed it. "I don't want you to ever think of me as a horrible mother, okay?"

"Ma, are you kidding? I would never think that."

Her eyes brimmed with watery tears. "I'm so sorry, Sosie. I've always wanted to be a good mom to you, but sometimes it just gets so hard. It's like I get sucked into this hell I can't pull myself out of. It's like I can see myself sinking and as much as the logical part of me tries to claw its way out the farther I sink. I try to get back to you, though, I do. Please know I try. It's just that I can't sometimes. But this time … this time has been different. I've come out of it. Every time I thought about your face, it stirred something up on the inside. I love you so much I swear it healed me. I tried with all my might, and I willed it so. It was you, Sosie. It was all because of you that I got better." She got up and went to stir the soup. "Everything is going to be different this time for us. I know it."

I appeared at her side and put my arm around her. She leaned her head into me. "You're the best mother, always and no matter what. I love you."

"I love you more than anything else in this whole, wide world," she said.

****

And I know she meant it. Every word.

My mother might've been a lot of things, but she wasn't a liar or a quitter. She wouldn't have left me alone to face these rumors on my own. She wouldn't have gone away without an explanation, a note, something for me to cling to. Days before she died, we went to a local jewelry store in town and picked out matching necklaces, two solid gold hearts that hung on a dainty chain. It was more than she was able to spend, so she worked out a deal with the owner and agreed to pay a little each month until they were ours to take home. I would've had the necklace last week if my mother were still alive. She was changing. I could feel the difference, not just see it. Why would she go to such trouble if she were going to leave me in the end?

Outside the wind is gaining momentum, the rain coming down in sheets. My heart beats faster and faster, the anxiety building with how violent it all sounds. It's too late to leave, not that I would. I have no friends and nowhere to go. I never had any intention of leaving anyway.

Like most nights, I find my way to the liquor cabinet. My supply is dwindling, only one bottle of bourbon left. I pour a double into a dirty tumbler and drink nearly the entire glass in a few big gulps. Within minutes, my skin is buzzing, and my body and mind start to relax.

I lie down on the couch, seeking silence from the thousands of thoughts spinning through my head. My hair is still wet—my clothes, too—but the whiskey warms me. Suddenly, I've got the urge to talk, but there's no one to talk to now that my mother is gone. I don't know what else to do with myself, so I put some music on and blast the speakers in my living room until they're about to break while dancing to The Smiths.

The bass pumps up and down, moving my heart and my head deeply and profoundly. The music, the lyrics, and the beat, seep into the tiniest crevices of my soul and holds me there, daring me to not feel everything else that's wrong in my life.

I dance until I can't breathe. I dance until the sweat is dripping from my forehead and onto the floor. I dance until I feel absolutely nothing else.

I take a break to pour myself another drink, and the rest of the night continues on for hours—dance and drink, dance and drink, dance and drink—until I'm wasted, and collapsing on the living room's Persian rug.

Then, I do what I always do when I'm drinking. I call him. Every time I say I'm not going to, but it's inevitable. I don't bother turning the music down. It's still blaring when I put the battery back into my cell phone and dial his number. It rings twice before he answers.

"Hello?" Johnny says, but I only listen. I take in the sound of his voice, and try to gauge where he is, who he's with. "Hello? Sosie?" He waits some more. "Okay, I'm hanging up now. Call me when you actually want to say something."

"Wait," I manage.

"What do you want?"

"Who are you with?" I ask, instead of answering the question.

"Does it matter? Are you listening to The Smiths?"

"Yeah," I say. "Why do you care?"

Johnny pauses. "You're right. Why do I care? Sosie, you've got to stop. You've been acting crazy."

"Sorry, I didn't realize calling my ex–best friend was a crazy thing to do, but whatever." Emotion rises in my throat.

"No, calling isn't the problem. It's blocking your number so I pick up. It's … it's dumping a goddamn Slurpee on top of my mom's head the other night. You're lucky I even picked up the phone just now."

"But you basically hate your mom," I point out.

"But it's my mom." He groans. "Look, I answered just now, because I'm worried about you. Are you at home right now?"

"Yeah," I say. "Want to come over?"

"No, I don't want to come over," he says as if it's the last thing he'd ever do. "I left Long Beach hours ago, and you should've, too. This is a mess, Sosie. Do you have somewhere to go?"

"Yes," I say. "My boyfriend is about to come and pick me up any minute."

"Alrighty." He chuckles, drawing out the word.

"What's so funny?"

"You don't have a boyfriend," he says, incredulously.

"I do have a boyfriend," I insist. "Why am I even talking to you anyway? Why do you even care about where I'm going?"

"So many questions. You haven't changed a bit."

"This was a mistake. I shouldn't have called. Have a nice life, Johnny," I say, and hang up in his ear.

****

The summer before junior year, Johnny and I used to drive on the highway in his convertible BMW, just so we could blast The Smiths, and scream every lyric, as if that might help us connect with the music more. Sometimes I'd stand up and sing, purposefully wearing a short skirt, so the wind would hit the fabric on my thighs, and Johnny might take notice. I was trying to seduce him and also trying to live out a scene from one of my favorite novels, *The Perks of Being a Wallflower*.

Sometimes I'd say things like, "In that moment, didn't you just feel infinite?" Johnny had no idea I was quoting a line from a book and was always impressed with my ability to put words to what he was feeling. I'd try to look dreamy-eyed as I said it, sometimes biting my lower lip for emphasis.

"I totally feel infinite," Johnny would say in response.

One night, he turned the music down and put his hand on my thigh, rubbing his thumb in small circles along my freshly shaved skin. It was the first time he'd ever touched me like that.

"When I listen to The Smiths with you, I just feel…" He paused, trying to find the right words. "Like, we're stuck in this amazing, infinite moment together, and I wouldn't want to be anywhere else other than here with you."

I tried to keep myself from laughing. It was then that I realized how easily boys could be fooled. A short skirt, a quote from a book, and he melted into my hand like putty.

"I know what you mean," I said, playing into it. "Because I feel the exact same way."

"Can I take you somewhere? Somewhere where we can just be alone?"

"We're alone right now," I pointed out.

"Alone, alone," he said.

I was ready. I'd been waiting for this moment all summer. "Yeah," I said, trying to play it cool. "Sure."

Johnny pulled off at the next exit and began driving aimlessly around.

"Do you even know where you're going?"

"Of course," he said.

"Are you sure?" I asked.

"Yeah. Geez, stop worrying."

Johnny pulled into an abandoned gas station and parked the car in a dark spot near the back.

"Where are we right now?" I asked, nervous, uncertain, giddy.

"Can you do me a favor and for once just stop with all the questions? I just want to look at you, because I suddenly feel like I don't know you."

"You've known me since the first grade," I said.

"I've known *that* you, but this you suddenly looks different."

"How so?" I asked, anxious for his answer.

"Oh my God, just shut up." He took my face in his hands and gently kissed me. Then he pulled away to look at me.

"What?" I asked, suddenly self-conscious.

"Nothing. It's just … you're beautiful," he said, and kissed me again.

Soon his hands were in my hair, my hands in his hair, our tongues slipping into each other's mouths with fury. He touched my stomach lightly over my top and then inched his way underneath, lightly grazing my bare belly.

I kissed him harder and softly moaned, trying desperately to send the message that I wanted more. He received that message and slipped his hand into my bra. I watched him touch me as his eyes were closed. I watched him want me. Nothing had ever given me a bigger thrill.

"I like you," I whispered.

"I like you," he said back, his breathing heavier.

"No. I like you like *that,*" I told him as he stroked me.

"I know."

"You know?" I asked, pulling away.

He stopped, opened his eyes. He was annoyed. "C'mon, Sosie, don't ruin it. Just go with it. Be in the moment for once. I like you like that, too."

I brought him back to me and kissed him. Within seconds, we were back, back in the moment, and back to where we had left off. Soon he was groaning. I was groaning. We moved to the backseat, and he took my shirt off, and I took his off. His skin was smooth and soft, only a tiny trail of hair on his stomach. He pulled my skirt up and climbed on top of me. I was scared. I was a virgin, and I knew he wasn't.

"Is this okay?" he asked me, before going any further.

"Yeah. Just go slow, okay?"

Johnny stopped, ungrasping his hands from my hips. "Wait. Are you a virgin?"

"No. God no," I lied.

"Sosie, you can tell me."

"Shawn Aspen," I said.

"You fucked Shawn Aspen?"

"Yeah, I did, okay," I said, with conviction, hoping he'd drop the subject. "Just kiss me," I said, tilting my head up.

He met my lips and placed himself between my legs. He started to take off my underwear.

"Wait, do you have a condom?" I asked.

"Yeah, yeah, of course. Sorry."

He climbed to the front seat and got a condom from the glove compartment.

"Do you sleep with girls in your car all the time?"

"No," he said, exasperated as he slipped it on. "Are you going to ruin it again? Just stop talking already."

"Okay," I said softly as he pushed himself inside me.

The sex didn't last long and wasn't nearly as arousing as the foreplay had been. It was clumsy, sweaty, and cramped. When we finished just minutes later, he unfastened his parts from mine, pulling himself out with the wilted condom still on. I felt awkward. I could tell he felt awkward. I cringed, looking for evidence on the latex for any blood that might expose my lie. There wasn't any, but everything between my legs was burning and sore.

"What are you looking at?" he asked, stuffing himself back into his pants.

"Nothing," I said, pulling my skirt down. "God. It's not like I didn't just see your dick three seconds ago."

"Yeah, but that was when it was hard," he said, with an uncomfortable laugh.

We climbed into the front seat, and he started the car.

"That's it?" I asked.

He groaned and leaned over, giving me a quick peck on the lips.

We never talked about what happened between us, not that night on the drive home, or ever. Johnny pretended like it never happened, like he'd never been inside me, like I'd never seen his face when he came, and like he'd never seen my naked body. But he had, and I had. Even if he wanted to forget it all, it had happened.

Chapter Four

The alcohol is running low, and I'm starting to sober, so I take what's left of the bottle of Jack and stagger upstairs to my mother's writing desk where I know there's a secret stash of prescription pills. I plop down on her rickety swivel chair, the seat squeaking as my weight makes contact, and I reach underneath the drawer for a tiny copper key. "Gotcha," I say, as I slide it into the keyhole and turn it until there's a click. I tug at the drawer to open it, but something is stuck, preventing it from fully coming free. Slipping my hand into the crack, I pry around, frantic to get inside and reach the bottles of pills, the gold, which I know will keep me numb and not feeling the things I don't want to feel. "Come on, you son of a bitch," I snarl, as I force my hand in deeper, yanking out what's in its way.

A photograph, a bent and creased in half photograph of my mother. She's standing on the glossy green lawn of a two-story grey colonial, and she's with a man. He's got his arm around her, on her hip, and she's turning into him the same way she used to turn toward my father when they were young.

I swallow hard, a lump in the back of my throat as I study it. Even in my muddled, half-wasted brain, I know in the pit of my stomach that I've discovered something I wasn't meant to see. Her writing desk was sacred, off limits, her safe space. She used to say, "It's the only place in this entire house that's only mine." She didn't even like me sitting on her desk chair. I remember plopping down on it once after getting home late from a football game, chatting and going on and on, rambling about whatever bonehead thing Johnny had done. I'd noticed her becoming nervous, her eyes glued to me, watching my every move while she drummed her hands against her thighs and waited for me to finish talking. "Do you mind coming over here?" she asked, once I came up for air, patting the side of the bed next to her.

I never knew about her secret stash of pills, or that she kept them in there. That is, until she was gone, and after I went searching for answers, a note or journal, anything that might give me a clue about what happened. I never found anything, and had long given up trying to.

My eyes squint, trying to focus my blurry vision, and trying to see if I recognize this burly man with his wooly beard and broad shoulders who's got his hands on my mother. I don't, but I recognize the house. It's a house just several blocks away on Waverly Place that my mother used to drive past, even when she had to go out of her way to do so. It was her dream house, or so she'd tell me. "Look at the house," she'd say, stars in her eyes. "Those charming white shutters and wrap around porch. Doesn't it look like something out of *Steel Magnolias*?" I'd glance up from my phone, give a weak nod of acknowledgment, and continue with whatever text message I'd been in the middle of sending.

I never cared to take in the details of the house before, but suddenly there's urgency, a burning in my chest that tingles all the way down to my fingertips to go and see it, and to find something, anything that might tell me something about my mother and what this picture means. Maybe I hope she'll be there somehow, not in the flesh, but in spirit, sending me a sign.

I stuff the photograph into my pajama pants pocket and retrieve the pills from the drawer. My lips are eager as I swig the whiskey from the bottle and slip a few pills into my mouth. They burn as they make their way down my throat. Teetering, I stand up, kicking the desk chair out of the way. I grab the pill bottle with one hand and the nearly empty bottle of Jack with the other. I'm going to that house for answers.

But I don't make it out of my mother's room before the light flickers, bright then dim, bright then dim, until the power goes out all together. The wind outside sounds like a choir of whistlers, hissing back and forth, each time getting louder then softer. I wobble over to my mother's bedroom window and peer out, but there's nothing on the other side, just a backdrop of pure blackness. I hear the branches on trees lashing about, but I can't see them. Absolutely nothing but darkness stares back at me. My fingertips touch the glass, longing to go outside, like a grounded child who's been punished from recess. I collapse to the floor, my body hitting the ground in a thud, tears of frustration streaming down my hot cheeks.

My cell phone buzzes in my pocket, and I pray it's not my father following up to see if I've gone to stay at a friend's house. Then again, who am I kidding? According to his crappy daddy standards, he's more than surpassed his fatherly duties for the week when he took time out of his important life to call the cops when he couldn't reach me or when he, gasp, had to call out of work. He's probably sitting in his hotel room in London, having a bottle of red wine until he passes out cold, and thinking about what fuck up I am.

I glance at my phone. It's not my father or Johnny. It's a text message from a number I don't recognize. For a split second, I consider ignoring it, but there's a far-fetched hope in the back of my mind that hopes its Nolan. I don't know why. There's nothing to give me any indication that it could be. He probably doesn't even know my name or who I am, but hope has a funny way of playing tricks on my brain, especially when I've been drinking and taking pills.

In the darkness where I sit on the dusty floor, my

phone illuminates the room. I click into the message, and turn the sound all the way up. There's the haunting sound of the crunching. Crunch. Crunch. Crunch. I know instantly it's Shira's video from the bathroom. But this time I see images, someone's feet, leather tattered work boots, and they're trudging through heavy weeds and dead leaves. The camera shifts to the man's face, but only for a moment. He's got a black mustache, and pitted skin like craters on the moon. He's not saying anything at first. There's only breathing, rapid gasps like he's nervous and trying to take in more air to steady himself. The footage moves to a mangled car.

A car I know, my mother's car.

It's totaled, the entire thing smashed like it went through a garbage compacter. Then, even though I know it's coming, the man says the words I'm dreading. "Wowza, that must've hurt. She's not so pretty anymore." My stomach lurches once I hear it, but nothing prepares me for what I see next.

It's her. She's wearing that red and yellow flowered dress that I can still picture her in, just as I had the night she died before she kissed me on the cheek and walked out the door forever, the flowy fabric fluttering behind her as she got into her car and left. But the dress looks nothing like my memories. It's ripped apart and filthy, parts of it burned, and exposing her bra and the bare, bloodied skin on her décolleté. The camera shifts some more, closes in on an image I never should've seen, something that's bound to haunt me for the rest of my life.

"No, no, no, no," I wail, throwing my phone across the room with such force that it hits the wall, and explodes into a million pieces. I'm seething, hysterical, and my entire head is on fire. I'm shrieking as I sit there in the dark, like I'm in the middle of a horror flick, and a masked murderer has just discovered where I'm hiding. I don't realize I'm still screaming until my voice gives out, my mouth still open but nothing coming out anymore.

There's disbelief in my utter panic, like I can't believe what I've just seen. I don't know what sick person would send something so horrific to me, but if I ever find out, I'll wrap my hands around their throat until they stop breathing.

Outside the wind is howling, and storm sirens wail through the air. All I want is to get away from myself, this house, my life, but this storm is bringing everything to a halt, trapping me in this hell. Because there's no other escape, I choke down more pills while the tears pour down my cheeks, and then after a while, stumble back to my mother's writing desk for a pen and paper. I light dozens of tea lights around the room, on the floor around her bed, on her dresser, bedside table, desk, and then sit down to write.

Dear Dad,

I know what you're thinking. You're somehow thinking that this is your fault, but it's not. There was nothing you could've said or done to save me or change this final act. I can't live without my mother. I've tried and I can't, plain and simple. These last few months have been a battle, a battle of my mind, and a battle to defend her. As much as I want to stay and fight to preserve her memory, I've realized I don't have it in me to. I'm much too fragile, and I'm much too weak. All I want now is to be wherever she is. I'm sorry for hurting you, but I have to go. Hope someday you understand.

Love,

Sosie

I fold the letter and gaze around the room, taking in the scene. There's something so Shakespearian about it, the way the candles create such a dramatic and creepy ambiance, the way the wind resonates like an orchestra, slamming into the roof and windowpanes.

I lay down on my mother's bed as the pills take effect. I feel like a poison laden Juliet waiting for her Romeo. The strangest things come to mind as I close my eyes. I see Mrs. Filipio and my father in bed and naked underneath the sheets. I can see her just as I had that day when I was seven years old, her honker nose and her sexed up hair, shrieking when she sees me, my father laying beside her with his hairy chest and gold chain around his neck, the room stinking of sweat.

Suddenly, I'm that little girl again, and I'm gutted, crushed. "I'm-I'm sorry," I'm saying, covering my eyes and running out.

I can hear Mrs. Filipio swearing under her breath. "Fuck, fuck, fucking shit," she's saying.

"Relax," I hear my father say. "She doesn't even know what she just saw."

"She fucking knows what she just saw, okay? She's not an idiot."

Mrs. Filipio was right. I did know what I saw. I locked myself in the downstairs bathroom, hot beads of sweat trickling down my back and on the bulb of my nose, crying and wondering if I should tell my mother or not. Mrs. Filipio knocked on the door, trying to explain, and trying to coax me out.

"Sosie, are you in there, honey? I know you're upset. Come on out, so we can talk," she said.

I couldn't breathe, and with each persistent knock, the room began to close in on me. It was summertime, and I climbed out the window in a desperate attempt to flee, falling hard onto my butt as I tumbled out the first story window, a bush breaking my fall. I lost my breath for a moment, the wind knocked out of me, but I didn't waste time. I started running as fast as

I could.

I ran for blocks and blocks with no idea where I was going. Tears were streaming down my face, a hot flood of wetness soaking my puffy cheeks and the front of my cotton sundress. I kept looking behind me, scared they would come looking for me at any moment, but when hours went by and no one came, I grew scared that no one cared if I was gone and even more petrified that no one loved me.

I sat on the curb of a random neighbor's lawn, waiting and waiting, my feet bare and dirty from not bothering to put any shoes on before I fled. The homeowner eventually opened the front door and discovered me, an old man with pants pulled up to his ribs and his shirt neatly tucked in. "Are you okay, girl?" he called out from the porch. "You need a Band-Aid? A glass of water?" It spooked me, left me feeling embarrassed, so I got up and sauntered home.

When I finally did walk in the door, hours after I'd run off, my mother was there, lazily lying on the couch and watching Wheel of Fortune. "Where were you?" she asked, her hair wrapped in a towel turban like she'd just showered. "Were you playing with Johnny?" The words were on the tip of my tongue. They were about to come tumbling out, but instead I found myself weakly nodding. I started for the stairs, in a rush to lock myself away in my bedroom so I could cry myself to sleep. "Your father left for a business trip," she called after me. I paused where I stood. "He won't be back for a few weeks."

That was the beginning of him being gone for good, of him leaving her and leaving us. The business trips got longer and longer, until the year I turned fourteen, and he eventually stopped coming home altogether, just a few hours here and there when he was in town for work.

I never did tell my mother about what I saw, but she eventually figured it out for herself when she was stripping the sheets on the bed weeks later and discovered one of Mrs. Filipio's spidery false eyelashes. Needless to say, Mrs. Filipio kept her distance from us after that, terrified of my crazy mother, and probably more terrified I'd spill the beans to Johnny. I never did, even though I thought about it many times over the years. I was too afraid he wouldn't believe me and end up hating me forever.

I shake myself out of the dream, my hand trembling as I stuff more pills into my mouth. Within minutes my lips are tingly and warm, and my brain gets fuzzy. My eyes start to close shortly after that, heavy and slow.

As I begin to slip away into the heaviest sleep of my life, the storm sirens outside have grown even louder than before. They sound like the devil and his posse coming to get me and take me away. I get scared, my body shaking, convulsing, maybe from fright, maybe because I'm dying. But suddenly, I don't want to die. I'm trying to speak, but there's no one there to help me. It's too late anyway. I'm slipping away. It feels out of body, like my ghost is hovering above my body, watching me struggle, but doing nothing about it.

Then, I manage to say something. "Help me," I croak. "Mom, please help me. Don't let me die."

Chapter Five

At first, I don't know if I'm alive or dead. My lips and eyes are glued shut from tears and vomit, and I'm trembling and cold. If I'm dead then I'm in hell because my mother isn't here, holding me.

I roll side-to-side, aching in pain and moaning. "Help me," I whimper, but the only response is the floor creaking. Somehow, I've ended up there. I cough, gasp for breath, and struggle to open my eyes. It's dark, and the candles have long burned out. "Mom?" I say, desperately, my head throbbing. "Mom, I'm scared." But no one is there. Then, as I'm calling out for her, the images of her lying in a mangled heap in that flowered dress comes flooding back. "No, no, no," I wail, curling up in the fetal position where I cry myself back to sleep.

When I awaken, light streams in from my bedroom window, laser precise, bright and concentrated into my eyes. I rub them, trying to get relief. My stomach grumbles for food, water, anything to settle it. I slowly brace myself onto my elbows and look around. Pools of dried vomit are all over the floor, and the whole room smells of urine. I force myself to stand, the sensation coming back into my arms and legs at once and feeling like a thousand spiders scurrying all over my skin. I change my clothes, find some bottled water, and drag myself down the steps, using the walls, railings, anything I can to keep myself upright.

The front window in the living room has been demolished. There's glass all over the soggy carpet and couches, and the wind is blowing in and rustling up the debris and dust into a cloud around me. I stand there, blankly in the empty frame of the window, letting the cold breeze hit my face, my bare feet standing atop the broken glass, and my mind barely processing what happened while I almost died.

It looks like an apocalypse outside. Cars are overturned, entire trees uprooted and split open, their branches and bark spattered all over the place. Homes have burned, and electrical-wire fires have corroded holes into the concrete, leaving everything smelling like a barbeque, rotting sewage, and metal all at the same time.

I put on a jacket and some shoes and go outside to the backyard. All of the windows along the back of the house are shattered, and the sun deck is cracked in half. The old tree house my father built crashed through the garage roof, destroying it along with my car that was parked inside. Shingles and aluminum siding exploded all the way into my next-door neighbor's yard.

Everything's a mess, and nearly everything around me is destroyed. But as I stand there looking at it all, I find myself smiling, pleased. Finally, the world staring back at me reflects the world that's been living inside me for the last few months. Maybe it's the end of the world, but I don't care. A world with so much destruction is a world I can exist in. In a haze, I go back inside for my messenger bag, grab the picture of my mother and the mysterious man in front of the grey house, and set out to finish what I started the other night. I'm going to see that house.

A neighbor who I've never spoken to is in his front yard picking up broken branches and putting them in an industrial-sized garbage bag. He's wearing a rain parka with the hood tied tightly in a bow, his face barely peaking out.

"That hurricane was something else," he says, as I walk by. His voice comes out husky, his cheeks red and chapped like an old sailor who's spent his life out at sea.

"It was," I say, stopping to talk for a moment.

"Damage all over the place. You know the water came up, right up over the boardwalk on Long Beach and busted it all up. Destroyed it. The eye must've hit it just right."

"Must've," I repeat, like an echo.

"And the subway stations in the city—flooded. Did you see that on the news?"

"Nope."

He chuckles. "Me neither. Still ain't got no power, but my buddy told me about it. Boy, oh boy. That'll cost a pretty penny to fix, not to mention how long it'll take. You know, they're saying the boardwalk could take a year, maybe more, to repair," he says, shaking his head in pity. "What a shame, what a shame."

"I'd like to go see it," I say.

"What's that?" he asks, shouting over the garbage bag that's rustling in the wind.

"The boardwalk in Long Beach."

"Good luck with that! Ain't no cars getting in or out of Long Beach right now. Totally shut down. Dunzo. Streets are flooded with sand and sea. And you shouldn't walk there, not with these wires and all sorts of other stuff lying about. I doubt you'll make it a few blocks before you have to turn right back around." He goes back to cleaning up the branches, and I start to walk away. "You're not thinking of going there now, are ya?"

"No. Not yet," I murmur. "I've got something to take care of first, but after. Definitely after."

The boardwalk was always a special place for my mother and I. Every summer, on opening weekend, we'd pack a cooler, lather ourselves up in sunscreen, and spend the day on the beach. When we got too hot from the sun, we'd take a walk along the boardwalk where we'd stop for ice cream from the Mr. Softee truck and get cherry dipped vanilla cones. Then, as we ate our ice cream, we'd stop to sit on a bench and people watch, making up stories about what we imagined these people's lives were like. My mother would say, "That girl in the neon green bathing suit over there. What's her story?" And I'd say something like, "She's waiting for her boyfriend to pick her up. He's probably going to propose tonight, but she doesn't want to get married. She secretly wants to run away and be a movie star." My mother would laugh, a hearty cackle in the back of her throat while she tilted her head back. "You are most definitely my daughter," she'd say. "Because that's precisely what I was thinking."

Even though there's probably nothing left of the boardwalk, I want to see it. I need to. I need to see anything that'll bring her back to me.

"Well, be careful," the neighbor says, looking concerned. "You know there are trees falling on people. Trees! Can you imagine? Some girl about your age was out walking her dog, you know just checking things out after the storm, and bam! Tree falls right on her and kills her instantly." He claps his hands in front of his face for emphasis. "You really should just go home, if you're smart."

I don't heed his advice and instead start making my way toward the house on Waverly Place. I'm hoping there will be answers there, someone to talk to who might be able to tell me who the man with his arms wrapped around my mother is. My heart thumps in my chest, the anticipation of who might live there or what I might discover, is almost too much for my still bleary brain. While I walk, the branches above crack against the persisting wind. It doesn't take me long to become paranoid and preoccupied with thoughts of falling trees. With every snap, I imagine myself like the Wicked Witch of the West, legs sticking out from underneath a giant tree trunk, dead and smushed, and how my caved in skull might look when the rescuers come and roll the tree off. Soon, I'm running and jumping over broken branches, dodging between flipped over cars, hopping over live wires, manic, and trying to get away from the images flooding my head.

I leap over a broken post, my shoes coming down in a squishy thud, slowed by a tugging, a nipping at my heels. "Get off," I wail, convinced the ground is trapping me, taking me down into a sinkhole. "Leave me alone!" I trip and fall, my hands and knees stuck in the mud and muck. A little brown dog stares into my eyes, wagging its tail. He noses me in the face, urging me to get up. "Tippy," I whisper, as I pet the little dog. "I've missed you. Where's mom? Take me to her."

"Charlie!" a man yells, running over and scooping up the dog. "I'm so sorry. He always wiggles out of his collar. Are you okay?"

"I'm okay," I mumble.

I get up, brush myself off, and discover I'm standing at the end of the street where the grey house resides. Rubbing my eyes, I focus harder, trying to concentrate my dazed mind, but as I peer into the distance, staring back at me is a shell of what the house used to look like. Half of the house is burned, black with soot, including those lovely white shutters, while the other half has a giant tree branch that's crashed straight through the front door. It's empty, abandoned, no signs of life or anyone to speak to. My head is pounding, my heart, too. "This can't be happening," I whisper, as I walk in a trance toward it.

I stop on the scorched grass out front, my knees weak as I stare at the demolished house in front of me. "Where are you, Mom?" I ask, losing it, and bursting into tears. "What are you trying to tell me?" The only answer is the whistle of the wind through a torn curtain hanging out of a second story window. My eyes make their way up to it, and I watch it blowing. In a haze, I stand there, staring at it for I don't know how long, but it's long enough for the sound of the whistle to turn into a crunch and for the images of my mother from the video to come flooding back. "No, go away, go away," I say, shaking my head all around, trying desperately to rid myself of the vision. It finally floats away, leaves me alone, but I'm not at peace. I'm far from peaceful.

The neighborhood is quiet, everyone still gone, as I enter the demolished house through a burnt-out window on the first floor. Maybe she's here somehow, somewhere in these walls in another photograph, a piece of clothing, anything that might give me a clue about what the picture meant.

My feet crush through broken glass and soot as I make my way around a small bedroom. There's a crib covered in black ash, and broken knickknacks all over the place. I bend down and pick up what's left of a ceramic figurine of a mother holding a child. I stand up and examine it, my fingers gently touching the faded glass. Beneath the crack of a door there's movement, steps, as the door slowly creaks open. Adrenaline rushes up my spine, and I make a break for the window.

"Hey, stop. Wait, wait!" someone yells. I'm about to climb through the window, make my escape, when my leg is jerked from behind, pulling me back inside. "It's okay, just wait," a boy tells me, as he catches his breath. He's about my age, and he's staring straight into me with his brown doe-like eyes. There's a kindness to him, gentleness in the way he helps me to my feet. "Are you all right?"

"Who are you?" I dust off my hands on the sides of my jeans. "Do you live here?"

His eyes widen, and he chuckles. "Shouldn't I be asking you the same thing?" He waits for me to answer, but I remain silent. "No, I don't live here, haven't in years, but I used to. I'm just here to see what's left of my childhood home. Call me nostalgic," he jokes, but I don't laugh.

"Do you know who lives here now?"

"No, I'm sorry," he says, apologetically. "Not anymore."

"Me," I say. "My name is Angie Anders, and I live here, and you're trespassing on my property. You should go," I warn, but he doesn't budge. "Leave or I'm calling the cops."

"If this is your property than why did you run?" he asks, and I roll my eyes. "I happen to know for a fact that's a lie anyway. You're Sosie Friedman. What's up, Sosie, I'm Jamie Roland." He extends his hand to me, but I cross my arms across my chest instead.

"Listen, if you think you know me from some segment you saw on the local news station or from some gossip around town, you don't know shit, okay?"

"Wow." He scratches his temple, his eyebrows raised. "You don't have to be so hostile. I'm a friend."

"I don't even know you," I snap. "I've got to go. Now would you please just let me leave?" I start for the window, but he stops me.

"Wait, Sosie." The way he says my name, the softness in the tone of his voice as he speaks, gives me pause. "I don't know you from any news reports, okay? I knew your mother." I swallow hard and turn around to face him. It's what I've been waiting for, but a shiver of fear washes over me. "Your mother and my father were dating, in love, before she died. I'm sorry about your mom dying," he offers.

Instinctively, I touch my messenger bag where

the photograph of her is tucked away. I unzip the bag and take it out, my hand trembling as I hand it to him. "I found this in my mother's writing desk. Is this your father?" I ask.

"Yes, that's my dad," he says, holding the picture up. "I think that was taken right after my mom and I moved out of here, across town." He takes a closer look. "Yeah, he's got that beard, and he only rocked it for one summer. That beard used to piss my mom off so much." He laughs. He hands the photograph back to me, and I put it in my bag.

"What's his name?"

"Samuel Roland, but everyone just calls him Sam."

My face wilts. I'd heard that name before. I'd heard it when my mother whispered it into the phone receiver late one night the summer before she died.

****

"I don't know what to do anymore, Sammy. You're the only one who really knows me," I heard her say on that balmy night, as she cupped her hand over the phone, speaking softly. She was lying in bed, her back propped up on a pillow, reading glasses on. When she saw me, she quickly hung up. "I've got to go," she said, and put the phone down.

"Who were you just talking to?" I asked accusingly, standing there in my pajamas.

"My therapist, Sosie, not that it's any of your business."

There were other instances, too. Once when she was outside gardening, I'd watched her from the window as she made phone calls from the cordless telephone in between watering the rows of tomato vines. I'd become curious when I saw her conversing so animatedly. I picked up the phone in the kitchen and listened in, hearing her say, "Sammy, I miss you, but I can't make it on Wednesday. Sosie has a piano concert. Forgive me." There was a long pause, a sigh. Before anyone responded, my mother said, "Sosie? Did you pick up the phone? Please hang it up now." I was startled and quickly did as I was told.

Then there was the time when she locked herself in the bathroom with the phone on the night I saw my father with Mrs. Filipio. "Sammy," I heard her saying. "He left again. This time for weeks."

Each time I'd pushed my curiosity away. I never questioned her. I didn't feel I had a reason to. We told each other everything. No secrets, only truth. She used to say, "You can count on me, Sosie. I know your father isn't around, and he's off doing whatever he does, but we don't need him. All we need is you and me." She'd clasp our hands together and kiss my forehead. "I'd never lie to you, and I'd never leave you. Not like him."

"No," I say, shaking my head at Jamie. "My mother wasn't dating anyone. She would have told me if she was, especially if it was serious. I just don't see how it's possible."

"It's possible," he assures me. "Look, if it makes you feel any better, I didn't know about them either until last summer. My dad and I had a complicated relationship up until recently. Bad divorce when I was a kid," he explains. "Anyway, when my dad came back into my life, that's when I met your mom, and no, I didn't know her long, but I know she wasn't the monster people are saying she was. She was a good person."

"She was the best person I've ever known," I whisper, my voice trailing off. "If your dad doesn't live here anymore, where is he?"

"Michigan. Sold the house and moved there after your mom passed away. He said everything reminded him of her, and he needed to get away. They had too many hopes and dreams for their future. Sosie, your mom wanted to give you a little sister."

I back up slowly, my hand out to stop him. "No. No, you're lying. This isn't what it seems. It isn't what you're saying. You're fucking with me. Are you the one who sent me that video of my mother? You're the one, aren't you?" I lurch at him, pounding my fists into his chest, about to make good on my word and wrap my hands around his throat. He holds my hands apart, his strength surprising me. "Get off me. Leave me alone. Stay away," I scream, and run away, leaping out the window in which I came.

Chapter Six

I run all the way to the boardwalk in Long Beach, Jamie's voice in my head the whole time, his words on an ominous loop, torturing me. "Sosie, your mom wanted to give you a little sister." I keep hearing him say it, over and over again.

"Push it away," I tell myself. "He's lying. It's not true. Don't believe a word."

My feet are soaking wet and heavy from the sand that covers the roadways and sidewalks. I shiver through my paper-thin jacket, but keep running toward the only significant place left where I might find her, hear her, reach her.

"Hey! Hey! You can't do that!" A man calls out as I duck underneath yellow caution tape and step onto the wooden planks of the boardwalk. "Hey, you! Stop right there!"

I take my first step, and my foot slips beneath me, the slats like pieces to a Jenga tower that are about to collapse into a crisscrossed heap. Through gaping holes in the wood, the sea comes crashing up, still angry and violent, like it's looking for a fight. Water sprays me in the face, blinding me. I wipe it away, ready for retaliation and willing to face this demon, but I lose my balance for a moment, swaying side to side. Digging my heels in, I catch myself, my arms out like a tightrope walker. When I'm steady on my feet, I pull out the photograph from my bag and hold it to my chest. "Where are you mom?" I scream, the picture clutched tightly to my heart. "This is killing me. I need you," I sob. "I know you'd never lie to me. You promised you'd never lie."

"Hey, get out of there, or I'm calling the cops!" The man appears, closer now but behind the safety of a railing. "What are you trying to do, get yourself killed?"

His shouting shifts my attention, and I lose balance again. I reach for something to grab onto, but when I do, the picture is whisked out of my hand and eaten by the ocean. "No!" I wail, almost leaping off the side as I watch it disappear.

"That's it, I'm calling the cops," the man threatens, pulling out a cell phone.

I quickly scoot back underneath the tape and take off in the other direction, running until the boardwalk is nowhere in sight.

Up ahead, Red Cross volunteers stand outside an old church, giving out bagged lunches and supplies. People line up around the block, and I get in line, too, mostly because I don't want to be alone or go home. I could cry, but numbness consumes me. I'm too tired and spent.

As I wait my turn, conversations buzz around me—some have no power, some have cars that have floated away, and some have houses that are flooded and have lost everything. I keep to myself, and they don't know I've lost everything, too, just in a different way.

A lady with a friendly, warm smile hands me my brown bag and bottle of water when I get to the front of the line. I take it from her and linger. Question marks float in her eyes, and she shifts uncomfortably on her feet as I stand there, fighting the urge to give her a hug. She has no idea how badly I need one. "Need anything else?" she asks.

I say nothing and instead shuffle away.

A few stars peak behind the lingering storm clouds and the sky has now turned dark. I stop and sit on a nearby bench. I gobble the sandwich in three greedy bites then swig the water down my throat. I hadn't realized how hungry I was. My stomach gurgles and aches from the shock of being fed. When my belly settles, I slog about town, kicking an empty plastic bottle with my soaking wet shoe. Each time I think of going home, a clammy sweat beads on the back of my neck and a wave of panic shoots through my chest. I can't return to that dark and empty house where the visions from the video are bound to come rushing back.

I kick the plastic bottle again, dead inside, lost. A voice rings in the back of my head. "Party at 185 Park Place!" My head tilts in thought. Would it be completely crazy to go?

****

I can't recall how I got there, but I somehow find myself at the corner of Park Place and Long Beach Boulevard. I creep for a while with no direction, no plan. Then, something catches my eye.

In front of a five-story, salmon colored apartment building sits a crumpled bicycle identical to Nolan's. I slowly make my way over to it, my eyes scouring every which way before I approach it. There's barely anything left of it, just a bent frame and busted wheels still fashioned to bike rack that's somehow managed to survive, but I can still see parts of the unique yellow spokes. I glance up at the building number overhead. 185. Sure enough, though the numbers are tilted and askew, the paint rusted and weathered.

"You look like you could use a smoke." My heart jumps to my throat. No one was there a minute before, but now a girl appears behind me, and my eyes struggle to focus on her face in the dark.

I squint, the streetlamps blinding me when I realize it's Nolan's friend, the girl with the flowy red hair.

She holds out a pack of cigarettes in front of her. "You want?" she asks, with a lighter in her other hand, ready to go.

"Sure." I put the cigarette up to my mouth, my hand shaking with shock that she's here in the flesh, and that I hadn't heard her coming. She lights it for me, and I inhale deeply. "Thanks for this," I say, savoring every puff of glorious nicotine. "I needed it. Badly."

"No worries." She shrugs, casually.

She's even prettier up close with her golden-brown eyes, accentuated with a simple flick of black cat-eye liner, and these adorable freckles that run along the bridge of her turned up nose. She's the type of girl who could probably have any guy she wants or steal your boyfriend if she wanted to. She's that pretty, that cool. She smokes her cigarette, sucking on it, and then twisting it between her middle and pointer finger that are painted in deep purple nail polish.

"I'm Sosie, by the way," I announce, between puffs.

"Casey." She grabs my hand for a sturdy handshake. "This is all so crazy, right?"

"The hurricane?"

"Yeah, the hurricane, what else?" She blows smoke into a doughnut shape. I watch her form, impressed. "You live around here?"

"Sort of," I answer. "But more west."

"Wasn't as bad over there, no?"

"Not this bad."

"You should've seen it two days ago. This is an improvement by a long shot. The National Guard was in here with their tanks and shit, trying to clean up. It's been an insane couple of days. Still don't have any running water." Casey sucks hard on her cigarette again. "Did you walk all the way here from the west side?" she asks, eyeing my feet.

"Yep."

"You're insane!" she exclaims.

"I didn't have much of a choice. My car was crushed by a tree house, and from what I've been told, no cars are getting in or out of here."

"It's true." She chokes on smoke while she's talking. "But a tree house?" she asks, cracking up. "I'm sorry, I'm sorry, I don't mean to laugh, but that's seriously crazy! My car is probably somewhere in Montauk by now. Hope insurance will cover it, or I'm totally screwed." She finishes the last bit of her cigarette. "Did you see the boats? There are literal boats on people's lawns and shit. They got swept up from the docks, and landed all over Long Beach in the most random places. Can you believe that?"

I stomp on the butt of my cigarette, and before I know it, she's ready with another for the both of us.

"You sure?" I ask, before accepting.

"Course. So, why'd you walk all the way over here from the west side?" she asks.

"Just wanted to check out the boardwalk." Jamie's voice resounds in my head again, and my mother's expression in the photograph flashes in front of me. I close my eyes and push it away, all the way down to the pit of my soul. "I heard it was demolished, but I wanted to see for myself. Hey, you don't happen to know whose bike this is, do you?"

"I think you mean, was? Ha!" She jokes, as she kicks what's left of the busted tire. "I guess that's what you get for leaving your precious baby outside before a hurricane hits. Idiot. Anyway, yeah, it's this kid, Nolan Sawyer's. He stays with my friend Terry from time to time. Terry lives across the hall from me," she explains. "Why, you know Nolan?"

"Sort of," I say, without elaborating.

"I was just about to go upstairs, actually. I think he's there." Her eyes linger on me. "He owes me a smoke. Do you want to come up and say hey?"

I swallow hard. This is it. "Sure," I say, nonchalantly.

Casey takes me through the lobby of the building. I hold my breath to keep from gagging on the smell of rotten sewage and sour seawater that permeates the air. Huge buckets are set up all around and collecting water that's leaking from the ceiling. We step over piles of ripped up carpet and heavy polyester drapes covered in sand that are lying in heaps all over the place.

"Sorry, we have to take the stairs," Casey explains, opening a door to a dark stairwell. "Elevator's still out. Luckily, the lobby and the first three floors are running on a generator." She glances back at me as she climbs two stairs at a time, and I struggle to keep up. Smoking two measly cigarettes has left me out of breath. "I'm on three by the way. So's Terry."

We stop at Casey's apartment first. It's a tiny studio, with a mattress, no bedframe or formal bedding, sitting in the middle of the room. She has a small efficiency kitchen, just a two-burner stove, and a small sink and mini fridge.

"Welcome, to my lovely abode." She takes her coat off to reveal voluptuous breasts and a tiny waist accentuated by a tight, V-neck sweater. "Here, let me give you the grand tour," she says, sarcastically. "Here's my bedroom, bathroom, and kitchen. There, done."

"You're lucky you're right by the beach, though," I point out.

"Yeah, it was cool until about three days ago. Go on, sit down," she urges. I look at my options: her unmade bed or a dilapidated beanie chair. I choose the beanie chair and plop down. "Take your coat off," she instructs. I do as I'm told, praying I look halfway presentable. I got dressed in such a daze this morning.

"Want something to drink? I think all I've got is semi-stale beer."

"Semi-stale beer sounds amazing," I answer, as she retrieves a couple of beers from the mini fridge and pops the tops off with a bottle opener. She hands me one, and I start guzzling it right away.

She holds out her bottle, waiting for me to finish. "Geez. Cheers," she says, clinking her bottle to mine while it's still up to my lips.

"Sorry, so thirsty."

"Hey, what size shoes do you wear?" she asks, staring at my soaking wet feet.

"Seven and a half."

"I had a feeling." She walks over to a closet, and begins digging through a pile of mismatched shoes. "Here we go," she says, retrieving a pair of beaten up Doc Martens. She tosses them to me, and then goes to lie down on her bed. "Sorry, they're ancient, but you can't walk all the way back to the west side in those things."

"Are you sure?" I ask.

"One hundred percent. This whole hurricane thing's got me feeling all charitable and shit."

I remove my wet socks and Chuck Taylors, and put the boots on. They feel glorious and dry. "Thank you," I say. Something catches my eye on the wall. "Hey, do you cross-stitch?" A framed embroidery design is displayed next to her bed.

"My sister," she says. "She sells them in SoHo at these art fairs they have on the weekends. They all have little sayings or song quotes. She's made me a bunch. That's just one of them."

I get up to get a closer look. In a little, round wooden frame, there's an intricate stitching of a polka dot bowtie with a tiny Polaroid camera as the center knot. Beneath the needlework is a song quote in cursive writing. I know the phrase immediately. "You must be a Simon and Garfunkel fan."

"Huge." Her lips purse together. "I'm impressed. I don't think any of my friends even knows who Simon and Garfunkel is."

"I collect their old vinyls." I explain. "And I've read every single thing ever written about them. It's really Garfunkel's fault they broke up, not Simon's, contrary to popular belief. Everyone just assumes it was Paul's fault because he's the one who went on to have a successful solo career. Sorry, I'm, like, totally obsessed with them." My fingertips lightly trace across the stitching. *"America* happens to be one of my favorite songs." I can almost hear the melody playing in my head.

"Same!" She splays across the bed to give me a high five. "I have a feeling we're going to get along very well." After we slap hands, she rolls onto her back, stretching. I can't stop looking at how she makes such a simple thing look so sensual. "So, how long have you known Nolan?" she suddenly asks.

"Not too long, actually. He's in my AP English Lit class at school," I explain, sitting back down on the beanie chair.

"Oh, so you're one of his high school friends," she says. "He doesn't have many over there, from what I hear. He's always saying that everyone sucks at Bolton Academy."

"Everyone does suck," I say, rolling my eyes.

She giggles. "Bolton Academy, though. You fancy," she jokes.

"It's all my father's doing. He went there, and spending an obscene amount of money on my high school education makes him feel like less of a shitty dad. I hate it there, though, for the record."

"Ugh. I feel you. I hated high school, too,

graduated three years ago." She checks me out up and down. "So, you like him?" she asks.

"Who?"

"Nolan. Duh."

I swallow hard, not expecting her to be so direct. "Kind of." I feel an obligation to be honest, though, I'm not sure why. "I mean. I don't really know him." She doesn't say anything for a moment, and I start itching with paranoia. "Shit. I didn't mean to … like, I'm not trying to steal anyone's boyfriend here. Is he your boyfriend or something? Oh my God, I'm literally so embarrassed. You've been so nice to me with the beer and boots and everything, and here I am acting like a total asshole."

"Whoa. Relax," she interrupts, before I escalate any more. "He's not my boyfriend. He's like a younger brother to me. He's a baby. "Do you ever smoke pot? Because I feel like some pot would make a world of difference for you. You're wound super, super tight."

"I've only smoked a couple of times," I tell her. "I'm more of a prescription pill popper."

"Seriously?" She looks a little horrified. I nod, owning it. "You high school girls start younger and younger, I swear. Just so you know, I'm not about any pill popping life." She's serious, firm. "I'm more of an organic, you know, stuff grown from the ground sort of girl."

"Don't worry, I don't have anything on me. Plus, I'm trying to turn over a new leaf anyway." Flashbacks from a couple nights earlier come barreling back. I see myself stuffing pills into my mouth, chugging it down with booze. I get a sickening feeling in back of my throat, remembering.

"Hey. Do you want to go see what those assholes are doing or what?" She stands up and puts out her hand, helping me out of the chair. Butterflies skip inside my belly. It's now or never. "I'm just warning you, Terry is kind of a douche, so if he acts like a total ass, you can't say I didn't warn you. Whatever. You'll see for yourself."

We walk across the hall, and Casey knocks three times on Terry's door. A few seconds later the peephole makes a sliding sound as someone peers out. Casey rolls her eyes, and knocks again.

"I can see the light shining through, and I can hear you breathing," Casey says.

The lock clicks, and Terry opens the door, wearing nothing but a towel.

"You're such a loud mouth breather," she tells him. "You're like a grizzly bear."

"Deviated septum," he says, leaning against the doorframe. "Hello to you, too."

He's grinning wide, his perfect teeth on full display. I can tell he's cocky, like the kind of guy who lost his virginity when he was fifteen to his hot tenth grade math teacher, cocky. He stretches a little, his abs flexing.

"What are you up to?" Casey asks.

"Well, I was just in the middle of giving myself a sponge bath," he boasts, running his hands through his sandy colored hair.

"That would explain the dry hair," Casey says, unimpressed. "Giving yourself a sponge bath with what exactly?"

"A wash cloth and Poland Spring," he answers proudly, again with a flashy smile.

"So, you're wasting your precious bottled water on washing your dick? You would. Are you going to invite us in or not?" she asks, drumming her fingers along the door.

He slinks away from the doorframe and motions for us to come in. "And you are?" he asks, as I step into the apartment.

"Sosie," I say, putting my hand out to shake.

He holds the towel around his waist closed and gives me an air kiss on the cheek instead. "I'd shake your hand, but then my towel might fall off."

"Ew. You're such a creeper," Casey says, making a gagging noise, as she pushes me along down the hallway.

As we walk in, Nolan is at the end of the hall, sitting on a couch, and bending over a coffee table. Our eyes meet. He squints like he's trying to get a closer look, and then quickly looks away.

My heart drops and I feel like an idiot. "Hey," I say, waving to him. "What's up?"

"Nolan's rolling a joint, if you guys wanna have a quick smoke," Terry says.

"You wanna have a smoke?" Casey asks me.

"Uh, I don't know," I start to say, but Casey is already dragging me over to where Nolan is.

Terry briefly goes into the bathroom, and then reemerges wearing a pair of gym shorts and nothing else. I follow suit as Casey sits down on a loveseat across from the boys. Terry stretches his arms across the back of the couch like he's the king of a castle, as his potent aftershave wafts through the air. I rub my nose.

"I haven't seen you guys in a few days," Casey says. "Probably because you were sitting here finishing the dime bag I bought, but were too greedy to share with me. That's fucked up."

"C'mon, Case. We finished that bag forever ago. You know that," Terry says. "And we're sharing our stuff with you right now, so be happy."

"Be happy," Casey, repeats sarcastically.

"Whatever, Terry."

Nolan ignores them both and lights the joint. He's in no rush, taking a long toke, before passing it to Terry.

"Are you going to share that or not?" Casey asks.

Terry starts to hand it to her, and then holds it above her head so she can't reach. "I haven't decided yet."

"Plenty for everyone," Nolan says, his eyes meeting mine, but only for a second. Terry is still withholding from Casey. "Just let her have it, Terry."

Terry hands it to Casey and she takes a hit. "Yeah. Don't be an asshole, Terry." Casey holds the smoke in her mouth, and then lets it out into his face. When she finishes, she passes it to me. I put it up to my lips, and inhale deep.

"Man, I just wanna get out there and ride again," Terry says, taking the joint from between my fingers before I'm finished. "The other day was epic."

"I didn't tell you, but we rode the most incredible waves the other day," Casey tells me. "Right before the hurricane hit."

I open my mouth to speak, about to disclose that I saw them goofing off on the local news, but I glance at Nolan and change my mind. "No way," I say, instead. "Isn't that sort of dangerous?"

"Oh, yeah, of course," Terry agrees. "But it was also fucking awesome."

"I haven't surfed waves that big since Cali two years ago," Nolan says, his eyes already bloodshot, his southern drawl extra slow and extra thick.

"It was amazing. The swells were over our heads. But it was freezing. Just so, so cold," Terry tells me. "I froze my balls off, but it was worth it, because I'll probably never surf like that again in my entire life. I just want to relive that shit over and over."

"We didn't tell her the funniest part," Casey pipes in. Terry smirks as if he knows what's coming. "So, we're down on the beach, we've got our surfboards and everything, wet suits on, and other people are down there too, like, taking pictures and stuff. No one was really listening to the warnings or sirens or anything yet. And there were news reporters and stuff, you know, covering the storm, doing their thing, and all of the sudden, Terry comes up behind this news lady and starts, like, gyrating and sticking his tongue out. Poor lady didn't even realize what was happening until the camera guy started screaming, like, 'Get outta the shot. Get outta the shot, asshole!' Then, Terry's, like, "Party at 185 Park Place!" They all bust out laughing as they remember. "Then, Terry had all these randoms show up the day after the storm looking for a party!" Casey tells me, cracking up.

I'm willing my cheeks from getting red with embarrassment. "That's so crazy," I say. "Who even does that?"

"Right?" she agrees, laughing.

Terry's focus shifts to me. "So, how do you two know each other?" he asks, motioning to Casey and me.

"Sosie and I have been friends forever," Casey quickly says. Our eyes lock, I smile a little, and she gives me a brisk nod to let me know she's got my back.

"And I sort of know Nolan," I say. "We have a class together at Bolton Academy."

"Shit. You're in high school, too?" Terry asks, getting out some cigarette papers from a drawer in the coffee table. "Listen, you can smoke with us, but I don't want to get caught up in any parental drama, if you know what I mean. You weren't here, if anyone asks when you go home tonight. Got it?"

"No, she's cool, Terry," Casey assures. "Relax."

"You don't have to worry," I tell him. "My dad's

in London right now and doesn't give a shit about me anyway, and my mom died four months ago."

It gets quiet for a moment. They all look at each other, no one knowing what to say.

"So, what class do you guys have together?" Casey asks, changing the subject.

"AP English Lit," I answer.

"AP English Lit, no shit." Terry laughs, clearly amused. "My boy's a writer, didn't even know." Terry picks through the marijuana flowers and selects the good bits in the center of the cigarette papers. "Is he any good?"

"He's actually a very good writer," I answer. "He wrote an awesome poem about the ocean."

Terry rolls the joint, but stops just short of licking the paper to seal it. "A poem about the ocean? How sweet. Never knew you were some beatnik, homo-type," Terry jokes, but Nolan doesn't laugh. "I think if I remember correctly, I might've caught you writing something a couple of weeks back, now that I think of it. You left it in the bathroom next to the can. I guess you do your best work there." Terry pats Nolan on the back.

Nolan looks furious, mortified. He suddenly gets up and leaves the room.

I immediately regret saying anything, and I feel like a total fool for being here in the first place. I look to Casey, and she's mouthing, "It's okay," but it doesn't make me feel any better.

"Oh, come on, come back. Don't be so fucking sensitive. I'm joking around," Terry calls after him, but Nolan walks out the front door, slamming it behind him. We're all silent for a few moments. "He takes shit so seriously, I swear to God. Whatever, he'll be back later. He always comes back when Larry's around."

"Larry's his mom's new husband," Casey

explains. "Nolan hates his guts."

"You know, I should really get going," I say, standing up. "I have so much to clean up at my place. It's really bad over there, and I never meant to be gone this long."

"No, don't be silly," Casey says, trying to send me a silent message with her eyes. I pretend not to notice. "Hang out for a little bit. C'mon, it's pitch black out there. There aren't any streetlights or anything. You can't leave now."

"No seriously, I should go. I'll be fine. I know the way." I start for the door, but the buzz kicks in as soon as I'm up and moving. I concentrate on walking straight, even.

Casey gets up and follows me. "What are you doing, Sosie? Are you leaving because of him?" she whispers, when we're out of Terry's earshot. "C'mon, he always does this. He's just being moody. He's high and probably just tired. C'mon, stay. Please?"

"We've got whiskey," Terry announces from the couch. He has three tumblers sitting in front of him on the coffee table, and full bottle of Jack Daniels.

My palms begin to sweat at the sight of it. I never can resist Tennessee whiskey, and my supply is dry back at home. I groan, weakening.

"Do we have a taker?" Casey teases, as she see's me losing the mental battle. "I think we have a taker, folks."

"How can I say no to Jack?" I concede.

Chapter Seven

One drink turns into two drinks, and so on and so forth until we finish the bottle between the three of us. I pass out on the couch, and when I wake up, Casey and Terry are nowhere to be found. My bladder is full, panging and heavy. I stand up, bleary eyed, and go looking for somewhere to relieve myself. Half asleep, I push the bathroom door open.

"Can you give me a minute?" Nolan says, as he stands at the toilet, his back to me.

"Oh my God." I cover my eyes, mortified. "I am so, so sorry."

"Can you, like, leave?" he asks, giving it a good shake and zipping up his pants.

"Oh my God, I'm an idiot. Why am I still standing here? Yeah, yeah, of course. I'm sorry." I cringe as I shut the door behind me.

He emerges seconds later.

"I'm so sorry," I begin. "The light was off, and I just assumed no one was in there, and then I didn't even see you at first, and I thought you left hours ago, and I had way, way, way too much to drink..."

He's changed his clothes and is wearing a fresh white t-shirt, slim fit black jeans, and a gold watch on his wrist. His body shifts, ever so slightly, and a delicious and clean musky scent drifts my way.

"It's okay, I'm done. It's all yours," he says, a hint of annoyance in his tone. I start for the bathroom, and am about to close the door behind me. "I'm warning you, you can't flush the toilet, and there's still no water. It's pretty rank in there."

"Thanks for the warning." I shut the door behind me and exhale. "Oh my God, fuck my life," I whisper. "I'm an idiot, a fucking idiot."

He's right. The bathroom does reek of piss, so much so that I retch a little. And it's filthy. Little nasty hairs are all over the floor. There are dirty towels not hung up and slung over the sink. The toilet bowl is filled to the brim with yellow waste. I hold my breath as I hurry up and do my business.

When I finish, I ease the door open as quietly as possible and tiptoe down the hall with every intention of slipping out the front door, escaping unnoticed.

"If you're going to Casey's, she's, um, busy," Nolan's voice says, as I put my hand on the doorknob. I reluctantly turn around, and he's standing there, smoking a cigarette. "Want one?" he asks.

My stomach flip-flops that he's actually talking to me, and my tongue feels pasted in my mouth. "I'm good. It's late. I should really get going."

"You sure? At least have a smoke before your trek home."

He looks so sexy, slender muscles squeezed into his t-shirt, and that accent is so charming, inviting.

"I guess one won't hurt." I follow him down the hall, sitting across from him on the couch, my heart racing as he hands me a cigarette and chivalrously lights it for me. "Thank you," I say. "So, what do you mean Casey's busy?"

Nolan tries to hide a smile. "Listen, it's not my place to say."

"Is she with Terry?"

"Yep."

"And see, I sort of thought…"

"What? That they hated each other?" he asks, and I nod. "Yeah. They like to pretend they hate each other, but really, they can't stay away from each other. They're one of those couples that are sort of like, can't live with 'em, can't live without 'em. Know what I mean?"

"So they're a couple? Like, dating?"

"Oh, yeah. For some time now."

"Wow, didn't see that coming." The nicotine is starting to sober me, steadying my scrambled brain. I suck on the cigarette harder, my lips pursing around it tight. "I love American Spirit by the way."

"I've been smoking these since I was fourteen," he tells me, proudly. "My older brother bought me my first pack."

He's gazing at me, this time in my eyes. Instinctively, I begin fiddling with my hair. "Where are you from?" I ask. "The first time I ever heard you speak was in Mr. Russo's class the other day when you read your poem … which I loved by the way."

"I think you might've mentioned that a couple of times," he interjects with a laugh.

"Sorry, I didn't mean to be a total fangirl, but I really did like it," I joke. "But your accent took me by surprise. So where? Kentucky? North Carolina?"

He rolls his eyes but good-naturedly. "What's with all you Yankees always talking about my accent and asking where I'm from? Georgia. Peachtree City, Georgia."

"How did a good ol' country boy like you end up in Long Island at Bolton Academy?"

"It's a very long story for another time. Hey, do you want to go to a party with me?" he asks, changing the subject.

"Like, right now? What time is it?"

"Eh. It's only one-thirty."

"You want to go to a party now?" I ask, incredulously. "I'm guessing you don't have a curfew."

"Naw. My mom pretty much lets me do what I want, long as I stay out of her hair."

"Where would we even go to a party now?

Nothing's open, and everything's destroyed out there."

"Do you trust me?"

"Should I?" I ask, biting my lip.

"Absolutely," he says, with a grin.

****

Nolan leads the way outside in the pitch black. We dodge flooding, uprooted poles, wires, sand, and strewn branches. All of it is more sinister in the darkness than in the daylight. The side streets are the worst, with houses either torn apart or burned to the ground. We can't even get down some of the roads because there's so much garbage and debris. Casey was right about the boats. Boats—entire boats and pieces of boats—litter multiple lawns, turned on their sides like beached whales. We walk past the Long Island Railroad at the Long Beach station, and it sits idly on the tracks, dark, abandoned, and lonely.

"Where are we going, by the way?" I ask. "I know you said a party, but the farther we get from Terry's place, the worse it's getting out here." Tension mounts in my gut. "Hold on a second." I stop, waiting for him to notice. He turns around. "Are you taking me somewhere to murder me? Because, just so you know, I might look small and meager, but I'm fully capable of messing you up. I've got nails. And teeth."

"Why do I actually believe you?" Nolan ponders with a chuckle. "And no, I'm not taking you somewhere to murder you. I'm taking you to a warehouse on East Broadway for the best party ever, so relax. We're almost there." I wrap my jacket around me tighter, my shoulders shivering. "You cold?" He starts to take off his black leather jacket.

"No, no, I'm all right," I say, stopping him. "But that's a badass jacket."

"Was my brothers. Hey, watch your step." He

steers me away from a wire I'm about to step on, his hand on the small of my back.

I can't help it, a smile sweeps across my cheeks as I relish his touch.

We arrive at the warehouse party, the plain industrial building coming out of nowhere, glowing from the inside out like a beacon in the night.

Nolan escorts me inside, and there are hundreds of people of all ages, most in yesterday's clothes, who look like they haven't showered in a week, sand stuck to the grease on their faces and hairlines. It's like everyone who didn't escape Long Beach before the hurricane has gathered in this cold, cement building to forget about what little is left of their homes and lives. There isn't any electricity, so everyone has brought whatever battery-operated flashlights and lanterns they own, propping them up on old crates, along with lit candles in mason jars. The candlelight brings a peaceful and warm glow to the dingy surroundings, making it feel like a concert where people hold up lighters when a really good song starts playing. Despite the demolition of their town, everyone's in good spirits as they drink cheap cans of beer and sway to the music of impromptu bands, playing songs that everyone loves like *Heart of Gold* and *Sweet Caroline*.

"You were right. This is the best party ever," I tell Nolan, shouting over the noise.

"And you doubted me," he teases. "It's been happening for the last three nights now. It starts at 8 PM and goes until the next morning. Some people sleep here. They just put sleeping bags down wherever and fall asleep with all the noise going on around them. Isn't that crazy?"

"I guess for some people it's better than going home," I say, my voice trailing off.

"Do you want a beer?" he asks.

"Is anyone checking IDs?"

"Naw, not at all. Nobody's driving, because of the roads being shut down and whatnot, so everyone is being really cool about things."

"I'd love one."

I stay put while Nolan goes to a cooler to retrieve some beers. Two acoustic guitar players and a drummer have set up a three-man band off in a corner and are playing a soulful rendition of *The Sound of Silence*. A small crowd gathers around them, arms wrapped around each other as they sway and sing along to the harmonies.

"PBR?" Nolan appears, placing a cold beer in my hand.

I crack open the top, the cold liquid dripping all over my hand as I take a sip. "Ah, that's the good stuff."

"Nothing like a cold PBR."

"That's right!" I nudge him with my elbow. "I forgot you country folks love your PBR."

"You're not wrong, but how does a New Yorker like you even know that?"

"C'mon. One out of every three country songs has a PBR reference, am I right?" He smiles. "You know I'm right."

Nolan puts his hand over his mouth, chuckling. "Nice observation," he says, genuinely impressed. "But I wouldn't take you for a country music lover."

"I'm not, but my mother was," I say. "So, what's this place, like, when it's not the setting for the best party ever?"

"I think someone said it used to be a furniture warehouse or something like that, but it's been abandoned for years."

"I'm surprised the cops let this go on, you know. Seems like sort of a fire hazard with all the candles and stuff."

"You kidding me? The cops are here partying with the rest of us. All the rules sort of went out the window after the hurricane."

My eyes wander about the room as I sip my ice-cold beer, Nolan's head bopping along to the music in my peripheral vision. I close my eyes, taking in the harmonies and this solitary, peaceful moment where, for once, I'm not thinking of my mother or my pain. When I open them, my eyes meet his, and he half smiles, one side of his mouth turned up, a dimple revealing itself for the first time. It's unexplainable, this connection I feel to him, like we're kindred spirits. My heart recognized his from the very beginning, from the first time in class when I heard his poem. I reach over to grab his hand, but I'm pushed from behind instead, my head jerking forward in a whiplash.

"Are you Sosie Friedman?" A girl steps forward from her posse of five other teenage girls. All of them have heavily applied make-up with matching red lipstick and thick black eyeliner. She waits for me to answer, two of her friends snickering behind her. "Are you Sosie Friedman?" she asks again, this time more demanding. She runs her tongue along her top lip, revealing a mouthful of crowded teeth.

"Answer the question," one of her friends shouts on her behalf, while the rest huddle, heads together like they're conspiring.

"Why? Do you go to Bolton Academy or something?" I ask.

"Do we look some boujee ass bitches to you?" her friend retorts. "Are you Sosie Friedman or not?"

I think about saying no, and I think about lying and running away, but before I know it, words are coming out. "Yeah. Why?"

"I'm Laura Markle," the girl with the snaggled teeth says. She pauses to give me a minute. "Laura Markle," she says, again with more conviction, but I stare at her blankly. "My little brother was Bradley Markle," she says, suddenly bursting into tears. Her friends nervously glance at each other, like her breaking down wasn't part of the plan. "Does that even mean anything to you?" she barely spits out.

Laura's loudmouth friend appears at her side for support. "Your mother murdered her little brother. She drove the wrong way on purpose, and Bradley died because of it. Why don't you tell her you're sorry or something?"

A small group of people turns around to see what's going on, but quickly looks away or at the floor, not wanting to get involved.

"Because my mother didn't murder her little brother. It was an accident. I'm sorry about your little brother," I tell Laura. "But it wasn't my mother's fault."

"Oh, no. I know this bitch didn't just say that," Laura's friend barks to the clique behind her in an attempt to fire them up, but they all stare wide-eyed and unsure, watching us go back and forth.

Nolan comes forward and stands between Laura's friend and me. "Everybody just relax," he says, making a human barrier between us. "There's no need for this to get out of control, okay?"

But it's too late for that. My adrenaline is amped, and I'm wound too tight. I crane my neck to talk around the length of his body like he's not even there. "My mother didn't kill anyone!" I scream. "It was an accident! For the last fucking time, it was an accident! And anyone who doesn't believe that needs to get a fucking life!"

Without another word, Laura's friend grabs my

arm, her nails digging into my skin. I look down at my flesh that's turning white from her gripping me so hard. She's got a wild look in her eyes, and her friends are surrounding us in a huddle, as she drags me out of the warehouse. People are gawking, but doing nothing. Nolan fades farther and farther away, as a stranger, some man, blocks him from helping me. I'm fighting Laura's friend, lashing my arm away, trying to pull her hair, but at some point I give up and helplessly let them take me outside without protest. I listen to the crowds of voices wilt into the background as she hauls me onto the curb like a piece of garbage.

"Stay away, do you hear me?" Laura shouts, as her friend tries to kick me, but Laura stops her. "Just stay the fuck away."

****

"Stay away from her!" My mother screamed at Mrs. Filipio. "Just stay the fuck away."

When I was eight years old Mrs. Filipio and Johnny found me walking home by myself from school after my mother forgot to pick me up. It was a chilly afternoon in the late fall, when the days are long and grey and it turns to dusk in the late afternoon rather than dinnertime. I was crossing a busy intersection, shaking with fear as I waited for the walk sign to flash.

"Sosie, honey, what are you doing?" Mrs. Filipio asked, pulling up along side me, Johnny in the front passenger seat. "Get in the car this minute before you get hit by a car."

"I can't. My mom said I'm not supposed to take rides from strangers," I grumbled, the light changing, while my feet picked up speed. Seeing her face, hearing her voice, left me riddled with anxiety and anger after discovering her with my father a year earlier.

"I'm not a stranger, honey, I'm your neighbor.

You know that, so go on and get in," she said, appearing at the next intersection, her hazard lights on while she waited for me. Her window was cracked, as she blew smoke from her thin cigarette out the car window.

I stood there on the busy road, cold and scared, my back aching from carrying my heavy book bag for miles. Johnny was munching on cookies out of a white bakery bag and sipping orange juice from a straw.

"C'mon, we've got snicker doodles," he said. Johnny reached over her seat and sweetly handed me one. I accepted, my tummy aching with hunger, and reluctantly climbed into the back seat.

Mrs. Filipio stole a glance at me from the rearview and winked, while I slouched down in response and sulked out the window.

When we got to my house, Mrs. Filipio pulled up into my driveway, my mother's car nowhere in sight or any sign of her. Still, I hopped out, trudged to the front door, and knocked anyway, hopeful she was somehow inside.

"C'mon, Sosie," Johnny called out from the car after a few minutes of me standing on the porch. "We can play Uker at my house."

I paused, knowing the new rule. I was no longer allowed to play with Johnny. The only time we saw each other was if it was at school or if we got together in secret when my mother was passed out sleeping. After the false eyelash incident, it was forbidden otherwise.

Mrs. Filipio stepped out of her car, the engine still running, as she glided to the front door, her kitten heels clicking against the cement. When she reached me, she put her arm around me. I shook her away, snatching my arm like she had cooties. "It's no secret you hate me. I know that," she whispered. "But your mom isn't home, and I can't let you sit out here in the cold by yourself."

"Don't call me honey," I warned.

Hours went by at Johnny's house, with us sitting in the living room, a card table set up, while we played game after game of Uker. Nickelodeon played in the background. Every few minutes, I'd wander to the front window and gaze across the street, checking to see if my mother had gotten home yet. "She's still not home," Johnny deadpanned. "You've checked at least a thousand times. C'mon, let's play Go Fish," he said, already sorting cards for the next game.

My mother's car didn't pull into the driveway until after eight in the evening. The break lights turned off and she stumbled out, slamming the car door and slogging up the porch steps then into the house. Minutes later, she reemerged, the screen door flying open, screaming my name at the top of her lungs as she ran out onto the front lawn. "Sosie! Where are you? Someone call the police! Call the police! My daughter is gone!"

I abandoned Johnny and our game, running outside without my coat or shoes on. "It's okay. It's okay, Mom, I'm over here! I'm okay! I'm just here playing with Johnny."

Mrs. Filipio followed me out onto the porch. Johnny too. My mother's eyes shifted to me, then to Johnny, and then to Mrs. Filipio. In a snap, she transformed into a possessed beast and came barreling across the street, a car almost hitting her. It slammed on its breaks, the tires screeching, and I covered my eyes, absolutely sure she'd been smashed. But when I peeked, she hadn't been hit at all. Instead, she marched up to me and yanked my arm.

"Stay away from my fucking kid," she shouted at Mrs. Filipio, getting in her face. She was an incensed woman. A woman who would've walked through fire. A woman scorned. "Stay away! Do you hear me?"

She had a day's worth of alcohol on her breath as she dragged me all the way home, Johnny wilting farther away as we crossed the street to our house.

"Ouch, you're hurting me," I wailed in pain, but she didn't hear me because she was too busy calling me a traitor, telling me I'd betrayed her in a way a daughter should never betray a mother.

My heart was broken when she went into her bedroom, locked the door, and didn't re-emerge until the next afternoon. I sat on a stool in the kitchen all night and into the next day, waiting for her, petrified about what else she might say and worried she was still mad at me.

When she did come to, she was still in her silk pajamas, and it was one thirty in the afternoon. I was quiet, afraid to speak as she made coffee and toast and acted like nothing happened. She even kissed me on the forehead.

I never dared speak a word of it after that moment. I was just happy she loved me again.

Chapter Eight

I sit alone, numb, while the music from the warehouse plays in the background, this time a pathetic rendition of *New York, New York*. Even though the vocals are weak and off key, Frank Sinatra gets me every time and reminds me of my mother. We used to sing it acapella in the car when we drove into the city from Long Island. The second we saw the New York City skyline appear in the distance as we drove across the bridge, my mother would start singing the, *'Bah ba-bada–ba, Bah ba-bada-ba'* part, and I'd roll my eyes, because I knew what came next, my mother saying, "Take it away, Sos! You know you want to!" And she was right. I never could resist belting out the first few verses. I'd sing it with so much gusto that I swore I could be a Broadway star if I wasn't so tone deaf.

After we were through singing, though, without fail, my mother would sigh and become melancholy. To humor her, I'd ask what was wrong even though I knew the answer, and for the hundredth time, she'd tell me the story of how it was playing in a little piano bar in the theater district called *Don't Tell Mama's* when she fell in love with my father. She'd recall how they'd danced close, whispering their dreams into each other's ears. With wistfulness in her eyes, she'd tell me about how it was the first time she'd ever felt inspired to do more with her life and to not settle for being another pretty girl from a small, mediocre town in Pennsylvania. She was twenty-four on that fateful night, and it was then she decided to take a chance on love and New York, not knowing both would end up slowly killing her.

The song from the warehouse ends, and is replaced with the far-off sounds of laughter and chattering voices. I hadn't noticed Nolan standing in front of me, hands deep in the pockets of his leather jacket, brow furrowed in worry.

"Are you okay?" he asks.

"It depends on what you mean by okay. I'm alive, so right there, that's a win," I say, sarcastically. "But okay? Not really."

"Those girls were rabid, my God." I say nothing, clutch my knees to my chest. Nolan bends down beside me. "Look, I tried to help. I'm sorry."

"It's fine," I mumble. "I saw. There wasn't anything you could do. At least you tried. It's more than I can say for all those other people in there. Those girls could've been pummeling me with a baseball bat, and they wouldn't have done anything. I'm so sick of this shitty Island."

"Was it true?" he asks, quietly. "I mean, I've heard the rumors at school and all, but is it true? I want to hear it from you. Whatever you tell me I'll believe."

"Did you even hear what I was saying in there?" I snap. "No, it's not true. It's all lies, rumors created by people who love drama. My mother got into a car accident, plain and simple. Her medication was wrong, and she shouldn't have gotten in that car, but she didn't know what she was doing. I should've stopped her, but I didn't know. I didn't know she was going to die. That all those people were going to die," I say, my voice rising with emotion, my pain escalating by the second. "How could I have known? How could I have possibly known that all this was going to transpire?" The images from the video start coming back. I wince and swat them away. Then, a crunching vibrates into my ears, like a loud speaker shrieking on full volume. I'm rocking back and forth, trying to shake it all away, trying to rid myself.

Nolan swallows hard. "It's okay. It's okay, Sosie. I'm sorry you've been put through the ringer. And I'm sorry your mom died." My emotion halts, and I stop and stare at him, curious, confused to hear it said out loud. Suddenly, I can't catch my breath. The air escapes my lungs. I hold my breath, unable to stop. "Are you okay? Sosie, Sosie," he says, shaking me. I can't answer. "Nod your head if you're all right?" The breath returns to my chest in a burst, and I take in the air, in and out, several times. "There you go. There you go."

"I'm sorry," I whisper.

"No, just breathe. Don't explain. Just relax, breathe."

I close my eyes and try to calm down. "I'm okay, I'm okay," I finally say after a few moments.

He takes a fresh pack of cigarettes out of his pocket and hands me one. I light it and take a puff. "Better?" he asks. I nod. We're silent for a while, smoking, each alone in our thoughts. "I left Georgia and moved to Long Beach because my mom dragged me all the way here to marry a guy she met online."

"Seriously?"

"Seriously. They were dating for two months, didn't even know much about the guy or that it was even that serious. I just knew she was suddenly always smiling when she was looking at her phone. Then one day, my mom comes home from work and surprises me with plane tickets to New York and promises to take me to see the Statue of Liberty and stuff, but when we got here, she flipped the script. It was a wedding."

"Whoa. Plot twist," I say, blown away.

"Tell me about it. Then, I was forced to move into this guy's house, and my mom thinks he's a great guy because she suddenly doesn't have to work anymore and because he pays for some fancy school for me to go to. Anyway, I can't stand him, so I crash at Terry's place whenever he lets me. I mean, I practically live there."

"Terry's cool with that?"

"Oh, yeah, for sure. Beneath that asshole exterior, he's actually a pretty decent guy."

"So, what's so bad about him?" I ask. "Your stepdad, that is."

"Naw, don't call him that," he says, shaking his head. "He's just Larry. I don't know, he doesn't get me, you know? I've always been sort of a free spirit, and he's super uptight, straight laced and stuff, works on Wall Street, shit like that. He hates that I paint my nails. He hates my long hair. The other day, he was like, 'Go take that nail polish off. You look like a fag.' I was just like, whatever dude. I didn't even say anything, just left. Haven't been home since."

"What does your mom say?"

"She just makes excuses for him, you know?" he says, his voice trailing off. "My older brother was smart, though. He refused to move, but man, I miss him like crazy."

"Sorry, that really sucks."

"Don't be sorry. It's all good." He stares off into the distance, eyes squinty while he smokes his cigarette, chiseled jawline perfectly complimenting his brood.

"Hey. Thanks," I say, playfully bumping my shoulder into his.

"For what?"

"For making me feel like I'm not the only one with an f'ed up family."

"Anytime," he says, with a chuckle.

"I'm glad you ended up in Mr. Russo's class with me, you know, for what it's worth. I know it might sound weird, but your poem was exactly what I needed to hear that day."

His cheeks turn a faint shade of pink and he looks away. "Hey, enough about me. It's your turn. Tell me something about your mom."

"Like what?"

"I don't know. What was she like?"

"What was she like?" I repeat, mulling over the question, enjoying the words, and the thoughts it evokes. A smile washes across my face.

"Three words to describe her," he says. "Go."

"Okay," I say, trying to think. "Ah! This is so hard. My mother was a very complex person." I pause. "Whimsical. She had this amazing sense of humor, and she was so creative. She was a writer, by the way."

"Makes sense, with you taking AP English and all. What kinds of stuff did she write?"

"Children's books," I answer. "Okay, I've got another one. Impulsive. My mother was a very fly-by-the-seat-of-your-pants kind of person. She didn't think about things before she did them. She was the type to just go all in, balls out. She did stuff without worrying. God, I wish I could be more like that."

"Don't get distracted," he reminds me. "You have one more."

"Ferocious," I say. "She loved ferociously. She hated even more ferociously, my father in particular. And she dreamed ferociously. My mom was such a dreamer." I'm wistful, nostalgic for her. "I'm a dreamer, too. She used to say, 'For god sakes, Sosie, never fall in love with another dreamer. There isn't room for two dreamers in a relationship. Dreamers are never settled. They're always changing their minds. They wander and wander, always thinking there's something better just around the corner. One person has to be the sensible one. Find a sensible man.'"

"But sensible is boring. Sensible is Larry," he says, and we both laugh. "You miss her very much. I can hear it in your voice when you talk about her."

"So much that it's hard to breathe sometimes." He slides his arm around me, and I stare at my hands in my lap. "It just hurts, you know, people being so wrong about her, like not just those girls in there, but everyone. They have no idea who my mother really was. I just wish there was some way to make everyone understand, to make everyone see that she'd never hurt anyone like that on purpose. I need to make them see. I just don't know how yet."

"If she was here right now, what would you ask her?"

The picture of my mother and Sam, the way he had his hands on her, the things Jamie told me, there's a burning inside to know the truth, but I'm not ready to talk about it. Even thinking about it leaves me lightheaded. "God. I really don't know. There's just too much to choose from," I say, instead. "Mostly, I'm just scared that I'm going to need her in the future, and she's not going to be here. She's never coming back, Nolan. Ever."

"She's with you every moment," he tells me. "Even now. She'll never really leave you."

The way his eyes blink, filled with pity, empathy for my pain reflects my brokenness. He has no idea the turmoil I'm in or what I know. Or what I fear most. Warm tears streak my cheeks, and I blot them away with the sleeve of my dirty jacket.

"I'm sorry. I can't do this." I jump to my feet. "I've got to go. I don't know what I'm even doing here. I'm sorry."

"Sosie, wait. Where are you going?"

"I don't know. I just need to get out of here." I take off running, but he's right behind, trying to stop me. "No, please, just let me go."

"Sosie," he says, grabbing my bicep. "Please just

wait a second, okay?" I try to wrestle my arm away, but his fingers melt deeper into my skin. "Where are you going? It's the middle of the night. There aren't any trains or anything. Some streets you can't even get down. Come here." He pulls me in, wrapping me in a one-armed hug, my cheek pressed against his collarbone. I close my eyes and sink into the embrace. He pulls away for a moment, holding my shoulders as he assesses me. "Sosie, you just fell asleep standing up. C'mon, you're exhausted. You can hardly keep your eyes open. You need some sleep." My eyes are heavy, already starting to close again. "You can crash on Terry's couch. C'mon, he won't mind." He leads me down the block, his arm draped around my shoulder.

"Thanks for taking care of me," I murmur. "I haven't had anyone looking out for me in a long time."

"Me neither," he says.

Chapter Nine

I wake up on Terry's couch, underneath an afghan that smells of stale body odor and laying on a throw pillow covered in yellow nicotine stains. Still, it's the most decent nights sleep I've gotten in I don't know how long. A breeze blows into the third-floor window, chilling me through the thin blanket but offering a welcomed burst of fresh air. I stretch, kicking my feet over the side of the couch, my boots still on. I consider taking them off, but my last real shower was days ago.

"How'd you sleep?" Nolan appears, sitting on the couch across from me.

I spring up, heart thumping in my ears. "Great," I say. "I feel like I've been sleeping forever. What time is it?"

"Three o'clock."

"Three o'clock? You've got to be kidding." I rub my eyes. "Please tell me last night was a bad dream."

"Wish I could, but nope, it happened," he says with a sympathetic smile. "But lucky for you, today is a new day."

"Yeah. Lucky for me."

Nolan is cleaned up, fully dressed, and drinking a bottle of Gatorade. "Want a sip?"

"Please."

He leans across the coffee table and hands me the bottle.

My mouth is parched. I take a sip, and then another.

"Your lips are blue now," he teases.

"So are yours."

The daylight has brought a strangeness to our dynamic from the night before. The conversation isn't coming as easily, and we're both a little more guarded without the liquid courage.

"I saw Terry and Casey this morning," he says, changing the subject. "We're gonna go grab some grub at The Inn if you want to join. Casey heard they're open and serving food. Only place in all of Long Beach that's open."

As I open my mouth to answer, a humming of voices echo in the hallway, before the apartment door unlocks and Casey and Terry stroll in. Casey can't stop smiling, and Terry struts like a guy who just got laid.

"What the fuck is up?" Casey sings, as they invade our conversation without apology.

Terry plops down on the couch next to me. He smells like sex, grime, and bad breath. I inch away. "What are you kids up to?" he asks. "You slept here last night?"

"Yeah. I hope that's okay. I was so tired, and I just sort of crashed on the couch."

"Mi casa, es su casa," he proclaims. "Did you guys … you know?"

"No," Nolan says, sternly. "I slept here," he says, patting the ragged loveseat opposite of me.

Casey walks over and makes herself comfortable on Terry's lap.

He starts rubbing her thigh, going from the outside to the inside, lingering when his hand grazes the inside.

She giggles, lets out a little breathy sound, and I wonder if this is how all their foreplay starts.

"So, you guys went to the warehouse last night? How was it?" she asks, flinging her auburn hair behind her shoulders and sticking her boobs out in the process.

Of course, Terry takes notice, his eyes ogling her without shame.

"It was fun if your idea of a good time is getting

jumped by a girl-gang in hooker make-up," I deadpan.

"Whoa, whoa, whoa, what? You guys got jumped?" she asks, leaning forward, eyes wide, like we've just given her a golden nugget of gossip. "I heard there's been some crime happening, and that the police are gonna start cracking down, but I didn't realize people were getting jumped. That's intense. What happened?"

"These girls from another school came out of nowhere and just started running their mouths and stuff," I explain. "They were saying all kinds of crap about my mom. Stuff that's just blatantly lies. Anyway, I had to stick up for my mom. I did what I had to do, but they didn't like that and tried to push me around."

"What were they saying about your mom?" Terry asks. "Did you have to cut a bitch?"

"Was it about how she got into that accident and killed that kid?" Casey asks, and the whole room gets quiet. It's like everyone has stopped breathing, like we all took our last breath the moment she said what she did. Her hand instinctively goes to her mouth, her fingers slightly trembling. "I didn't mean to say it like that," she tries to explain.

"I-I didn't realize you knew about that," I stammer.

Before I say any more, Nolan swoops in and comes to my defense. "Listen, whatever you heard on the news, whatever they're saying, it's all lies," Nolan tells her. "Let go of everything you know or heard, okay?"

"I'm sorry, Sosie, I didn't mean it like that," Casey says, talking quickly, in damage control mode. "I just meant—"

Her voice resonates, her lips move, but I'm not listening. After last night, a switch has flipped. I'm numb, like I could be poked with a thousand daggers and not feel a thing. "It's fine. I shouldn't be surprised.

Everyone on this shit-hole island knows the story. I'll never escape it. I just wish I could run away to someplace where no one knows my story."

A goofy, stupid grin washes over Terry's face, and he puts his pointer finger in the air like he's having a light bulb moment. "I know a way we can make that happen. What would you guys say to getting the fuck out of dodge and heading to Virginia Beach?"

"No, no, shut up. Not that again," Casey tells him. "Don't even think about it," she says, waving her finger at him. "I already told you no."

"Oh, c'mon." Terry wraps his arms around Casey's waist. "Sosie wants to get the hell out of here, and I think we could all use a change of scenery, right? It's a perfect plan, babe."

"I'm down for Virginia Beach," Nolan says. "I mean, I'll have to tell my mom some bullshit story about where I'm going, but that shouldn't be a problem, especially since school's still shut down."

"Would you still want to go if it involves stealing a car?" Casey asks Nolan. "Because this genius right here wants to steal a car." Casey rolls her eyes. "It's a legit plan until it involves grand larceny, right?"

"Oh, c'mon, don't be such a scaredy cat," Terry tells her, turning her body to face him. "It'll be fine. Sven won't mind. I promise. Just think, we could go down to beach and check out the surf. It'll be cold as hell, but the waves will be huge after the hurricane, and I'm itching for a ride so bad. Babe, you are too. I know you are. We can get out of this dump for a couple of days, have a beer, relax, surf. Sosie needs to get away, too. Didn't you hear what she just said? It'll be good for all of us. This place is like a ghost town anyway. It's a mess, and there's nothing going on."

Nolan seems excited by the idea. "Be lying if I

said I wasn't jonesing for a ride."

"Right, dude? Right?" Terry says, getting more excited by the second. "What do you say, babe?" he asks, nose nuzzling her neck. His hand grazes her hip in a sexual way that makes it uncomfortable to watch.

She gets caught up for a moment and Eskimo kisses him back. Then she abruptly pulls herself out of his clutch. "No, you guys. No. I'm sorry, but this is just such a bad idea on so many levels. Sven will one hundred percent not be okay with you stealing his car, and I can just see it snowballing into a total disaster."

"*Borrowing*," Terry corrects her. "Stop calling it stealing. We're borrowing Sven's car."

"Okay, can someone tell me who Sven is?" I ask, getting lost in the logistics of it all.

"Sven's Terry's next-door neighbor," Nolan says. "He's in Punta Cana on vacation."

"Lucky son of a bitch left before all this hurricane bullshit went down, and won't be back til next week," Terry adds. "I can't believe I didn't think of this before."

"So how would we do it, steal, borrow, whatever?" I ask.

Terry shoots me a million-dollar grin.

"Sven basically has a man crush on this jackass," Casey pipes in, explaining for him. "He takes care of Sven's cats when he goes away, so Terry's got keys to his apartment, but I really think it's because Sven's secretly hoping Terry will walk into his apartment one night and crawl into bed with him."

"That's assuming I haven't already," Terry teases her. She punches him in the arm. "Jokes, babe, just jokes. He's a good-looking dude, though, I won't even lie." He turns his attention back to us. "Listen to how perfect this is. We went for a walk this morning and saw his car parked on Hudson. I don't know how, but somehow there was no damage. Nada. Zip. The whole block was untouched. Then, I found his keys hanging by his front door. He'd never know, and we'd be back long before he gets home. It's basically a perfect plan. And he hasn't called to check in once."

"The bridge is still shut down. We can't even get out of Long Beach if we wanted to," Casey reminds him.

"I think they just opened it back up this morning," Nolan says. "That's what I heard anyway. I don't know, I kind of think this is brilliant. What do you think?" he asks me. "Could be good for you."

"What do I think?" I mull for a moment, my eyes wandering over to the open window in Terry's living room. The drapes whistle against the wind, the air hissing through the fabric, the same way the curtains had when I'd gone to see the grey house on Waverly Place, Sam's old house. I'm transported back to that moment, and how I stood outside, looking up at the window, the fear I'd felt deep in my heart for what I might find.

Suddenly, I realize, I'm no longer afraid. The game has changed, and the warehouse was the final blow. There's a titanium shield wrapped around my heart where the fear used to live. I'm calloused and unafraid.

Jamie's voice echoes in my head. "*Michigan. Sold the house, and moved there after your mom passed away.*" I swallow hard, knowing what I must do. The only way out of this hell I've been living, the only way to really know the truth is if I somehow get to Michigan and get to Sam. I need to see his face in the flesh. I need to hear his voice when I confront him about her. And I need a car. Terry's got a plan to go to Virginia Beach, but we may need to take a detour first or not get there at all. No one needs to know that yet, though.

I slowly turn my attention back to the group who

is anxiously waiting on my opinion. Casey's biting her lip, Nolan's squinting like he's trying to read what I'm thinking, and Terry's pumped up and rubbing his hands together. "I don't surf, but I'm in for a beer and a change of scenery. What are we waiting for? Let's do it."

"Yes!" Terry says, giving me a high five that stings my palm. "That's what I'm talking about!"

"What about you, Casey? Are you in?" I ask.

"It'll just be a couple of days, Case," Terry promises her. "And we'll be back way before he gets home. We're in the clear, babe."

"You guys suck," Casey says, not hiding her annoyance. "I'm in, but if we get arrested, I'm blaming it all on you fuckheads."

****

Before we head out on our road trip, we grab a bite at The Inn on Beech Street. The four of us settle into a corner booth in a private little nook at the back of the place. Nolan and I sit on one side of the booth, Casey and Terry on the other. The restaurant still has signs of damage. Tiny remnants of debris and sand scatter the floor. The cushions on our seats are damp and musty smelling from water damage. Broken windows all over the place have been patched with Saran wrap. The one waitress taking care of the whole restaurant, a haggard woman with frizzy hair and permanent frown lines around her mouth, scribbles down orders in a pocket-size notebook, only taking a break to wipe the sweat from her forehead. It takes her several minutes to get to our table, and when she does, she doesn't greet us with a friendly hello or smile, but instead just stares and waits.

"What'll it be?" she asks, pen and paper ready and loaded. We all hesitate. "Kitchen's only partially running, so all I can do for ya is a cheese pizza, small or large, or Italian heroes. We don't got no soda, just bottled water," she says, without looking up. "So, what'll it be?" Each of us waits for someone else to speak up. She zeroes in on me. "Are you going to order something or not?"

"I guess we'll take a large cheese pizza?" I say, scanning the group for approval. Casey shrugs, and the boys nod. "And four waters, please."

"Four?" she asks.

"Yeah, four," I answer.

"Whatever," she grumbles, putting the pen behind her ear. "Pizza might take a few, so don't blame me if it's cold when it gets here," she adds before disappearing through a swinging kitchen door.

"You said they had buffalo wings," Casey complains to Terry.

"I thought they did," Terry says, but Casey still isn't happy. She sits there pouting, a pissed-off puss on her face. "What do you want me to do, go out back and kill some chickens so you can have buffalo wings?"

While Terry and Casey bicker, a girl around my age and her mother sit at a nearby table. I know they're mother and daughter because they have identical profiles, same nose, same chin, and the same mousy brown hair. They remind me of my mother and me. Munching on breadsticks, the girl digs into a pat of butter over and over with each bite.

The mother's back is to me, but the daughter's eyes keep glinting my way while she says something to her through a full mouth of food. A few seconds go by. The mother glances over her shoulder nonchalantly, and then leans forward and says something to her daughter.

The waitress appears with the waters and sits them down on the table in front of me. I dole them out one by one.

I take a sip of mine and swish it around like mouthwash. "See, that table over there? The one with that girl and that lady in the burgundy sweater?" Casey nods, the boys not listening and deep in conversation about waxing surfboards. "I think they're talking about me. Maybe I'm crazy, but I swear I just saw that woman turn around, look right at me, and then say something to her daughter."

The woman swings her body around again, pretends to squint at a clock on the wall, steals a peak at me once more, and then turns back to her daughter. "See!" I say to Casey. "Did you just see that? She looked right at me."

"Whoa. I actually did see that. Are you sure you don't know them from somewhere or something?"

"Not at all. I've never seen either of them before in my life. But how much do you want to bet they were at the warehouse last night and saw my drama with that group of girls? There were a bunch of people just standing around and, like, staring at the girls putting their hands on me but doing nothing about it." Casey's eyes are fixed on me while I talk, her eyes skimming over my hair, face, and clothes like she's lost in thought. "Are you even listening to me?"

"Have you ever thought about changing your look? I'm sorry, I don't mean to offend, but it's, like, in my DNA to enjoy a good makeover. I can't help myself. My mom and grandma are beauticians," she explains. "Hear me out. You're always saying how you can't escape this stigma, and how everywhere you go, people are calling you out about all the stuff with your mom. Well, why not switching up your hair or something so people don't recognize you?"

My ears perk, and I raise an eyebrow, listening.

"When I dyed my hair red, it literally changed my

life. Red hair is exotic as fuck these days, and it would look phenom on your skin tone."

I run my fingers along the strands of my long, stringy hair. "You know, you might have a point ... but red? I guess it might look cool."

"Large cheese," the waitress says, appearing with our pizza and a stack of napkins.

The pizza is steaming hot, the aroma of spices and cheese filling the air.

My mouth salivates. "We're going to need some more plates," I tell her, and she leaves to go and get them.

A few seconds later, she reappears with more plates, setting them down on the table in front of us, the cheap porcelain clanking together like chimes.

We devour the pizza, none of us speaking while we stuff our faces, and burn our mouths with the doughy and cheesy goodness. My belly is full, warm, and satisfied by the time I finish.

After a few minutes, the waitress comes back to pick up the empty plates and glasses. She rips off the bill from her notepad, and lays it down on the table. "Cash only. You can pay at the front, or leave exact change on the table," she announces, and then walks away.

Casey is digging through her purse, and the boys in their pockets.

I open my bag and pull out a wad of cash. "I got it. It's on me." I place a twenty-dollar bill on the table. A smirk cracks across my chapped lips. "What do you guys say, should we get the hell out of Long Beach already?"

Chapter Ten

After lunch, we take Sven's car. We don't waste time. All of us agreeing it's best to get out of Long Beach as soon as possible. Casey and I assume the responsibilities of the domestic matters back at the apartments, like leaving plenty of food and water out for Timber, Sven's mangy cat, and cracking a window open in case she wants to roam.

After locking up Sven's place, we stop at Casey's apartment and then Terry's to grab a few things for the road trip. We stuff sweatshirts, t-shirts, underwear, socks, and bathing suits into a couple of large duffle bags and then go and meet up with the guys a few blocks away. When we get there, Nolan and Terry are loading the surfboards onto the roof rack of Sven's old car with Nolan making sure the boards are secure by tightening the straps and buckles. There are three piled on top of each other, fins up and neatly stacked.

Terry leans against the rusted car, pleased, anxious, amped, while he spins the key ring around his clubbed pointer finger. "Fuckin' Virginia, baby." He flashes a broad, white smile and then greets Casey with a sloppy kiss.

"Gonna be epic times, epic times, ya'll," Nolan agrees.

"The water's probably going to be freezing," Casey grumbles. "And I didn't pack your wet suit. Couldn't find it."

"Nonsense. Don't need it. All I need is the ocean." Terry hooks Casey's head into his bicep as he pulls her in close for another kiss.

"Timber's all set," Casey informs him. "We put out food and water, and left the hall light on for her."

"Okay, so who's driving?" Nolan asks, as he

tosses the bags into the trunk and slams it shut.

"Not it," Casey declares. "I'm not driving with the boards on top of the car like that. I'll crash us into a tree."

"Can't," Terry says. "There's a warrant out for my arrest."

"What the hell?" Casey asks, pulling away from his hug. "You can't be serious."

"Driving with a suspended license will do that to you," he replies, and she glares at him. "It never occurred to you that I don't have a car for a reason?"

"I wouldn't mind driving," I offer.

"Good, because I don't have my license yet," Nolan says, tossing me the keys.

I climb into the driver's seat, and we're on the road by 6 PM. Terry dictates the plan: drive a few hours to Philadelphia and stay at his buddy's place that has electricity and running water. In the morning, we'll have a quick shower and be back on the road before the sun comes up. If all goes according to plan, we'll arrive in Virginia Beach sometime in the afternoon the next day.

Or so they think.

I'm not sure how I'm going to get to Sam in Michigan yet, but all I do know is that I need to get to him somehow, some way. I'll have to figure out the details later.

Terry can taste the salt of the ocean; he can feel it stinging his skin. At least that's what he won't stop talking about. He's going to catch a wave, have a beer in some little bar that plays nothing but Grateful Dead, take a nap in the car, and then do it all over again before we head back to Long Beach. Nolan and Casey join in on the chatter, Nolan from his position next to me in the front passenger seat, and Casey in the back with her legs draped over Terry's lap.

Their voices jump as they bounce musings off each other of what the beach will be like once we get there. Guilt starts creeping in. Am I sabotaging the first real friendships I've had in forever by duping them into going somewhere that isn't what they planned? Will I have to steal a car in the middle of the night and leave them somewhere without a ride? I shake off the worry, trying not to think about it.

At least not yet.

While they chat, I crack open my window and let the crisp air hit my face as we cross the Long Beach Bridge, dark water below us, while some shitty pop music plays on the radio. My mind wanders the farther we get from Long Island, and I finally have the space to think about my mother, and everything that's happened in the last few days. I think about Sam, and who he is, what he might tell me, and what they were to each other. I think about how I almost died, the picture I discovered, and how I found Nolan. I think about everything—except the video. I still can't bear it. I know there will be answers soon. I just need to hang on a little longer.

"Why are you so quiet, Sosie?" Casey asks, leaning forward into the center console between my seat and Nolan's. "What, you're not pumped about leaving Long Beach? You haven't said a word."

"I'm pumped," I respond, half-heartedly. "I just have a lot on my mind, that's all. Plus, I've never surfed before."

"I'll show you how," Nolan promises, and my heart sinks a little further. "Once you get up, there's nothing to it."

We aren't an hour into the trip, when Casey starts shifting in her seat. She crosses and uncrosses her legs, huffing and puffing, restless.

"I'm sorry, I can't take it anymore. You guys, I

have to pee," she finally admits.

"Come on," Terry groans. "We're barely out of New York."

"I drank so much water at lunch. What do you want me to do, pee my pants? Ugh. I might have a UTI."

"If I had a dollar for every time you might have a UTI," Terry says.

"Fuck off, Terry." Casey's eyes scan the road. "Look, Wal-Mart, in one mile," she says, reading a sign. "You've got to stop, Sosie. If I don't find a bathroom soon, I'll seriously have an accident."

I swing the car into a parking spot at the Super Wal-Mart, and I can't help noticing how different the world looks outside of Long Beach, and somewhere in a little place called Linden, New Jersey. People come and go as they please, not paralyzed by the aftershocks of the hurricane or stifled by the clean up. It's like nothing happened here. Lights blaze from the streetlights and inside the store. No branches hang askew, crumpled by the wind. There's not so much as a discarded wrapper in the pristine parking lot and there certainly aren't any overturned cars or boats. The hurricane aftermath that's held us hostage for the last few days in Long Island is completely absent in Linden. This place is a real-life Tomorrowland.

The four of us walk through the automatic doors at Super Wal-Mart, into the Disneyland of the mega shopping experience. On cue, a helpful greeter, a woman in her mid-seventies, makes her way over to us, offering up a sale paper and a welcoming snaggled-toothed grin.

"Where's the bathroom?" Casey blurts out, interrupting the woman as she begins her spiel about the specials and sales going on.

"We also have a Mickey D's here," the greeter continues, not hearing Casey. "And Subway. Two footlongs for five bucks today. Tuna's the special."

"Is there a bathroom?" I ask, on Casey's behalf. "My friend needs to go, like, now."

"Oh, I'm sorry, of course there is," the greeter says. "Right over passed the cash registers."

Casey tears off to find the bathroom, and Terry decides to look for the cartons of cigarettes, while Nolan and I wander around. Aisle by aisle, Nolan and I walk about selecting our items. He gets an economy-sized jar of off-brand peanut butter, and I get a box of Nilla Wafers. It feels natural, like we're together, and just an average couple out for an evening shopping trip. I like walking with him this way, me pushing the cart, him walking slightly ahead.

We turn down the personal hygiene aisle, and I zero in on the boxes of hair dye. Cherry Crush, Mahogany Sunrise, Red Velvet—there are dozens of colors to choose from. I pick up one of the boxes and read the back, my finger running across each word as I scan the directions and ingredients.

"What do you think?" I ask Nolan. "This one's organic, made out of Henna." I hold the box called Red Copper next to my face and grin, jutting my chin out and trying to be adorable. "Casey thinks I need to make a change."

"Whatever makes you happy," he replies. "But I don't think you need to change anything."

A smile washes across my face. "Well, thanks," I say, bashfully. "But I feel like a new look is exactly what I need. Like, it'll give me a fresh start, you know? After last night, I just want to start over. When those girls were yelling at me and saying all that crap about my mom, and then I was sitting outside by myself on the curb, something shifted on the inside. I feel different now. I just want to shed the old me. It feels right."

"I can understand that," he agrees. "But if you want my humble opinion, you should try not to let what people say about you affect you so much, especially if what they're saying isn't true." He pauses. "I mean, I know that's easier said than done."

"Yeah. It is," I say, and I can feel a wall of defensiveness rising up inside me and between us, like a line has been drawn in the sand and he crossed it. "Especially if you couldn't possibly understand what I'm going through because your mom isn't dead. Maybe your mom sucks, but at least she's alive. You shouldn't speak on things that you don't know a goddamn thing about."

"My bad," he says, taking a step back, hands up like he doesn't want any trouble. "I was just trying to help, be a friend. I thought we were cool, but I guess not." He takes his stuff out of the cart, and walks away.

I instantly regret lashing out, but I don't try to stop him. The anger still boils in my belly.

I select the perfect box of hair-dye, pick up some toiletries, new underwear, protein bars, and anything else I might need for the road after I eventually break from the group. Then, I meet up with everyone outside where they're waiting for me at the car.

"Finally," Terry says, stomping on his cigarette and eyeing my bags. "What did you do, buy the whole store? Let's go. Don't want to keep my buddy waiting."

I crank the car and glance at Nolan who's still sour, staring out the passenger window, mouth tense and hard. After stopping at a nearby gas station, we get back on the highway and drive until we reach Philadelphia a little after 10 PM.

"Are you sure he's home?" Casey asks, as I park in front of Terry's friend's house.

"It looks a little deserted," I agree, surveying the house.

There aren't any cars in the driveway, and all the shades inside the house are drawn.

"Of course he's home," Terry answers. "I just spoke to him a few hours ago. He's expecting us. C'mon." Terry hops out of the car and pops the trunk open. We all get out after him, each of us a little unsure. "Catch," he says, tossing me the Wal-Mart shopping bags. We follow him up to the front door where he knocks several times and then rings the doorbell.

"See, Terry. I told you, nobody's home," Casey says, arms crossed over her chest, wearing a dirty look. "It's totally dead in there."

"He's home, okay? Just relax for a goddamn second." The three of us lock eyes while Terry wipes the sweat from his forehead, searching around the various planters and mailbox for a key.

Music and flashing lights explode through the dense trees from the house next door. There's laughter and the charred smokiness of a bonfire wafting in the cool air.

"Are you sure it's this house, and not the one next door?" I suggest. "Sounds like a party or something going on over there."

"I'm sure, okay?" Terry snaps. He tries one more spot, underneath an outdoor mat that says *Home Sweet Home*, and finally locates a key. He holds it up and sneers. "See, haters," he says, waving it in front of Casey's face. "And you doubted me."

We walk into the house and Terry turns on a living room light. An overhead fan starts rotating above us, thick dust spewing every which way from the old blades. I cough, waving the grime out of my face.

"Does your friend live here with his Grandma or something?" Casey asks, picking up a round doily from a coffee table and laughing at it. "Because this place feels ancient."

I'm still coughing, and it's getting throatier and more aggressive by the second. "Sorry. I'm allergic to dust mites," I say, between chokes.

"Sosie can't even breathe," Casey says. I sit down on a wobbly armchair to catch my breath, its legs almost giving way beneath me. Casey busts out laughing. "Seriously, where even are we right now?"

"Why don't you guys be a little more grateful?" Terry reprimands. "Someone is giving you a place to stay for free, and all you can do is make fun of it?"

"God. Sorry," Casey says, pretending to zip up her mouth and throw away the key. "You don't have to be so uptight."

"We can't take any of the rooms upstairs," Terry continues. "Don't know why, but there's a bedroom on the first floor, so me and Casey will stay there, and Sosie, you can sleep on the couch in here, and Nolan, you'll have to take the couch in the basement downstairs." Nolan nods, but looks less than thrilled. Terry walks over to coffee table where there's a scribbled note and starts reading aloud. *"At Party next door. Come over and have a drink and smoke if you wanna hang."* Terry waits for one of us to say something. Everyone looks exhausted, spent. "Well? Do you guys wanna check it out?"

We all hesitate, no one wanting to be the party pooper. I clear my throat. "I'm down," I finally say, even though it's the last thing I feel like doing. There might be an opportunity to put my plan to see Sam into action, and I need to seize every chance I get. "I could definitely use a beer right about now."

After we change our clothes and get situated in our sleeping arrangements, Terry leads the way through a thick, wooded area that separates his friend's house from the neighbor's next door. The moonlight and stars shine through the trees, illuminating a path for us as we make the short trek between houses. My legs itch from scrapes, and I'm covered in dirt once we emerge from the clearing and discover the party of fifty people or more.

It's going full throttle outside, with people partying across acres of dead grass and around a burning fire pit. They throw back drinks, goof off, and take turns rolling down mini hills as they—totally wasted—crack up at one another.

We push our way inside, and Terry and Casey set out to find Terry's friend. Nolan, still ignoring me, tags along with them. Techno beats ring in my ears as people in the living room play drinking games, stripping away clothes layer by layer in between shots of Tequila and dirty dancing. In the kitchen, girls in slutty tank tops and tight jeans drink beer out of funnels and kegs while they take turns cheering each other on.

I drink beer after beer out of a red Solo cup, huddled in a tight doorway alone. Somewhere in between my third or fourth beer and a shot of Tequila, I push my way into a dining room, feeling buzzed and chatty and looking for someone to talk to. I run into Casey and Terry who are off in a corner, talking with a wormy looking guy with acne and scrawny arms. Casey spots me and dashes over, wrapping her arms around my neck like she hasn't seen me in days, her entire weight barreling into me, almost knocking me over.

"This is Terry's friend," she spits, two inches from my face, slurring her words.

"Ryan," he says, taking my hand and lightly kissing it.

I squirm my hand away, and stuff them into the back of my jeans pockets. "Hey. I'm Sosie."

"Well, nice to meet you, Sosie. Do you want to roll?"

"I'm sorry, what?"

Casey's watching me with excited anticipation, waiting for me to answer while Terry licks her neck like a kitten. "Didn't you say you were a pill popper?" she chides. "Seriously, she told me that the other day."

"Yeah, but not that kind of pill popper. Like, a pain pill popper," I say, as if it's not as bad.

Terry, Casey, and Ryan laugh in unison. "I thought you were more bad ass than that," Casey says.

"Nope, I guess I'm not," I snip. "But hey, I thought you were only into the stuff grown from the ground. Isn't that what you told me the other day?"

"I am. I don't mess with pills and shit, but we're not talking about me. We're talking about you." Terry pulls her into him and gives her a deep, tonguey kiss. "Sorry, guys. I gotta run. I've got some business to take care of," she says, as Terry leads her away and up a set of stairs nearby.

"So, do you want to?" Ryan shouts in my ear once they're gone.

"Do I want to what?"

"Do you want to roll?" I shake my head no. "Really?" he asks, a little disappointed.

"Sorry," I offer, with a shrug.

"Do you want another beer at least?" I nod. "Be right back. Stay here, okay?"

Ryan goes to get me a beer, and seconds later I spot Nolan on the other side of the room, glassy eyed and cheeks pink and warm. I exhale when I see his face. We make our way across the room, both too buzzed to remember we're mad at the other. Nolan's slightly unsteady on his feet, and I am too, the beer and shots taking effect once my legs are in motion.

"Can I talk to you?" I ask, taking his hand.

Without answering, he leads me through the

kitchen, out a flimsy side door, and into the backyard where people are gathered around a dying down fire pit.

"I love that smell," I say, sniffing the smoky aroma. "The smell of wood burning always reminds me of my grandmother's house when I was a little girl." I collapse onto the grass in front of the warm bonfire and yank his arm to sit down next to me. He settles in, and I lay my head on his shoulder. "I'm sorry for snapping at you earlier."

"Naw, don't be sorry. Don't even worry about that," he assures me. "I overstepped a boundary."

I snuggle up closer to him, pulling his bicep into my cheek. His body stiffens in response. "So you forgive me?" I ask.

"You kidding me? Of course, I do," he says. "We're friends, right?"

I let go of his arm, of my head that's been snuggled so tightly into him. "I like you," I suddenly blurt out, but the laughter of a giddy couple pressed up against a fence in between kisses, interrupts my confession. Nolan focuses on them, his eyes glued with intention. "Did you hear what I just said?" I shake his arm a little. "I *like* you."

"Sosie," he begins and then stops.

"I like you," I repeat in the sexiest voice I can conjure up, and then without thinking, I lean in and kiss him, a slow, soft pillowy kiss. While my lips are still pressed to his, I wait for the moment when he might pull me in closer, reciprocate my feelings, but it doesn't happen.

"No, Sosie, no," he mumbles, instead pulling away. "I'm sorry." He gets up from the grass.

I leap to my feet, the blood rushing to my head and making me dizzy. "What's wrong? What did I do wrong?"

"Nothing, Sosie."

"I didn't?" I ask, hopeful again and going in for another kiss.

"No, please don't do that." He holds me back by the shoulders.

"I don't get it. Why don't you want me to kiss you?"

"Sosie, I care for you, I really do, but I'm sorry. I mean, I think you're a beautiful girl, but I care for you as a friend. That's it. That's as far as it goes."

He really is sorry. I can see it in the way the tiny lines around his eyes appear when he's worried, and the way he's using his hair to avoid looking at me. It doesn't make it any less devastating.

"You know what?" I snarl, walking away. "Fuck you. Just … fuck you."

It's time to take control of this road trip and get to Sam. No more playing around. I go back inside the house. Ryan waits with two beers in either hand. "I thought you took off on me," he shouts over the music.

"Never," I say, taking one of the beers from him, and chugging it in three big gulps. "I changed my mind. I want to roll." His eyes narrow and a curly smile washes over his face.

He takes a small, round pill out of his pocket and places it on my tongue. I make eye contact as I sip from his beer to wash it down.

The next thing I know, I'm dancing freely and recklessly to the base of the pumping stereo. I whip my hair and head around, thrusting to the beat of the music. Whenever I look at Ryan, he jumps, too, holding one of my hands up in the air, joining in on my freestyle dance, eyes closed, blitzed out, and smiling.

"You know Molly now," he screams over the music, when we're both sweaty.

"Molly? Who's Molly?" I ask.

"You met her about twenty minutes ago. The pill," he tells me with a chuckle.

As we dance, the people around us whirl in and out, bumping into me, bumping into him, bouncing us back to each other on every other beat of the music.

I giggle uncontrollably. Soon, I'm tingly all over, fuzzy, and happy beyond any happiness I've ever felt. In that moment, it seems like the best decision I've ever made. Ryan and I keep dancing closer and closer, the sweat from his forehead dripping all over me. My arms are wrapped around his neck, my face buzzing, lips vibrating. I keep kissing him to bring the feeling back into my mouth and tongue. He starts to look less wormy, and his bony body starts to feel like the softest pillow I've ever slept on. Every time he touches me feels more intense than the last. I suddenly get the urge to feel my skin against his, so I take my shirt off—I take it off in the middle of the party—in front of everyone and dance in only my bra. Ryan gropes me all over in front of countless people, but I don't care. He doesn't care, either.

"Get a room, you disgusting whore," some girl yells at me, dumping a beer on top of my head. But the beer feels amazing, and I lick up whatever's dripping down my face and into my mouth.

"Can we go somewhere?" I shout into his ear, my lips lightly grazing his cheek. "Like some place we can be alone?" I bite my lip, and he runs his hands over my hips.

He takes me upstairs to the second floor of the house. I laugh the whole way, clutching my shirt to my bare belly as I follow him. He turns a light on in a dinky bathroom, closes the door behind us, and locks it. Without a word, he reaches around my back and unhooks my bra, exposing my bare skin. I grab his face between my hands and kiss him, his hands groping and squeezing every inch of me. His fingertips start moving farther and farther down my stomach, lightly grazing like a tickly spider, until they reach the top button of my jeans.

"No," I whisper, moving his hand away and back onto my hip. "Not that, okay?"

"I thought you wanted…" he starts to say, but I smash my lips back into his before he can finish. I run my hands through the back of his hair, and his breathing gets heavier, more urgent. He grabs my waist, and thrusts himself into me over my clothes. I touch him, the hardness under his jeans. He groans and lightly bites my lower lip. I kiss him again and reach my hand around to his back pocket where the drugs are tucked away, but his jeans sag on his skinny torso, and I can't quite get to them. "Hey, what are you doing?" he asks, moving my hand back to the front of his pants. I comply for a moment, he groans again, and then I sweep back around, this time digging farther down. The plastic bag grazes my fingertips, but he takes hold of my wrist. "Hey, stay here," he says, guiding my hand into his jeans, and slipping it inside his boxers. He's throbbing, craning his neck into mine as he drives himself against my hand. I'm about to pull away, when he suddenly starts moaning, and getting his cloudy, rancid stickiness all over my palm and his jeans. When he finishes, he doubles over onto the floor in the fetal position, drifting off into a blissful nap.

It all ends so suddenly that I stand there in shock for a moment, afraid to move or make a sound. My feet are planted on the dirty mosaic tiles, and I have to remind myself to breathe. I hold my messy hand out in front of me, enveloped in shame like a heavy blanket that I can't escape. I push the feeling down, away, deep into a space inside so undiscovered that I didn't know it existed, and instead, focus on my plan, what needs to be done:

stealing the drugs and somehow getting them into Casey, Terry, and Nolan, so I can distract them and take the car tonight. Hopefully, the pills will make them lethargic enough that they pass out cold and sleep into the next day. By the time they wake up, I'll be long gone, and there will be nothing they can do.

I'm like a robot as I wash my hands in the sink and put my bra and shirt back on. When I'm sure he's in a sound sleep, I reach into his pocket, take out his plastic baggie of drugs and empty several into my palm before stuffing them into my jeans pocket. Without a sound, I ease them back where I found them.

"What are you doing?" he murmurs, coming to for a brief moment.

I freeze while he rotates to his other side and passes out cold again, snoring. When it's safe, I slip out of the bathroom, turning the lock from the inside, shutting the door behind me. Halfway down the stairs, I pause and watch Nolan walk around the crowded living room, head searching every which way. His eyes are about to make their way up to where I stand, when I duck back up the steps and find my way into a small office, then shut the door behind me. Within seconds, someone is banging on the door.

"Open the fucking door!"

I rush over and lock it, my back against the door while I wait for whoever's on the other side to leave. When it's quiet, I flip the light on. A desktop computer stares back at me. "Kismet," I say, walking over to it and settling into a comfy chair. A screensaver of a turtle floats in the ocean, its head bobbing along in the water. I move the mouse around and click on a search engine in the right-hand corner, then type in *Samuel Roland, Michigan.* The first hit is an antique shop called *Roland's Hobby Shop* in Frankenmuth, Michigan. I click on it.

In the *About Us* section, there's a small picture of an old woman and man standing beside a middle-aged man with salt-and-pepper hair and a thin smile who I recognize as Sam from my mother's photograph.

The accompanying paragraph talks about how the shop is the oldest store to stay open and never close for the last fifty years in Michigan. The people in the picture are the original owners, Thomas and Clara Roland, and the new owner, Samuel Roland. There's a special note from Sam, talking about how he recently has taken over the shop after his parents' deaths and how he's excited to have relocated to Michigan from Long Island. He now looks forward to starting this new chapter of his life in Frankenmuth.

I take a post-it note from a pad on the desk and jot down the phone number and address, and then get up to leave. When I open the door, Nolan is standing there.

"How long have you been here?" I ask.

"Not very long, but I've been looking all over for you. Are you okay?" he asks. "Listen, I didn't mean to hurt…"

"It's fine," I say, interrupting him. "Look, let's just forget about what happened before, okay? My buzz is wearing off, and I'm way too mortified to ever even think about that again."

"Fine by me." He pauses. "Hey, do you know where Ryan is? We were about to head back to his place, but no one can find him. I saw you with him earlier."

"Not a clue," I lie, glancing over at the bathroom where I left him. The door is still closed, and the light's still on. "Actually, I saw him with some girl. I think he might've mentioned that they were going to her house or something."

Casey and Terry appear, Casey with black mascara smeared all over her cheeks, and Terry with purple hickeys covering his neck.

"Where's Ryan?" Terry asks.

"He went home with some girl," Nolan informs him.

"The only girl I saw him with is Sosie," Terry says.

"If you must know, after you guys went upstairs, he started talking to some girl and totally ditched me," I say, staring at the floor, trying to seem wounded.

"That doesn't sound like Ryan," Terry challenges.

"Whatever, babe. Who even cares?" Casey says, stroking his bicep. "We've got keys to his place. I'm sure he won't mind that we went back without him. Let's just go."

"Actually, I was hoping to have just one more beer before we leave," I say. "I'm so wired for some reason. It'll help me sleep."

"One more? You're a beast!" Casey says. "I think I'm all set with this buzz I've already got going on."

"C'mon, what's one more little beer," I say, tugging at her hand. "The beer is so weak, it's practically water. If I don't get a good night of sleep, I won't be able to stay awake on the road tomorrow. What do you say, guys, one more before we go?" I ask Nolan and Terry. "Pretty please?"

"I guess one more won't hurt," Nolan agrees. "But just one, all right?"

Down the hall, a guy is leaning against the bathroom door where Ryan is locked away, banging a closed fist into the wood. "Open up, I gotta piss," he begs, as he clutches his crotch.

A girl saunters up beside him. "Good luck with that. That bathroom's been locked for the last forty-five minutes. There's another one downstairs."

Adrenaline rushes up my spine, as I think of Ryan in there passed out on the floor. "Why don't we go downstairs and get that beer?" I suggest to the group, and they all follow me back to the living room on the first floor.

"Let's make this quick," Terry says. "I'm fading."

"No problem," I say. "You guys stay here. I'll grab the drinks."

"I'll help you," Nolan offers. "You can't carry it all by yourself."

Casey and Terry find a couple of empty spots on the couch, and Nolan follows me into the kitchen where the keg is. I pat the front pocket of my jeans where I placed Ryan's drugs, my hand trembling with nerves as I grab the first Solo cup and fill it up with beer from the spout. Nolan is creeping over my shoulder, his breath close enough to feel. I hand the first cup to him without slipping anything into it. It's too risky. A part of me is relieved that I haven't betrayed him, but worried I could be sabotaging my plan. I'll look for another opportunity later. He takes a sip, and his attention shifts to two guys having a loud, drunken conversation. Whatever they're saying he's amused, laughing along with them, caught up in the banter. I grab two more beers and saunter over to the kitchen counter. Glancing over my shoulder, I take a few pills out of my pocket and slip them into each beer, swishing it in a circle. I'm panicky while I wait, shaking, my heart plip-plopping, a palpitation so intense it leaves me lightheaded. I have no idea if I'm doing the right thing as I watch the tiny pills float at the top, as they slowly become absorbed little by little, each fiber dissipating tiny bits at a time until it evaporates completely.

Nolan appears, and I hold my chest, nearly jumping out of my skin. "Sorry, you startled me."

"Hey, you're missing one," he says.

My hands are full," I quickly say. "Can you grab it for me?"

Nolan fills up another Solo cup with foamy beer, and we head back to where Terry and Casey are waiting on the couch.

"Here you go." I hand the first laced beer to Casey, and then the second to Terry. A lump forms in my throat as I watch each of them take their first sip. Casey kisses the foam off Terry's lips, and then they each take another drink.

Every few seconds I peak at the staircase, on edge that Ryan could walk down at any moment, but he never does. While Casey and Terry drink their beers, I raise my cup in the air to Nolan. "Cheers to friends," I say with a smile. "We're in this together, right?"

Chapter Eleven

As soon as we finish our beers, I hurry everyone along back to Ryan's house before the pills start taking effect. But somehow, Terry and Casey defy the odds, and the drugs do nothing other than making them extremely horny. Instead of passing out cold as planned, they retire to their designated room, and proceed to have session after session of loud, raucous sex.

An hour goes by, and they're still going at it, keeping Nolan and I awake and chatting on the couch. I would've made my escape by now, but Nolan is showing no signs of retiring to sleep. Every time there's a lull in the conversation, he changes the subject and starts talking about something else. I watch the door, unable to relax, paranoid Ryan's going to walk in at any moment and confront me, all the while longing to get going to Michigan.

Casey moans for the umpteenth time, and Nolan waits for her to quiet down before speaking. "So where'd you go after you left me outside?" he asks. My eyes are fixed on the door. "Sosie?"

I shake myself out of a fog. "Nowhere. I mean. Don't worry about it, okay? It's all good." The anxiety is building, creeping up my spine, making my hair stand on end. I feel like I'm a bomb that's about to detonate. I need to get out of here. "I'm sorry, Nolan. I can't lie to you any longer. I'm leaving tonight." I get up from the couch and start gathering up my things. "I'm taking the car and driving to Michigan. You can come along if you want or you can stay here with them." I pause for a moment and realize the whole house is suddenly quiet, no more moaning or squeaking bed.

Nolan blinks over and over, a deep furrow between his brows. "Sosie, are you still drunk? You're talking crazy. I think you need some sleep."

"I'm not drunk, and I'm dead serious. I'm leaving."

"You want to drive to Michigan? Why? What the hell's in Michigan?"

"This guy who might have some information about my mother and her death." I roam around the house, talking fast, rummaging through drawers, stuffing whatever loose cash is lying around into my messenger bag. "Look. It's a long, complicated story, but basically before the hurricane, I found this picture of my mother, and she was with a man—a man I've never seen before in my life—and he had his arms wrapped around her. He may have been dating my mother in secret before she died. I need to go to him. He works at this antique shop in a place called Frankenmuth."

"Sosie, slow down," he says, calmly. "None of this is making any sense. "We've already got plans. We're going to Virginia Beach in the morning. You can call whoever this guy is on the way or something."

"No, no, no." I'm shaking my head, the madness rising. "I need to speak to him in person. I'm going to his store. I need to see his face, his expression when I ask about her. He needs to see me in the flesh, standing in front of him, so he can't lie."

"Was this your plan all along?" Nolan's eyes scan mine, back and forth, back and forth. "To hijack our trip?"

"No," I lie.

"But you were just going to take Sven's car and leave us stranded here without any ride?"

I bite my lip. "I didn't think that far into it. Look. Something hit me earlier when we were driving over the Long Beach Bridge. That's the bridge my mother was on just before she died." I look deep into his eyes. "I'm not okay, Nolan. In here," I say, pointing to my heart. "And I need to be okay. I can't live like this anymore. There's stuff I need to know, settle within myself to really heal. I'm sorry if this is a lot … if I'm a lot, but I've got to go."

He licks his lips, tilts his head back, and looks at the ceiling. "I know you're not okay," he says softly and pauses. "I can't let you go alone. I want to go with you."

It takes everything inside me to not run into his arms, throw myself into his clutches, and kiss him. "Well, then we've got to go now. We're running out of time." I continue rummaging through the house. I open a drawer, and inside, tucked away, is a beautiful brooch with a mother-of-pearl butterfly. I pick it up, hold it to my décolletage, and then put it back in its place.

"I can't leave without them, though," Nolan says. "We've got to take them with us. Terry's been too good to me, giving me a place to stay whenever I need it, taking me under his wing. I can't just leave him here with no ride. It wouldn't be right."

"They'll never go for it. Terry's got his heart set on Virginia Beach. Didn't you hear everything he was saying in the car?"

"You're right," Nolan agrees. "They'll never go for it … willingly." He takes a step toward me. "Unless they have no choice."

"What are we going to do? Handcuff them and throw them in the back of the car? Be realistic."

"C'mon, those two are dead to the world in there, guaranteed. Didn't you hear that grand finale? We'll get them in the car, they can sleep off their sex coma while we drive through the night to Michigan, and by the time they wake up, we'll be more than halfway there, and there'll be nothing they can do about it. It'll be fine. We'll tell him we're going to Virginia Beach after you take care of some business in Michigan."

"I don't know," I say, still not convinced. "Terry is going to be so pissed."

"I'll take care of Terry. Don't worry about him."

I peak down the hall to Terry and Casey's bedroom. All is quiet and calm. "Are you sure about this?" I ask.

"Sure as I'll ever be," he says, and extends his hand.

Nolan and I tiptoe down the hall and into the bedroom where Casey and Terry are out cold, their bodies intertwined in a tiny twin bed. Terry's mouth hangs wide open, sheets tangled between his hairy legs, and Casey's head is stuck in Terry's armpit while she drools all over his chest. The whole room reeks like a bar, bad breath, and sweaty sex. I walk over to the side of the bed Casey's sleeping on and gently sit her up.

"Get off me, Terry. I'm sleeping," she slurs as I slip her t-shirt on over her lacy black bra. Her head flops forward then backward as she desperately tries to lie down. I let her, and then while she's on her back, I glide her leggings back onto her thin, shapely legs, before pulling them up and over her waist.

Nolan pulls on Terry's boxers, shoving him around every which way.

"Hey, Bro. Wazzup," Terry says, coming through for a second and going in for a kiss. "Love you, man."

Nolan and I can't help but crack up. "This is fucked up on so many levels," I say.

"No. Fucked up would be leaving them here in the middle of nowhere without a ride."

We finish getting them dressed, gather up the rest of our stuff, and then take them out to Sven's car one by one, wrapping their arms around either of our necks and helping them as they stagger into the backseat of the car.

"I've never seen Terry so smashed," Nolan says, peaking at the backseat where they're both snoring.

"He drank a lot," I inform him. "Both of them did." I start up the ignition, but pause before pulling out of the driveway. "I have no idea how to get to Michigan. Do you?"

"Terry, wake up," Nolan yells, balling up an old hamburger wrapper from the floor and throwing it at his head. "We don't know how to get to Michigan. We need your navigation skills."

"Are you insane?" I ask him.

"There's a map in the glove compartment," Terry mumbles and starts snoozing again.

Nolan turns on the dome light overhead, retrieves the map, and unfolds it in front of me. He locates where we are and traces the route from Philadelphia to Michigan with his finger. It takes him a minute to pinpoint Frankenmuth. "And it looks like we get on the highway just a few miles from here."

I rest my hand on his forearm. "Hey. Thank you."

His cheeks flush pink, and then he turns his attention to Terry and Casey. "Do you guys want to drive to Michigan?" he shouts. Casey groans something inaudible in response. "I think that's a yes. I'm going to take that as a yes."

We stop at a gas station before leaving Philadelphia and load up on energy drinks, snacks, and other supplies. My heart races with excitement and anticipation, and I can't stop talking. I'm bubbly, over sharing. I'm gabbing on and on about me, about my mother, and about anything else that crosses my mind.

Nolan is a captivated audience, eyes wide and enthralled in my stories, his only interjections a brief comment or directions.

Hours go by this way, nothing but the open road,

our ears popping from the altitude as we navigate through the mountains, no signal on the radio, and only my lengthy narratives and deepest thoughts. I tell him about how my mother used to sunbathe topless in the backyard in the summertime and how she'd adopt a French accent, roll her hair up into a turban with a scarf, wear cat-eye shaped sunglasses, and sip lemonade out of a mason jar with a straw. I'd watched her from inside the house, while lounging on the sofa and catching up on a summer read. She'd yell to me from the yard, "My love, won't you play that Brigitte Bardot song for me one more time." I'd get up and open the windows a little wider so she could hear it better, crank up the volume, and play *Moi Je Jou* for the hundredth time. It didn't matter how many times she heard it, she always wanted to hear it again. She leaned back on her plastic beach chair, face to the sun, as she let herself be transported to a different place, a different life, somewhere in Paris, or maybe Portofino.

"Your mother sounds like a character," he remarks. "I would've loved to have met her. You've told me lots of stories about your mom, but you haven't mentioned much about your dad."

"That's because there's really not much to tell," I say. "My dad's never really been around for me. He cheated on my mother a billion times, one of his mistresses being our slutty neighbor across the street. He tore my family apart a long time ago and is literally the cause of my mother going crazy. Now he works constantly to avoid me, leaves me to take care of myself, and tries to make up for it by buying me whatever I want, and giving me however much money I ask for. Period. The end. Not much else to tell."

Before we delve any deeper, there's a rumbling from the backseat. It's Casey, and she's awake, stretching and croaking.

"Babe, get off," she says to Terry, breaking free from underneath the weight of his arm. He turns over on his side and rests his forehead on the window, passing out again with his cheek smashed against the glass. "Holy shit, you guys, I'm so nauseous right now." She rolls the window down. "I might throw up." She sticks her head out like a panting dog, and the car fills with brisk, November air. After a few moments, she rolls the window back up and relaxes into her seat.

"Better?" I ask.

"Barely," she answers, in a husky, tired voice. "How long was I sleeping?"

"'Bout four hours," Nolan replies.

"What time is it now?"

"Seven o'clock," I tell her.

The early morning sun shines into the car, bright and inviting, but blinding Casey. She covers her eyes with her forearm.

"I don't even remember getting in this car. I barely remember anything from last night, either. I must've drank more than I thought." Her words come out slow, hesitant, as if she's trying to piece everything together. "It's seven o'clock? What time did we leave?"

"3 AM," I say.

"Whoa. I don't even remember that." She pauses. "Oh my God, you guys, I have to pee really bad."

"Should I stop?" I ask, Nolan.

"Yes, you should stop," she answers for him. "I need to pee, and I need a coffee. My head is pounding."

We're still in Pennsylvania, and somewhere in the middle of a two-hundred-and-seventy-mile stretch of road on the Pennsylvania Turnpike. Right outside of Pittsburgh, according to the map, but there isn't much else around other than farmland and woodland with cows and horses grazing in between thick stretches of forest. There certainly isn't anywhere to stop for a decent coffee or semi-clean bathroom. A vending machine in a dingy rest stop that spits out watered down cappuccino into a paper cup and a toilet that isn't the great outdoors is the most we can hope for.

I pull off of the highway, watching Casey from the rearview mirror as her forehead crinkles in confusion. Terry rouses in the backseat, too, grumbling and yawning.

I park in front of a rest stop, a small building made out of a series of cement slabs. It looks like a dungeon or the type of place where if you're in the wrong place at the wrong time, you might find yourself missing and thrown away into the surrounding wilderness. Truck drivers flock out front, smoking and taking turns using the men's side of the restroom. The door swings open and closed while they glance into our car, eyeing whatever fresh meat is about to get out.

"Where are we?" Casey pipes up, craning her neck to search for clues. My armpits begin to sweat. "A sign over there just said Pittsburgh. Why are we in Pittsburgh?"

Terry, still groggy and fluctuating between a state of wakefulness and sleep, remains silent.

Nolan and I are both quiet. The only sound is the car hiccupping as it idles in the parking spot.

"Why are we still in Pennsylvania? Shouldn't we be near Virginia by now?" Casey demands, her voice rising higher and higher with every question. Casey shakes Terry's arm. "Wake up, Terry. Wake up."

"What?" he mutters, aggravated but now cognizant, and sitting up.

"We're nowhere near Virginia Beach," she informs him. "We've been driving for hours, and we're still in Pennsylvania."

"You assholes," he exclaims. "You got us lost?"

"Okay, everyone just relax," Nolan says. "If you'd just give us a chance to clarify what's happening, I promise it'll all make sense in a minute." Casey shakes her head in disbelief, almost as if she knows whatever he's about to say next is going to be bullshit. "We're not lost, but we're not on our way to Virginia Beach … yet. We're making a quick detour first."

"A quick detour to where?" Casey asks.

"Michigan."

"Michigan?" she asks, as if there are a thousand more questions, but her brain can't process it all at once.

"Nolan, what the hell?" Terry asks, his voice full of bro-code disgust.

"Look, everyone just be cool," Nolan says, trying to diffuse the unfolding confrontation. "Sosie has to take care of some stuff in Michigan, but it's not gonna take long, and then we'll head to the beach right after. It'll set us back a day, tops."

"Oh. My. God." Casey draws the words out for dramatic effect. "We don't have a few days! Are you kidding me? We're on a tight schedule. This was supposed to be a quick trip before Sven gets back, but now we're suddenly wasting precious time going to Michigan? This is such bullshit. You never even asked us if we minded."

"Technically we did," Nolan points out, and I nod. "And we took your groans as a yes."

"You didn't ask us when we actually knew what the hell was going on!" Casey cries. "And you took it upon yourselves to leave in the middle of the night when the plan was to leave in the morning!"

"I can't believe you let her do this, bro," Terry growls, through a clenched jaw. "You're totally whipped by this girl for some reason. I don't get it. I just don't get it. She's not even hot."

"Watch your fucking mouth," Nolan warns him.

"Or what?" Terry taunts him, ready for whatever the repercussions might be. "Or you're going to punch me with your big, scary fist of painted nails?"

"Fuck you, Terry," I say, interrupting their argument before it goes any further. "For your information, I'm driving to Michigan because I need to speak to a man who might be able to give me some information about my mother's death."

"So I'm forced to go on your little Nancy Drew expedition? Do it on your own time," he retorts.

"Sosie's mom died, have some respect," Nolan says.

"Sorry, your mom died and everything, but literally all I've been hearing about since I met you is this same old sob story about your mom and how everyone's been picking on you. This might sound insensitive, but it's time to put on your big girl pants and start getting over it. At some point, everyone's moms are going to die. It's called the fucking circle of life. I should know, my mom died two years ago of cancer, but you didn't know that did you, because I'm not constantly blabbing on and on and on about it, am I? You can't go on feeling sorry for yourself for the rest of your life, and you can't drag everyone around you into the drama just because you're sad."

"You wouldn't understand," I whisper. "You couldn't possibly."

"I do understand," he says. "You don't own grief, Sosie."

Casey's eyes shift from me to Terry and then back to me, her breath shallow and forehead crinkled in worry.

"You're right, I don't own grief. I never said I did." He opens his mouth to speak, but I put my hand up to stop him. "And maybe your mom died, so you understand what it feels like to lose someone you love, but do you know what it feels like to see your mothers severed head lying on a dark road ten feet from the rest of her body? Do you know what it's like to be sent a video like that, because some heartless asshole recorded it so everyone could have a good laugh at your dead mother's expense? I guess I failed to mention the part about my mother being decapitated. Isn't that fucking dandy? To see the last expression your mom wore when she died. And do you want to know the most fucked up part of all? The part I can't seem to shake? She looked terrified. Her eyes…" My voice gets stuck in back of my throat, my shoulders trembling. "I could see it in her eyes that she was really fucking scared." After a moment, I dry my tears with the back of my hand and swallow hard. "Yeah, so maybe I might need a little closure, and there's this guy in Michigan who might be able to help me, that is, if you decide not to be a total asshole and will allow me to do that. So what's it going to be, Terry? Are you gonna let me do what I need to do in order to find a little peace, or are you gonna make me turn the car around and go to Virginia Beach right now because you need that beer and to feel the saltwater on your skin?"

Both Casey and Terry sit in silence, the blood drained from their peachy complexions. "I'm so sorry," Casey whispers. "I had no idea. Do whatever you need to do." She nudges Terry, and he curtly nods. "We'll get to Virginia Beach when we get there."

Chapter Twelve

We continue on our way to Michigan. Hours go by in silence. There's no talking, no music playing on the radio, only the sound of the tires hitting the pavement and the occasional hum of a semi riding next to us.

Finally, Nolan reaches over and turns the radio on. "Classic rock?" he asks, stopping on one of the only stations coming in.

"I hate classic rock," I say.

He turns the knob some more.

"Ooh, leave this song on," Casey pipes in from the back seat. Her mood has lightened, and she's embracing the road trip vibes. She's got the hood of her sweatshirt up, her pretty face peaking out from behind wispy pieces of her long, red hair. She looks grungy, yet sexy all at the same time, like every guy's fantasy of the girl next door. "Sosie loves this song, too, don't you, Sosie?"

We make eye contact through the rearview mirror, but I quickly turn my attention back to the road, sapped from my confession a few hours earlier and exhausted from the lack of sleep.

Casey sings along to the radio at the top of her lungs. She hooks her arm through Terry's and tries to get him to sway back and forth to the music.

He doesn't budge and instead sits stoic, like a statue made out of cement. "What is this shit?" Terry asks. "You can't honestly like this."

"Are you kidding me?" Casey answers. "This is only one of the greatest bands to have ever existed. You've never heard of Simon and Garfunkel? See, told you, Sosie. We're the only ones I know with good taste in music."

"Good taste in music. Yeah. Okay," he retorts.

Her eyes are still on me. She doesn't look away. It's like she's trying to send me a telepathic message. I'm receiving it, but I pretend not to. She's waiting for me to back her up, waiting for me to say something in defense of the band. I don't, the song ends, and the moment passes. She stares into her lap, hands folded.

I turn the radio down. "I'm thinking we'll be in Frankenmuth around three o'clock, maybe four, if we hit traffic."

"You planning on stopping by the shop today?" Nolan asks.

I nod. "Then I was thinking that we'll leave tomorrow, sometime in the morning or early afternoon," I announce for everyone to hear. "If it's okay, I thought we could get a hotel room tonight. Don't worry, though, it's on me. I'll put it on my dad's credit card."

"How far are we from Michigan right now?" Casey asks.

"About three more hours," I tell her.

"Three more? Fuck my life. I'm bored," Casey declares. "Is anyone else bored?"

"I am," Nolan raises his hand.

"Let's play a game!" Casey suggests.

"I have a better idea, why don't we all be quiet, or better yet, why don't we all take a nap? There, there, close your eyes and fall fast asleep." Terry pulls Casey over to him, trying to get her to rest her head on his chest.

She tears out of his grasp and instead bounces, animated and enthusiastic into the space between Nolan and me. "Hey, have you guys ever played Never Have I Ever?"

"Course," Nolan says. "Who hasn't?"

"Oh, God, you're such a child," Terry groans, already annoyed and resistant. "Why do you want to play that stupid game right now?"

"Because, duh, it's fun. Besides, what else are we going to do for the next three hours? Can't you just, like, humor me, or do you always have to be a dick?"

"You didn't have any complaints about my dick last night," Terry quips, not missing a beat.

"You're so vile sometimes," she tells him. "Sosie, have you ever played?"

"Yeah, but it was a long time ago, and I really don't remember the rules or whatever."

"It's easy," she explains. "Basically, each of us will take a turn and say something they've never done, like, 'Never have I ever been arrested,' and if anyone in the group has been arrested, like, for example Terry's been arrested, so he'd be the one to take a shot."

"Only one problem, babe. Can't play a drinking game without any booze," Terry says, pretending to play knock-knock on her head.

"Have you ever heard of using your fucking imagination, Terry?" she scolds.

"Imaginations are for children, much like this game," Terry says. "God. Why do you turn into a high school girl when you're around people who are younger than you? It's a character flaw, you know that, right?"

"Shut up, Terry," she says.

"Okay, if someone doesn't start the game soon, I'm going to pull over and leave you all on the side of the road," I threaten like a mother yelling at her bickering children.

"I'll go first," Casey says. She takes a long, deep breath, holds it, and then lets it out. "Okay, I got it. Never have I ever hooked up with someone and not known their name." After she speaks, she looks around eagerly, waiting for the consensus, waiting to hear our secrets.

"I have never," I admit.

"I have never," Nolan says.

Terry grins. "I have."

Casey grimaces. "Of course you have."

"But you made it so easy, babe."

"Tell the story," Casey instructs. "Now you have to tell us how it all went down."

"You mean, how she went down?" Terry jokes, and Casey punches him in the gut. "I mean, there's not much to tell. I was nineteen, I was modeling in Paris for a summer, and she was thirty-five. She didn't speak any English. We hooked up in the bathroom in some little bar after one of our photo shoots. She blew me," he clarifies. "It was amazing, and I never saw her again."

"Was she hot?" Casey asks.

"Yeah, obviously. She was a French model."

"Hotter than me?" she asks. "Wait, never mind. She was thirty-five? Whatever, she was old. Probably had a saggy ass."

"Nope, her ass was fine," he says, drawing out the last word.

"You guys, stop." I intervene before a full-blown argument breaks out. "I thought we were playing a game, not talking about every girl Terry's ever boned. Okay, it's my turn, right? Never have I ever stolen something and gotten caught."

"I have never," Casey says.

"I have never," Terry says. "That is, gotten caught."

"I have," Nolan says

"Really?" I ask, surprised, intrigued.

"It was back home in Georgia, and I was in the fifth grade. This girl Sheila, who I thought I was in love with, dared me to steal this, like, stupid little keychain from a gift shop while we were on a school field trip. So, to impress her, I put it in my pocket, you know? I was nervous as all hell, looking around after I did it and stuff, so worried someone was gonna see me, and she was there, like, looking at me just awestruck and so surprised that I had the guts to actually do it, and I could tell I got her, you know? She was all about me. So, there I was, in the store, keychain in my pocket, and I decided it was time to make my escape. So, I strut out of the store, Sheila trailing close behind. She's giggling, and then all of the sudden a worker at the store was all, 'Um, son, can we please see what's in your pocket?' and I was like, 'Oh, shit, it's over. My life is over,' and I start crying like a little baby. Sheila takes off, and I was left standing there alone with the store clerk, who then took me into the little room where they called my mom. Boy, did I ever get a whooping that night. My mama whipped me *bad*." Nolan winces at the memory, and then chuckles.

"What happened with Sheila?" Casey asks.

"Never spoke to me again," Nolan tells us.

"Aw. So cold," I say.

"Tell me about it."

"Okay, Terry, it's your turn," I say.

"I can't think of anything," Terry grumbles.

"Don't be a party pooper," Casey tells him. "Just think of something. It can be anything."

He thinks for a moment. "Okay. Never have I ever tried to kill myself," he says, the words flinging from his mouth, careless, random.

"I have never," Casey says.

"Nope," Nolan answers.

They wait for me. My mind is racing. Should I lie? Should I tell the truth and let them in on how screwed up I truly am? I contemplate. It's not like they haven't already had a preview. "I have," I confess.

"You don't have to tell the story," Casey offers, probably because she knows things are about to get awkward again.

"No, she has to tell the story like everyone else," Terry says. "Those are the rules, remember?"

"It's all good, I don't mind telling." I shrug. "About a week ago was when I did it, or tried to do it, I guess you could say. It was the night of the hurricane, the night I was anonymously sent that awful video of my mother. After I watched it, I just hit rock bottom. Something snapped inside me. So, I took a whole bunch of pills, drank a whole bunch of liquor, enough to kill a horse, and I just went to sleep. But instead of dying, I somehow woke up a couple of days later. I felt like total garbage, and it was the worst hangover of my life, but I was still alive. And little did I know, while I was supposed to be dying, the hurricane was happening all around me, and that alone could've very well killed me if all the poison I put into my body hadn't, but for some reason, I didn't die. For some really screwed up reason that even I don't understand yet, I lived. I guess I just wasn't meant to die, not then anyway. I don't know, maybe it was the universe telling me there's still some shit here that I need to take care of before I go. Like, going to see this guy in Michigan, for instance."

Nolan turns to me, but I keep my eyes fixed on the road ahead. He puts his hand over mine. "I'm glad you didn't die," he says, quietly. "Really glad." I turn the radio back on, scanning through the stations until I stop on a Fleetwood Mac song. It's perfect for this moment, dreamy and melancholy, and I hum along to it, letting my mind get swept away. Casey rolls the window down and puts her hand out into the breeze, rolling it in a wave along to the beat. I watch her, entranced by the way her hand moves through the wind, the motion soothing my soul.

The next thing I know, Nolan is shaking my arm,

grabbing the wheel with his other hand.

"What? What's wrong?' I ask.

"Sosie, I think you just fell asleep with your eyes open," he tells me.

"You were swerving all over the place," Terry says.

I blink, my eyes still open and stinging. "I fell asleep with my eyes open?" I ask, horrified at the haunting feeling of being present but not in control. I shake myself out of the doze. "I'm okay. I'm okay."

Lights flash in my rearview mirror, bright blue and red lights gaining on us with every second that passes.

"Sosie, there's a cop behind us!" Casey yelps from the backseat.

"I can see that. Fuck, what do I do?" I watch the cop car in the rearview as it gets closer and closer.

"Everyone just be calm," Nolan says. "Sosie, pull over to the shoulder. It's going to be okay."

"I'm so fucked," I mutter as I put my signal on and pull over, the wheels thumping over the speed humps in the road.

The officer parks behind us and gets out of his car, approaching from the passenger side door.

"Just be cool," Nolan reminds me in a soothing, soft voice.

"I'm trying," I say, but my adrenaline is pumping through me, rushing over me like a whirling tornado.

The officer knocks on the window. He tips his brown suede hat as a hello, then runs his finger along his well-groomed sideburn like he's trying to figure me out.

I stare at my reflection in his aviator sunglasses.

"Roll your window down, Sosie," Nolan says, coaching me.

I follow his instructions and give the officer a

weak smile.

"You were swerving back there and speeding," the officer says, not wasting any time with small talk. "Going twelve over, to be exact. Are you aware of that?"

"Yes," I croak. "I thought I saw an animal in the road, and I was trying not to hit it. I'm sorry. The speeding I wasn't aware of."

"License and registration."

I open the glove compartment and sift through the messy papers, until I locate a small leather binder. The officer leans into the car, suspicious, like he's sniffing.

"You been drinking?" he asks, a mint green Tic-tac falling out of his mouth, and onto Nolan's forearm as he speaks.

Nolan doesn't move a muscle, and the officer makes no attempt to pick it up.

"No, sir," I promise.

"Any drugs?" he asks.

"No, sir, no drugs."

"So, if I looked through this car right now, I wouldn't find anything?"

"No, sir, you wouldn't."

"License and registration." He reminds me, removing his sunglasses.

He's younger than I thought and dashingly handsome, once his eyes are revealed. I don't expect it, and for a moment, I'm taken with his aqua colored eyes and thick, black eyelashes. He seems to know what I'm thinking, perhaps no stranger to women getting caught up in the cop fantasy and his good looks, but everything about his demeanor tells me he's all business. The simple gold band he wears on his left ring finger a plausible reason.

My fingers tremble as I open up the leather binder, praying the registration is inside. It is, and I breathe a sigh of relief as I hand it to him.

"License as well," he says, getting impatient.

"I'm sorry. Of course." I lean over Nolan's knees and retrieve my purse from the space in front of his feet. "Sorry about that, officer," I say, handing him my license.

He holds up the registration and analyzes my license simultaneously. "This isn't your car," he says, the words coming out like a statement. I don't respond. "This isn't your car?" he repeats, this time as a question.

"No, sir, it isn't. It's my friend's car, and we're borrowing it," I say.

"We're?" he asks.

"Yes, my friends and I, sir."

Nolan nods as a sign of solidarity.

The officer looks skeptical as he makes eye contact with each of us, his brows furrowed. "I'm going to need you to step out of the vehicle, miss. Please wait until the traffic has cleared to get out."

The last car whizzes past and the road clears. I step out of the car and walk over to the officer who's standing near the back end of the vehicle. I'm completely sober, but there's no denying I'm in desperate need of sleep. My eyes, irritated and bloodshot, won't help my cause.

"Okay, miss," he says, his sunglasses perched back onto the bridge of his nose. "I'm going to have you go through a few tests for me, all right? If you haven't been drinking or doing any drugs, you should breeze right through, and if you have, then let there be no confusion, I'm going to arrest you. Do you understand that?" I glance at Casey, who's watching me with worried eyes from the back window. "Miss? Are you listening to me?"

"Yes," I answer, the words coming out breathy

and shallow. Terry directs Casey to turn around and not look at me. My eyes break away from them and back to the officer. "Yes, I understand."

"All right. First, I'm going to check your eyes," he tells me. "Keep your head still, and follow the stimulus only. The stimulus is going to be my pen. Do not move your head. Do you understand the instructions?" The way he speaks reminds me of a stage actor projecting his voice to the back of the auditorium. It's deep, enunciated, formal.

"Yes," I answer.

He takes a pen from behind his ear and holds it up, moving it back and forth as I follow with my tired, burning eyes, struggling to focus. When he finishes, he puts the pen back. "Very good. Okay, come and step right over here." He motions for me to follow him a little ways back, and I oblige like an obedient dog. He stares at me for a moment. "You know, you look a little different than the picture on your license."

"I do?" I ask, my hand instinctively touching the ends of my stringy hair. "Oh, you mean my hair? Yeah, that picture was taken two years ago."

"My wife changes her hair all the time, too. One day it's red, the next day blonde. Hell, she's even had pink streaks. Didn't care for that very much, to be honest. She can't do any of that stuff now, though, doctor's order. She's seven months pregnant," he explains. "Step over here. I need you to help me out, alrighty? Hold the end of this tape here real tight. Now lay it down, gently, gently," he says, guiding his end of the tape to the ground as I do the same. "Very good. Now here's what you're going to do. You're going to walk heel to toe, arms down at your sides, and count each step out loud, nine to be exact."

I nod and get into position on the line, my feet

coordinated in place.

"Wow, overachiever here," he says.

I take my first step to start, but he puts his arm out in front of my ribcage to block me. "Whoa, whoa, whoa, slow down. You didn't hear all the directions. When you get to nine, you're going to turn like this," he says, demonstrating the pivot. "Then walk nine steps back the other way. Got it?"

"Got it."

"And go."

I walk along the line, taking each step with great precaution and concentration, careful to not make a mistake. When I get to the end, I rotate, and walk back along the line the other way.

He doesn't take his eyes off me, but instead watches my feet, glances up at my face, then back to my feet. When I finish, he saunters over, hands on his hips.

"I've got good news." He takes off his sunglasses and pauses. "You, my friend, have successfully passed the series of field sobriety tests. I'm not even going to administer a Breathalyzer, because that's the first time in all my years patrolling this highway that anyone passed this test with such ease."

I can't help but smile ear to ear. "Thank you," I say. I glance back over to the car. Casey is watching me again. I quickly give a discreet thumb's up while the officer writes something down in his notebook.

"You can go and get back into your car now," he instructs me. "But don't turn the ignition on yet. Do you understand?" I nod. "I'm going to do a couple of things in my vehicle, run some information, but I'll come back over and let you know when you can go."

The officer goes back to his patrol car, and I repress the urge to skip as I make my way back to Sven's car. I hop into the driver seat.

"What happened? Oh my God, Sosie. We're all freaking out," Casey says.

"Everything's fine," I assure her. "He made me do a bunch of tests, but I passed with flying colors. And now he's just running some information real quick, but as soon as he finishes, we can go."

"Holy shit, thank you baby Jesus." Casey celebrates with a little happy dance in her seat, but then abruptly stops in the middle of it. "Wait a minute, did you just say that he's running some information? Oh my god, you guys, he's probably running the registration. Do you think he's running the registration? What if Sven reported his car missing by now?"

"Sven didn't report the car missing," Terry says. "He's in Punta Cana for another few days. There's no way."

Seconds later, the officer is back at the passenger's side window, knocking on it with his knuckles.

"Oh my God, oh my God, oh my God," Casey whispers.

Terry shushes her, and I roll the window down.

"Here you go, miss. All's well," the officer says, handing me the binder with Sven's registration and my license. "I'm doing you a favor today. I only wrote you a ticket for going five over, rather than twelve."

"Thank you so much," I say, sincerely.

"And since there doesn't seem to be anything awry with the car you're driving, it hasn't been reported as stolen or anything like that, I'm going to take your word that you have indeed borrowed this vehicle with the owner's permission. So, no ticket for that." He pauses. "And just a word of advice, you might want to update that picture on your license. It's a little outdated."

That's a little rude. Maybe I have been looking a

little rough these days—not the bubbly looking sixteen-year-old I once was two years ago—but life's been shitty lately. Heartache has a way of sapping your looks. The last thing I need is anyone rubbing it in. Still, I smile at the officer, thankful to be off the hook and anxious to get back on the road. "I'll keep that in mind."

The officer pats the roof of the car. "Be safe now."

Chapter Thirteen

Once the officer gets back into his car and leaves, I turn the ignition on, wait for the road to clear, and then merge back onto the highway.

"Eek. That was close," I say.

"Hey, do me a favor and turn around," Terry says. "We're going back to New York. I'm making an executive decision." I pretend not to hear as I crack open the last energy drink and take a big slurp. "Are you deaf? I said pull over right now. The only reason we're on this trip to begin with is because of me, and I've changed my mind. Sven needs his car. Road trip is over, and we're going back to Long Beach. Now turn around."

"We've been through this, Terry," Casey says, with an exhausted sigh. "We're on our way to Michigan. Sosie has stuff to take care of there, remember? It's important to her."

"Yeah, Casey's right," Nolan says. "Besides, it's just a couple more hours to go, and we should be there."

"What the fuck is wrong with you people?" Terry barks. "It's like I'm stuck in the fucking Twilight Zone? Are you all mental?"

"That's actually a real possibility," I say. "I mean, it wouldn't really surprise me if there was something mentally askew with all of us, right guys?"

"Totes," Casey agrees.

"Not the craziest thing I've ever heard," Nolan says.

"Fuck all of you," Terry says.

"Hey, take it easy, Terry," Casey says. "We're just joking around. Lighten up. No need to go off the deep end right now. Everything worked out back there. It's fine."

"Don't tell me to lighten up," Terry warns her.

"She could've gotten us all arrested just now. She was driving like a moron."

"I was tired," I admit. "But I think I just needed some fresh air, and one of these." I raise my can and take another sip. "But honestly, I'm good now. Fully awake and capable."

"She's fucking nuts," Terry says.

"Stop it," Casey says, under her breath.

"Why are you sticking up for this girl? Look, I get it, you want to play the big sister role or whatever, it gives your life purpose, but don't let it cloud your fucking judgment. She threw us in the back of this car while we were passed out to manipulate this trip. You can't deny that it's a totally psychotic thing to do. Like, it's not normal."

"I was a part of it, too," Nolan says. "It wasn't just Sosie."

"You don't get it. None of you get it. Do you understand how bad that could've been for me just now? Like I need to go to jail right now. If that had gone any differently, any differently at all, then I could've been locked up for a very long time. Do you understand that?"

Casey rolls her eyes, not moved. "You weren't going to go to jail. People don't go to jail for riding as a passenger with a suspended license, Terry. If the cops went around arresting everyone who ever rode in the backseat of a car with a revoked license, then there wouldn't be any room in jail for the people actually committing real crimes."

"You mean crimes like manslaughter?" he asks her, pointedly.

"Yeah, I guess," she agrees, without making the connection. "Crimes like manslaughter would probably constitute."

"I'm not worried about going to jail for driving

in the goddamn backseat of a car with a suspended license," he tells her. "I'm talking about going to jail for manslaughter, or the fact that I have a dime bag on me right now."

"You have a dime bag on you right now?" she asks, outraged. "And you didn't offer me any? I have a raging headache and you knew that!"

"Am I the only one paying attention to the fact that Terry may or may not have just admitted to killing someone?" Nolan asks.

"Nope, definitely heard that, too," I say.

"Terry didn't kill anyone," Casey says, dismissively.

"Actually, I did."

"You better be joking."

"I wish I was."

"So, you killed someone?" Casey asks, her voice starting to show worry.

"Yeah, I did."

"You fucker!" Casey exclaims, punching him in the bicep.

"What? Don't look so disgusted. What was I supposed to say? Hey, in high school I killed a kid by accident?"

"Yeah!" Casey shouts. "Don't you think I have a right to know if my boyfriend killed someone?"

"See? This is why I can't tell you anything. You just go crazy and get emotional. You don't even try to understand what the situation is. You just lose it."

"There you go, blaming me for your shit. Typical Terry."

"I'd explain everything to you if you'd just shut up for three seconds and let me speak. Holy shit," Terry says, exasperated. Casey is quiet, waiting. "I was seventeen. My buddies and I had gotten some pretty decent looking fakes, so we decided to go out to a bar and have a few drinks. We'd never done anything like that before. It was a pretty low-key night at first, we took a few shots, played some pool, had some beers, talked with some girls. As the night went on, I was really hitting it off with this pretty blonde. It's funny, because now I really can't even remember anything about her other than the fact that she was pretty and had long blonde hair. I can't even picture her face, really. My buddy had been talking to her, too, but I didn't know it. We were all drunk, really drunk, and one thing led to another, and my buddy and I started arguing. It was stupid. He pushed me, and I pushed him back. The bouncer kicked us out, but we continued to push each other around outside.

"I was laughing at him at first, because I thought no way he was this upset about some random girl, but then he swung at me and hit me in the chin. I was so pissed, hurt too, because he was my best friend since grade school. I swung back at him and got him good. The next thing I remember I was waking up in the hospital, my head pounding, and basically no memory of anything that happened.

"My parents were there. They were both crying, and that's when I found out what I'd done. When I punched him, I knocked him out, and he hit the ground, hit his head hard on the concrete. I didn't remember any of it. It was as if they were telling me a story about something they'd seen on the news, but none of it felt familiar to me. It wasn't until months later that I started to get memories back. Not complete memories, but flashes, you know?" Terry stops for a moment, and stares out the window blankly. "It wasn't anyone's fault. We were both drunk and stupid that night. That's it. It could've been me, you know? Just as easily as it was him, it could've been me."

"So, what happened to your friend?" Casey's voice is low, full of dread. "Did he live?"

"He was in a coma for a week, and then he died," Terry tells her.

"Did you go to jail?" Nolan asks.

"Not exactly. My dad's a judge in Wisconsin, and let's just say he figured shit out for me. I avoided jail by a sliver, a technicality, and got off easy with probation. They could prove he had an undetected heart condition that may have also contributed to his death. But the deal––the deal my dad made with me—was that I had to leave Wisconsin for good and I couldn't get into any more trouble for the rest of my life anywhere and for any reason. My dad told me he'd personally put me in the cell himself if I ever did."

"So you thought stealing a car was a good idea," Casey asks, sharply.

"I did that for you. You kept talking about how much fun you had when we went surfing before the hurricane, and I wanted to experience that with you all over again."

"You did it for me? Oh, okay," Casey says, sarcastically. "If you honestly believe that, then that makes you a total sociopath. This was all your idea. You talked me into it."

"I can't believe this girl. I just poured my heart out to you, and this is what I get."

"That's not all you get," Casey says. "You also get a big fuck you."

Casey crosses her arms over her chest and skulks down in her seat. She and Terry barely say another word to each other for the rest of the trip. None of us do. That is, until we make it to Michigan a few hours later, around four o'clock in the early evening.

****

Frankenmuth is a quaint Bavarian town, and we're greeted with a giant religious cross and a Jesus statue with the words *Jesus Saves* engraved in the stone. Everything about it feels safe, like the type of place where everyone knows everyone and the speed limit doesn't go beyond twenty-five. It's so small, we practically run into Sam's store as we drive around looking for somewhere to eat.

"There's Sam's shop." I point to it out the windshield, heart pounding in my ears as I lay eyes on it for the first time. I pull over and park in a space out front.

"Rolland's Hobby Shop?" Nolan asks. "That's it? You sure?"

"Yeah, I'm sure. Looks exactly like the picture I saw online. Hey, just give me a sec, okay? I'll be right back."

I get out of the car while everyone waits. Old-fashioned kerosene streetlights line the narrow road, already lit even though the sun hasn't fully set. The lights above illuminate the storefronts of homemade fudge shops, bakeries, and colorful candy stores. Everything has closed up early, perhaps because it's Sunday, including Sam's place, which has a friendly flip sign in the window, promising to be back soon.

My heart tingles as I peer into the dark window. There's a wooden table and chairs set up in the main storefront display with a scene set for high tea with an empty cake platter, ornately painted teacups, and a ceramic pot. A postcard rack and an old-fashioned cash register reside next to the table.

As I stand out front, shivering in the crisp, wide-open air, a part of me can't believe I'm really here, actually doing this. Although nerves are dancing around in my belly, being here feels right. A necessary means to an end.

"Sosie, you almost done?" Casey calls out from the car window. "What are you doing? Everything's closed, and we're starving."

I tear myself away from the store, from my wandering thoughts, and go back to the car.

Just down the road, we pull into a McDonalds that looks more like a Bavarian chalet than a fast food joint with its little brown shutters, mini clock tower peaking out from the center, and blue and white awnings. I opt for the drive-thru and treat everyone to burgers, fries, soda, and chicken nuggets, which we gobble up while sitting in the car. When we're done, we drive around, searching for somewhere to crash for the night, but there aren't any motels or anything remotely affordable, even after I drive the length of the town twice. There's only a grand hotel, which sprawls across acres of land, and advertises rooms for two hundred and fifty dollars from a sign written in German looking script. It's a little out of my price range even if I'll be paying with the credit card my father pays off.

I pull up to the valet stand, and a young, high school aged boy approaches the car, wearing a traditional knee-length lederhosen, complete with embroidered suspenders and brown loafers. I leave the car running and we all hop out.

"Welcome to the Bavarian Inn Lodge. Have you stayed with us before?" he asks, while the others go have a smoke at a nearby bench.

"Nope," I reply. "Not from around here."

"No kidding," he says, with a friendliness you only find in the Midwest. "Where ya from?"

"New York."

"Whereabouts?"

"Long Island."

"No kidding! You guys just got hit pretty bad

with Hurricane Sandy, didn't ya? Been watching it on the news."

"Yeah. Let's just say my friends and I needed to get away."

"Well, this is your place, and we're happy to have ya! My name is Brice, and I'll be taking care of your car. Tim over there will help you with your bags." Tim gives a weak nod from his perch inside the valet stand and then promptly goes back to texting on his cell phone.

"That's all right. Don't need any help with the bags. There's just a few, and I think I can manage."

"Well, alrighty then," he says. "Let me just take down your license plate information, so I can get you parked. It's ten bucks a day to valet, that okay?"

"Totally fine."

He jots down the information onto a card and then rips off the bottom portion, handing it to me. "Alrighty, so, whenever you want to get your car, just give that card to Kaley over there at the front desk, and she'll phone us right away." Kaley sits behind a window, tapping away at a computer at the front desk. She's wearing the female version of Brice's outfit. "Kaley can also get you checked into your room, so when we're done here, just head on over to her, and I probably shouldn't say this," he says, holding his hand up to his mouth like he's about to spill a juicy secret. "But I'm sure if you tell Kaley that you're visiting from New York after the hurricane, then she'll hook you up with a complimentary chicken dinner. We're famous for our chicken dinners, ya know."

"I didn't know that." Brice starts to jump into the driver's seat to park the car. "Oh, hey, wait," I say, stopping him.

"Sorry! Your bags. I'm so sorry." He retrieves the bags from the trunk and puts them on the sidewalk.

"You're sure you can manage those, because I can get—"

"No, no I'm fine. Actually, I wanted to ask if you've ever driven a car with surfboards attached to the hood?"

His eyes squint while he considers it. "Can't say I have. Don't do much surfing here in Michigan. Now tubing, we do a lot of that out on the lake in the summer time."

"Just make sure you park it somewhere with lots of space."

"Always do," he nods.

****

As promised Kaley hooks us up with a decent-sized room on the fourth floor and a coupon for a complimentary chicken dinner. The room, however, is hardly worth two hundred and fifty dollars. The whole place smells of blue toilet bowl cleaner, the carpet is soggy and musty, and one of us will have to sleep on a stiff rollaway bed.

Terry wastes no time claiming one of the double beds as he lies on his back, shoes off, feet stinking up the whole room, while looking up at the popcorn-spackled ceiling. "Gah. Why are we here? I just need to get back in the water." He groans. "Like, stat."

Nolan has designated himself the rollaway sleeper and sits atop the lumpy, pilling comforter.

"I need a manicure." Casey complains as she sits on the opposite bed from Terry, picking at her chipping nail polish.

"I'm going to take a walk," I announce. "I've got sea legs after that drive. Anyone want anything?"

"Nah," Casey says, preoccupied with her nails.

I go downstairs to the lobby and help myself to the complimentary cookies and hot apple cider that's set up on a table for guests. I find a cozy couch in front of a fireplace and start digging in.

"Nervous about tomorrow?" Nolan walks up, hands stuffed in his pockets.

I swallow a big bite of cookie. "I eat when I'm nervous," I explain, almost apologizing. "I'm not even hungry right now."

"I had to get out of that room."

Nolan sits down next to me. "Terry's feet?"

"You know it." He laughs as I stuff another cookie into my mouth. "Don't be nervous about tomorrow. Everything's going to be good, you'll see." He rubs my arm, and goosebumps prickle underneath my shirt. I want to hug him, to snuggle up against his collarbone, to have him wrap his hands around my waist and pull me into him while we sit in front of the cozy fire. He seems to sense my desperation, and abruptly lets go. My heart sinks. "Sosie, I feel like I need to explain something to you."

"If this is about last night, I really don't need you to. I already told you that."

"I know. It's just … there's some stuff about me that you don't know, and maybe if you did, then things would make more sense." He takes a deep breath and looks me in the eyes. "I'm gay, Sosie."

My mouth drops open. "Wow. Really?" I ask, stunned.

"Yeah. I don't know why I didn't just tell you that before. I'm not embarrassed about it or anything. Not anymore. I guess I just didn't know how to say it or something. You okay?"

"Yeah." I answer, but I'm still in shock. "I mean, you're right. Things definitely make more sense now."

"For the record, if I was straight, then you'd definitely be the first girl I'd, uh, bang. Is that how straight guys talk or just Terry?"

We laugh. "Thanks, I guess? It means a lot to at least know I'm bangable."

"You're totally bangable," he assures me and then gets serious. "There's something else, too. You remember when we were in the car, and whatnot, when you were telling us about, you know, trying to kill yourself?" I nod. "I should've said something at the time, but I guess I sort of chickened out. I've never told anyone this … but something similar happened to me. I tried to kill myself, too."

I tilt my head and bite my lip, seeing him in a new light. "And see I took you for a totally, well-adjusted human being."

"Naw, not even. We're all a little screwed up, I guess."

"When?"

"About two months ago," he replies. "Right around the time I started at Bolton Academy."

"Why did you do it?"

"I guess I just felt trapped in my life, and like I was all alone, and because I was missing my brother like crazy. When my mom forced me to move to New York, it all happened out of nowhere, and it was such a big change from where I came from in Georgia, you know? In Georgia, I had friends, a life I loved. Then I moved to Long Beach and suddenly I'm going to this fancy private school where I don't fit in at all, where I don't know anyone, and no one cares to know me. Then, one day in early September, everything just sort of bubbled over. My brother was supposed to come and visit for the weekend, and I was looking so forward to it, counting down the days. Then, he missed his flight, and I had this horrible day at school, and it all sort of hit me at once, I'm never going to make any real friends in New York and this loneliness is never going to lift. That's how it felt at the time, anyway. So, I came home and got some wire cutters from Larry's toolbox in the garage and cut the cord off of an old vacuum cleaner. Without even thinking, I fastened it around my neck and tried to hang myself from the banister. I didn't leave a note or anything. It was that impulsive. The next thing I knew, I was hanging by that cord, each moment fading farther and farther away, and I remember thinking, 'What the hell am I doing right now?' It felt surreal, and then, bam, the cord broke and I fell to the ground, gasping for breath. But the second I hit that floor, I realized I didn't want to die. I was just sad and pissed off with my new life in that moment. I was looking for a way out, but I didn't want to leave forever and never come back. I just wanted my old life back, ya know? I just wanted out of my current circumstances. After all that, I knew there was more for me, I knew there had to be more. So, right then and there, I made peace with my life and whatnot, and with God, and I told myself I just needed to get through high school, and then the first chance I got, I was going to get the hell out of New York and move back to Georgia. So, I dusted myself off and never spoke of it. I never told anyone. My mom and Larry never found out about it, either. The irony was, I had marks on my neck after, you know, like, ligature marks from the cord and whatnot, and Larry thought they were hickeys from a girl. For a week he went on and on, trying to guess who I'd been making out with. I just laughed it off, and let him go on thinking that." He chuckles for a moment, remembering. "He's so afraid I'm gay." He pauses and we both have a good laugh. "To him, it's, like, the worst thing ever. I think my mom knows about me, but she pretends not to. But ya know, I could easily hate my mom for all this, but I don't. Sure, she tore my brother and me apart, and totally shook up my life, but I still love her. Even when I had that cord wrapped around my neck, I loved her with all my heart." He thinks for a moment. "You know, it's taken me a long time to realize this, but everybody's just doing the best they can with what they have, you know?"

I'm quiet, thinking of my own mother, my life, and how I got here. "I know," I finally say.

"Look, everything is going to be good tomorrow, okay? Whatever happens, you've just got to keep an open heart and open mind. I never met your mom, but I know she loved you very much. How could she not?"

"Thank you." I smile. "Hey. You said a minute ago that you made peace with God?"

"Yep, I did."

"So, you believe in God, like, totally, completely?"

"Yeah, absolutely."

There's conviction in his answer, and it gives me pause, makes me think. "After everything that's happened in the last few months, I'm not sure what I believe or why I'm even still here."

"Sosie, you wouldn't be here if you weren't meant to be. At least that's what I believe anyway," he says. "You have a purpose, and maybe you don't know what that purpose is yet, but you have a purpose. The problem is, some people leave before they figure out what their purpose is."

"Well, I hope I figure out what my purpose is sooner than later."

"I believe you will."

"You know what's sort of crazy?" I ask. "Around the beginning of September, you know, about the time you said everything just sort of fell apart for you?" He nods. "That was a really bad time for me, too. I felt so alone. My mom was gone. My dad wasn't there for me. I literally had no one. If only we'd met sooner, talked to each other at school or something, found one another before now, maybe we could've saved each other from all that heartache."

"Maybe," he says, putting his arm around me. "But at least we found each other now. I'm happy you found me, Sosie."

Chapter Fourteen

I wake up extra early the next morning around 5 AM. Casey's curled up in bed next to me, Terry's passed out in the double next to us, and Nolan's on the rollaway still fully clothed, lying on top of the covers and softly snoring. I gather up my things and sneak into the bathroom to get ready.

It's been days since I've seen myself—really allowed myself to look at what's staring back at me. I slowly approach the mirror, one cautious foot at a time, and gaze at my reflection.

If it's possible to have aged ten years in only a few short days, I have. Drawn and skinny with sunken in collarbones, I touch the skin on my face and décolletage, pale, yet splotchy and red. Filth clings under my nails, as I touch the translucent skin along my jawline, and then run my fingers through my greasy light-brown hair. I'm a stranger—a caricature of a teenage, homeless runaway from one of my father's movies. If not for my almond-shaped hazel eyes emerging despite the purple veiny circles, I wouldn't have recognized myself at all.

I undress and run a warm bath, hoping it'll make me feel better and cleanse me of the beast from the mirror. I can't go to meet Sam looking this way. My mother would be horrified. She raised me to never go in public without looking my absolute best. If she caught me walking out the door for school with wet hair from a rushed shower, she'd march me back upstairs, and hand me a blow dryer and hairbrush, even if it meant I'd be late for class. All the same, when she was suffering in the throes of depression, she wouldn't dare leave the house or let anyone besides me see her looking unkempt. Instead, she'd send me out to run her errands while she holed up in the safety of our house and away from the preying neighbor's eyes. Appearances were one of the most important things to her.

When I step into the hot water, dirt dissipates from my feet, turning the clear water brown in an instant. I sit in the old tub, soaking in the steamy water for a long while before reaching over the side and grabbing the shopping bag that contains the hair coloring kit. I rip the package open and don't bother reading the directions as I shake the plastic bottle and douse my hair in the cold, stinging dye.

I swirl my hair up into a topknot, and then lie back in the tub, taking the opportunity to close my eyes and relax before one of the biggest days of my life. Sometime later, I awaken with my head slumped over the side of the bathtub, skull burning from the colorant. I submerge myself under water, allowing it to rinse its way out of my hair, letting my scalp cool off in the now lukewarm water.

I finish up with my bath, step out of the tub, and wrap myself in a fluffy, complimentary bathrobe. The water drains behind me, making a loud whistle sound, as I stand at the sink and brush my teeth with some of the travel toiletries I picked up while shopping.

I apply a little make-up, get dressed, and blow dry my hair with the courtesy hair-dryer provided by the hotel. When I'm done, I can't help reveling at the results. Casey was right. The red hair has totally transformed me. My hair is a glossy, coppery shade of scarlet-red, and the shaft down to the cuticles are revitalized to a shiny and luscious finish. My dull and snarled hair from an hour earlier is something of the past, and I can't help bouncing my new style around, pretending I'm a model in one of those L'Oreal shampoo commercials.

I'm mid hair flip when footsteps resonate at the bathroom door, followed by a light knock. It's Casey.

Her feet sound like a fairy, and she sneezes and then blesses herself. I drag myself away from the mirror and open the door.

"I have to pee," she says, wearing nothing but an oversized t-shirt, her knees knocked together in attempt to hold her bladder. She starts to yawn, but abruptly stops to check me out from head to toe. "Whoa. Girlfriend got a make-over," she says, eyes wide and alert.

"Who would've thought $8.99 from Wal-Mart could change my life in this way? I've got to hand it to you, though. You were right about the red hair. It's making me feel like a total bombshell right now."

"I can see why. It looks amazing on your skin tone, but I'm sure all that make-up you're wearing is helping, too."

I'm instantly self-conscious as I peek at my reflection. I've got a lot more make-up on than she's ever seen me wear, but the foundation and bronzer was necessary, considering how pale and spotty my skin had been earlier this morning. "I just put a little powder and concealer on. Nothing major."

"You put a little concealer and powder on, but you're also rocking the winged eyeliner, shiny pink lip-gloss, blush, and you're wearing my blouse that I was saving in case Terry took me out to dinner to make up for being an asshole."

"Sorry," I say, touching the top and running my hand against the chiffon fabric. "Do you mind? I really didn't have anything presentable to wear, and I want to look my best."

"I'm teasing you. It's fine. Plus, it looks better on you than on me. It's not made for someone with big ta-ta's like this." She sticks her chest out and holds her baggy t-shirt flush against her skin, displaying her goods with a confident grin.

I glance at the alarm clock. It's close to 8 AM. "Oh my God, I have to go. Tell the guys I'll be back in a few hours, okay? Wish me luck."

I leave the hotel room, get my car out of valet, and head straight into town. My plan is to get to Sam's shop around 8:30 AM, close to opening time, so I'll have a better chance at talking to him without anyone else around.

In the fantasies I've had, he's so thrilled to see me he closes up shop and asks me to grab coffee and breakfast from the bakery two doors down. There, he divulges everything he knows about my mother and what they were to one another as we snack on croissants and drink hot chocolate.

By 8:15 AM and slightly ahead of schedule, I pull into a parking spot across the street from *Rolland's Hobby Shop*. My pulse races as I wait in the idling car, watching the dark store from afar. Movement darkens the window, like shadows sweeping across the floor, but no one can be seen yet. Ten minutes later, the lights switch on, and the sign in the doorway reverses to read, *Open! Please Come In*. My palms sweat, clammy as I clutch the steering wheel and rest my head on my knuckles, taking deep breaths as I drum up the courage to get out and go inside.

And then, a figure. Sam.

He emerges from the store with a slow but steady stride, ceramic coffee cup in hand. He tilts his head up to the sky, like he's taking in the cool morning air and light. He's bigger in stature than he appeared in the picture with my mother, with broader shoulders and a thicker waist. He still has the same wooly beard. His hair is slightly longer and greyer now, the front fringe splitting into a center part on his forehead, and he's wearing a heavy flannel button down and work boots. Another man walks up, of similar appearance and stature, and greets him with a hearty handshake. The two converse, good naturedly, looking like they just stepped out of an Eddie Bauer ad.

His eyes suddenly break away from his friend and meet mine for a moment. Perhaps he could feel someone staring at him, stalking. I quickly look away, but I can still feel his gaze, even as I pretend to look for something in the glove compartment.

Nausea grips my belly as sweat pours off my forehead and armpits, the chiffon material of my top clinging to my damp skin. I put the air conditioning on even though it's thirty degrees outside, and I try to concentrate on my breathing and slowing down my throbbing chest.

You can do this. Now get it together and go talk to him.

When I glance back at the outside of the store, Sam and his friend are gone, and the outline of his silhouette is now behind the cash register.

My heart skips inside my chest. Without thinking, I put the car into drive, about to leave Sam's store and escape Michigan forever. But something stops me. Something inside won't let me leave. I turn the car off, get out, and cross the street.

An overhead bell dings as I walk in.

Sam stands behind the counter reading a newspaper, the coffee cup sitting in front of him. He looks up and our eyes meet, and in that moment I'm certain he has no idea who I am. "Good morning," he says, greeting me with a warm smile.

"Good morning."

He steps out from behind the register, hands in his pockets, chest hair sticking out the top of his shirt. "Can I help you find anything?" He holds my gaze, maintaining a smile.

My eyes scan over everything about him, taking in the details of what make him, him, his blue-green eyes that are a little too close together, his slightly crooked nose, his large hands, his baritone voice, his out-of-style jeans.

"I'm looking for a vase," I say, out of nowhere, my words taking me by surprise.

"A vase, eh?" He scratches his nose and then lights up. "Ah, yes, well, I don't know the particular type you had in mind, but I just got a beautiful glass blown vase in a few weeks back. It's gorgeous. Would you like to see it?"

"Sure."

He disappears to the back of the store where he searches for the vase. While I wait, the bell on the door rings, and the guy who'd been talking with Sam outside is back.

"Hey, Ron, back here," Sam calls from a kneeling position, as he rummages through a box.

I listen as their voices pick up where they left off.

"So, I just talked to the owner next door and they're not looking to sell anytime soon," Ron says.

"That's crazy. They haven't had more than ten customers in months," Sam says.

"But, I was thinking, we might be able to do a deal where we knock down that wall over there, because you don't really need it, it's just cutting off space, and that should give you a little bit more expansion. Honestly, I wouldn't worry too much, though. I have a feeling in a year they're going to change their minds. Maybe they're not ready to sell right now, but I can't imagine they'll stay afloat too much longer."

Sam is on his feet, the vase in his hand. I drum my hands along my thighs while I wait, and Sam glances over at me, taking notice.

"Listen, Ron, let me finish helping this young lady, but I'll swing by your shop later and we can talk more. That okay?"

"Sure thing," Ron says. "I'll be there until four. Jessi's got a piano recital tonight, so closing up shop a little early."

The man leaves, and Sam walks over to me, proudly carrying the vase. "This is the vase I was telling you about. She's a beaut, isn't she? It a gift?"

"Sort of."

He hands me the vase, and I pretend to be interested in it. I run my fingertips along the raised details in the glass.

"You from around here?" he asks.

"No, not from around here. From New York."

"You don't say. I lived in New York for years, many years. What parts?"

"Long Beach."

He becomes excited, animated. "I lived in Long Beach for a good portion of my life. My son still lives there. Beautiful town. But boy, oh boy, Hurricane Sandy," he muses. "That was rough. Were you around for that? My son said it was a nightmare. He and his mom still don't have power. What brings you to Frankenmuth?" He's firing so many questions the walls start to feel like they're closing in around me. "Family here?"

"No, no family here," I say, slowly. "Actually, I'm here to talk to you."

He looks confused, and then I see the moment where he see's her in me. His entire face contorts, changes. His eyes and mouth are sad, his loneliness palpable. He buckles at the mere thought of her.

"Sosie." His voice crackles in his throat.

He hugs me, my whole body stiffly engulfed in his giant arms as he starts crying. There are whimpers, sniffling, and I get the sense that if he allowed himself to let go completely, he'd end up lying on the ground, totally unhinged. His emotionality wipes me of my own as I politely wait for the embrace to be over. When he finally let's go of me, he steps away, his hands on his hips as he shrugs over and over.

"Wow, I can't believe you're here," he says. "Can't believe it's really you. I've seen pictures, but I didn't recognize you with the red hair."

"It's sort of a new development." I shrug.

"How did you find me?"

"I found a picture in my mother's writing desk. It was of you and my mother in front of the grey house on Waverly Place. And then, I actually met your son," I say. "It was after the hurricane. I guess you could say we ran into each other by accident. It's kind of a long story. I hope it's okay I'm here."

"Of course it is," he says, with deep sincerity. "Of course it is. Wow." He leans in as if he might hug me again but he instead ushers me to a dining table and chairs, the one I'd seen from the window last night. He pulls out a chair, and I sit down as he settles in across from me, hands folded on the table in front of him. "I'm really glad you came." His eyes well up again. "I'm sorry, it's just that you look so much like her. God, I miss her."

"Me too." We're both silent for a moment, reflective. "You loved her?"

"I loved her so much," he says, with conviction. "Still do."

"She loved you?"

"Yes." He smiles as if reliving a special moment he had with her. "She was my soulmate."

"She was mine, too," I whisper.

"*You* were her soulmate," he says, taking my hand. "God, she loved you so much."

When the moment feels appropriate, I gently slip my hand out of his grasp.

He takes the hint, unoffended, and folds his hands into his lap.

"Why did she keep you from me? All that time you two were together, why did she keep it all a secret?" He scratches his eyebrow, and I can tell he's trying to come up with the right thing to say. "No, don't," I say. "Don't. Don't sugar coat it. Just tell me the truth. Tell me in her words. What did she tell you the reason was?"

"I suppose she thought it would upset you," he finally concedes.

"You suppose?" I try not to sound interrogational, but it comes out that way anyhow. "Did she say that?"

"Well, she said on more than one occasion that you hated your father for ruining your family, and she didn't want you to blame her for it, too."

"How long were you two seeing each other?" I ask, like a journalist trying to get the nitty gritty details.

He thinks for a moment. "Fifteen years? Yeah, about fifteen years." I think about the pictures at my grandmother's house in Pennsylvania where I'm happily swinging on the hanging tire, my parents grinning at one another. I think about how their bodies were close, their hips always turned into one another. I think about how I'd often looked at those photographs longingly to go back to that time when my parents were in love. The revelation that Sam was in my mother's life even then stings me straight through the heart. "Sosie, I can see you're a little hurt by that news, but you must know, your mother tried very hard with your father for a very long time, but he was never faithful to her."

"And she wasn't faithful to him, either, it seems."

He's quiet, looking down. "Yes, but after a while, they had an understanding, an agreement."

"That's news to me."

He clears his throat uncomfortably. "I want to be open and honest with you. There's really no sense in lying at this point. Facts are facts, I guess, whether you like the sound of them or not."

"Well, that's sort of a convenient thing to say, isn't it?" I retort. "Facts are facts." I imitate him, doing my best impression of a big, burly man with a deep voice. "How about this? I don't like your facts." I feel my gut beginning to stir with agitation, the anger creeping over me.

He weakly smiles, like he's trying to save face. Like he doesn't appreciate where this is going. "Sosie, I know it's hard to understand, why she wouldn't want to let you in on all this, but I promise you, her intentions were in the right place."

"I'm not sure I agree with that. It kind of seems like she wanted to be the hero while I went on thinking everything was my dad's fault." The reality stings.

"No, no, that's not it at all," he says, firmly. "She was going to tell you about us. She was actually getting ready to tell you right before she died." His voice trails off.

I sense there's something else there, but he's guarding it and being careful. "Did you think she was well before her accident? Did you see any signs that would indicate anything was wrong?"

He looks wistfully out the window, thinking on it for a moment, before he takes in a deep breath and sighs. "No, not at all, actually. In fact, she'd been telling me that she finally beat it. She had dreams for the future. Personally, I never even entertained the thought it was anything but an accident. Sosie, I know there were some rumors around town that your mother intentionally caused that car accident. It's part of the reason I had to get away. I couldn't bear to hear the lies. But I don't ever want you to think she would do that, because she wouldn't. What I mean to say is, I know for a fact she'd never do it on purpose."

"But how can you possibly know for a fact?"

He closes his eyes and breathes deeply. When he opens them, he looks me right in the eyes. "Sosie, your mom really wanted to tell you herself, but since she's not here to, I guess I can tell you now. Your mom was pregnant." The moment he says the words, he extends his giant calloused paw to me, grabbing hold of my hand whether I like it or not. "Now, it was very new, she was only twelve weeks along or so, but she was so excited. She was going to tell you. God, she was so excited to tell you."

My brain is pumping in and out information faster than I can keep up with. I wince, feeling a pain shooting straight through my heart. A pain so severe, I'm sure my heart is about to stop beating. My mouth is dry as I open it to speak.

Sam squeezes my hand tighter. "Sosie, she felt the love for this new baby had saved her from her illness. The love she already had for this baby had completely transformed her and made her well. She told me as much. That's how I know she'd never leave intentionally. It just wouldn't make sense. That should give you some peace of mind."

In an instant, I'm transported back to the kitchen on the day she was making the matzo ball soup when I pushed the little voice inside down and away, the voice that was hesitant to believe her when she was suddenly acting okay. I can smell the broth boiling, feel my mother's arm around me as I stood at the stove with the wooden spoon, hear her melodic voice. *"Every time I thought about your face, it stirred something up on the inside. I love you so much that I swear it healed me. I tried with all my might, and I willed it so. It was you, Sosie, it was all because of you that I got better."* I can't breathe, and my hands shake.

"I know, I know, Sosie. It must be devastating to hear that you were going to have a little brother or sister, and now that chance is gone. It's been taken from you, and it isn't fair."

"What?" My face contorts, mouth drooping into a scowl.

"You know, if he was a boy, we were going to name him Cash, you know after Johnny Cash," he continues, somehow missing the fact that the mood has changed.

"My mother drove the wrong way," I whisper.

"Listen, Sosie, her medication was wrong. That damn doctor was always switching it up and getting her all out of whack. I'd been telling her for years to find a new doctor."

"But the night she left, she hugged me extra tight, kissed me on the cheek, and she had tears in her eyes. It always bothered me that she had tears in her eyes." A vision of my mother, just the way she was that night, flashes through my mind, her big brown eyes watering as she blots it away with her thin ring finger.

"You know, the hormones at the beginning of a pregnancy were really throwing her for a loop, making her extra emotional."

"She had a lot of secrets," I say. "She guarded them close to her chest, and she made me think I was the center of her universe, but really, she had this whole other life I knew nothing about."

Sam's forehead wrinkles in worry, his face twisted into a tragedy mask. "All I can tell you is that she was trying to protect you. She always had your best interest at the forefront of her mind."

"My mother could be very selfish." I think back to when I was a little girl and she was on her campaign to destroy Mrs. Filipio. How she forbade me from playing with Johnny, and how she'd watched me spend the whole summer by myself with no friends, catering to her every whim and playing her favorite French song while she sunbathed outside in the yard. She knew I longed for a friend. She watched me spend those sunny days alone on the couch reading, knowing I was incredibly lonely. It wasn't until many, many years later that she became okay with me spending time with Johnny and that was after she realized there was really no preventing it. But even then, I had to beg for her approval.

All the times over the last few years when she was in the throes of her depression, she expected me to take care of her and be at the house in case she needed something. I always dropped everything when she needed a refill on her medicine or when she was suddenly in the mood for her favorite Chinese food. She knew that. I spent all my time being there for her, living an isolated life without many friends and with most people thinking I was some kind of socially-awkward freak. She used to clasp our hands together and kiss my forehead, promising she'd never lie to me or leave me the way my father had. Then there's the time she gallivanted into my school, looking like she just stepped out of a psych ward with her hair all crazy, and how she screamed my name until I came out of class. When I asked her what she was doing there, she yelled that I'd gone to school without laying her pills out first.

His eyes scan mine back and forth, a worry

wrinkle between his brows. The intention is obvious: fix this, preserve her memory. But it's already out of his hands.

"She was the least selfish person I've ever met," he says.

Before my eyes, this big, strong man transforms into a pathetic little boy under my mother's spell. She's his puppeteer, even from the grave.

"You poor, poor man," I say, with sincere pity. "She's controlling you still. She's controlling how you remember her. You're only remembering the good parts, and you're overlooking all the bad stuff. That's the thing about dying suddenly. You're too busy grieving from the loss and shock of it. Your brain can't bear to see the bad parts were there all along, too." I think for a moment, the fog in front of my eyes beginning to lift. "I can see that now. Everything is clear."

He studies my expressions, my movements, like his mind is trying to make sense of how this conversation took such a hostile turn. "No. With your mom, there was only goodness and sickness. You're angry with her, but she wouldn't want this."

"Of course she wouldn't. It's the last thing she ever wanted." I pause, the realization hitting me profoundly. "She killed herself." Saying it out loud feels like a bag of bricks falling on top of my head. It's the one thing I never wanted to believe, but now that it's here, there's no pushing it away. "But she tried to make it look like an accident, because she didn't want anyone to think she was selfish. She wanted to preserve her memory, and if it was an accident, then no one could harbor any ill will toward her. She could control how we remembered her. That's why she didn't leave a note. She was hoping if it was shocking enough, then no one would ever question the accident part of it." The video, that horrifying image of her, creeps its way in. I'm sure she never meant for it to go that far. The narcissist in her would never have allowed it, but it certainly distorted my belief of her death, and therefore, worked to her advantage.

Sam doesn't take his eyes off me. His mouth parts, like he's opening it to speak, but no words come out.

"This whole time I thought everyone was against her, and me, but they were all right. I was wrong."

"No. No, you've got it all wrong." He speaks fast, rambled.

"She wanted to make everyone think that they'd saved her, but it was all part of the plan, the decoy. She was desperate for people to not know the truth."

"It was an accident," he shouts, slamming his fist into the table over and over, tears billowing in his eyes. He quickly gathers himself, taking a deep breath. "Your mother would never leave intentionally. Never. She was happy."

"No, she wasn't. I'm sorry, Sam, but she wasn't. She was never happy. Sure, she had moments where she felt happiness, but she was a chronically unhappy person. It wasn't all her fault. She was sick a lot, and she had a hard life. I know she tried, but she just wasn't capable of sustaining happiness. I think she eventually stopped trying to get better, and then it became a plan. A plan to die. If she perked up, it was because the plans were already set into motion."

I'm so in my own head that I don't realize I'm being ushered to the door by Sam. He's kicking me out in the same manner in which he welcomed me in, with sincerity. He's sincerely done with me. I stand in the doorway of the store, his burly chest blocking me from coming back in.

"I'm sorry, Sosie, but I need you to leave. I have

customers coming in."

There aren't any customers, not even one person walking around the streets outside. "Okay," I say, without protest.

He opens the door and all but pushes me out. "Take care of yourself. Goodbye, Sosie." He shuts the door and flips the sign to *Closed*.

Chapter Fifteen

Back at the hotel, a little after nine-thirty, everyone is showered and anxious to leave. Casey and Terry have made up. Casey lies on Terry's bed, resting her head in his chest while they watch old re-runs of *Cops*, and Nolan sits at the desk with the lamp on, doodling his name a hundred times on a mini notepad.

"How did it go?" Nolan asks, the moment I walk in.

"Eh. I'll tell you about it later." I avoid eye contact. The emotions are much too raw, and I'm still reeling from Sam's revelations and my own conclusions. For now, I push it to the back of my mind until I can get on the open road and have the space to think. "You guys ready to hit the road?"

We gather our things and head down to the lobby. Nolan, Casey, and Terry decide to wait outside for the car while I check out of the room with Kaley who's still working the front desk.

"So, these extra fees here are for taxes and valet services," Kaley says, using her French manicured acrylic nail to point to what she's talking about.

"That's fine." I barely glance at the receipt and scribble my name in the signature block.

"We hope you had a great stay, and we'll see you back again soon." She smiles and hands me my copy.

"Actually, I don't think I'll ever be coming back here again."

Her smile wilts, the tops of her cheeks deflating as her mouth relaxes into a flat line. "Well, I'm sorry to hear that, but we understand that New York isn't close. It'd be a trek to get out this way again."

"Nah, that's not really it. This place just didn't give me good vibes, you know?"

She still manages to smile a little. "Oh, well, I'm so sorry about those less than ideal vibes. Headed home now?"

"Nope. My friends and I are actually headed to Virginia Beach. Going to go surfing."

Casey appears in the entranceway, waving. "Cars here," she shouts.

"Have a safe trip," Kaley says before answering a blinking call from the hold line.

I meet the crew outside and hop into the car. Nolan is next to me in the passenger seat, and Casey and Terry are nestled up in the back again.

"Can you get that map for me?" I ask Nolan. He retrieves it from the glove compartment and takes care unfolding it in front of me. My eyes quickly scan it. "Looks like we need to get to M-83 South first. We'll be on that road for about a hundred miles or so."

"How long until we get to Virginia Beach?" Casey asks, picking at something in Terry's ear.

"Not sure," I say. "But a while."

"Like, how long is a while?" she asks, examining whatever it is that she's scraped off with her fingernail.

"About ten hours."

Soon, Frankenmuth fades into the background, and then Michigan altogether disappears. A few hours into the trip to Virginia Beach, we drive through Ohio, which looks much like Michigan but with browner farmland and more industrial smoke stacks.

There's something serene about the open road without any traffic. I can understand why Sam would leave New York and settle in Michigan. It's the place you go if you need a breath of fresh air, if you're in the mood for an easier and smoother existence, or if you need to recover from something horrific.

Sam left New York to get away from my

mother's memory, to get away from all the rumors and things that reminded him of her. It's hard to not feel sorry for him as I think back to our conversation, his sad, puppy dog eyes and the way he winced in pain when I spoke my truth.

As I drive along the smooth highway and take in the great, wide open, I imagine what Sam's doing at this very moment—probably pushing all the things I said far and away from his mind, trying to ignore the facts smack dab in front of his face. I know it, because it's what I'd been doing in the months since it happened, up until a few hours ago. He'll probably go on living out the rest of his days, pining over her, missing her, thinking of her. To be fair, even after all the revelations, I probably would, too.

"So, what does everyone want to do when we get to Virginia?" I ask, trying to get my mind on something else.

"Surf," Terry says, his tone deadpan.

"Okay, Captain Obvious," I reply. "What else?"

"Have a beer," he says.

"I could use a beer right now," I say.

"Me too," Nolan says, his head resting against the window in a weak attempt at a nap. "Hey, look." He spots a billboard off in the distance and sits up straight, reading the sign aloud. "*Red's Saloon.* We can get a beer at *Red's Saloon.* One mile. I bet they don't card at a Podunk bar like that."

"Oh my God, no," Casey says. "Can we just get to Virginia Beach already? This is getting annoying, you guys."

"Red's Saloon?" Terry inquires. "Sounds like a titty bar to me."

Casey punches him in the gut. "How would you know?"

"Sosie, what are you doing?" Nolan asks as I take the exit.

My lips curl into a smile. "C'mon, one beer never hurt anyone."

"It's like 11 AM," Casey whines. "I don't even want a beer right now."

"Good, then after the three of us have one, you can drive."

****

We walk into *Red's Saloon*, an old bar with dusty peanut shells covering the floor, and no other patrons, save a truck driver who's passed out at the bar with a shot of tequila still clutched in his chubby fist.

"What can I do you for?" a pretty bartender in her early twenties asks.

"I'll take a Corona."

"Don't got no Corona." Her tiny bee-stung breasts are pushed up in her strappy tank top. "We got Budweiser."

"Budweiser's cool."

"ID?"

I hand over the fake ID I use in emergencies, and she examines it. I can tell she knows it isn't me, but she doesn't probe.

"Budweiser it is." She bends over to retrieve a beer from the refrigerator.

"Do you guys want a Bud, too?" I ask the group.

"I was going to say that I wanted an orange juice and vodka, but whatever," Casey grumbles under her breath. I give her a look to not push it.

The guys shrug. They don't care. "Actually, four Buds," I tell the bartender.

"You got money to pay?" she asks, chewing on her cheek.

"Course," I say, a little offended.

"You driving?"

"My friend is driving. Any more questions?"

"Nope," she says, and plops a tin of peanuts in front of me.

A vintage jukebox sits in a dark corner, looking like it hasn't been played in years. "Does anyone have a quarter?"

"Jukebox is free," the waitress says, appearing with the beers. "Play as many songs as you'd like, but just do me a favor and don't play any Bon Jovi. Always reminds me of my asshole ex-boyfriend."

"Don't worry," I assure her. "I hate Bon Jovi."

I sip on my beer and saunter to the jukebox. I flip through the songbook twice before making my selection from the slim choices of cheesy Hootie and the Blowfish tunes mixed with a few decent number one hits. I punch in my song of choice, it starts playing, and I meander back over to the bar stool next to where Casey is plopped.

"Have you ever heard the term basic bitch?" Casey asks, as she sips her beer. "*Don't Stop Believin'* is totally something a basic bitch would choose from a jukebox. There wasn't any Zeppelin? Janis Joplin? You're better than this."

"What? I love Journey. You don't love Journey?"

"Yes!" the waitress exclaims. "I fucking love Journey!"

I start singing along to the music, and the waitress comes out from behind the bar and starts singing, too. She gets into it right away, and soon we're jumping around together, flipping our hair wildly, our arms around each other's shoulders, swaying to the music like we've been best friends since grammar school.

Nolan and Terry pour themselves free liquor when the waitress isn't paying attention, and Casey walks over to the jukebox, looking for something else to put on once my song is over.

When the song ends, the waitress sits down next to me on a bar stool and cracks open a beer for herself. "I haven't had that much fun since before I had my son," she says, still giddy. "I had a baby last year, you know. A little boy, and I'll tell ya one thing. Kids are no joke. Nobody tells you that you'll never sleep again once you have one. I haven't slept in fourteen months. I'm telling you the truth, too."

"What's his name?" I ask.

"Bailey. I named him after Baileys Irish Cream." She lets out a little snort when she laughs. "It's my favorite drink, but I actually liked the way it sounded with my boyfriend's last name, too. Brown. It's got a nice ring to it, doesn't it? Bailey Brown? Wanna see a picture?" She takes out her phone to show me. "Isn't he a little chunk? Look at those rolls!"

"He's really adorable," I concur.

She kisses the picture and then puts it away. "You're lucky you came in today. My boss is usually here, but he leaves me in charge on Wednesdays, so that's why I can sit here and chill like this right now. Like, I could never do this if he was here," she says, swigging her beer.

"Well, lucky me," I say, with a smile.

While I hang out with the bartender, Terry joins Casey over at the jukebox. He wraps his arms around her waist from behind and slowly runs his hand underneath her top, all over her belly and back. Her eyes close as she nuzzles into his neck and sways back and forth to the music. Nolan wanders over there, too, but keeps a safe distance at a booth nearby.

I finish the rest of my beer, and the waitress takes Casey's half a beer and places it in front of me. "You read my mind," I tell her.

"Son of a bitch," she says, looking every which way. "Morton left without paying again. He always slips out when I'm not paying attention. Now, I'm going to have to put my own money into the till or I'll be short. Son of bitch, asshole, prick."

"How much does he owe you?" I ask.

"Seven bucks!"

I reach into my pocket and place a five-dollar bill and two singles on the counter.

"No, no, you don't have to do that," she says.

"I want to. Really, I insist. You got distracted because of me, it's the least I can do."

"So, you didn't tell me where you're headed after this."

"Virginia Beach. My friends and I are headed down there to check out the surf. My friends surf. I don't," I clarify. "But they want to catch a few waves, and then after that, we'll head back to New York."

"I knew you weren't from around here. You have a unique look about you." She examines me, like she's trying to put her finger on what's different. "You're sort of mysterious. I think it's the red hair and the way you do your eyeliner like that, you know, with little wing that goes up? No one around here does that."

The more she drinks, the closer she talks. I can smell the yeast on her breath from the beer as it wafts onto my neck. I finish my beer, and she stands up to get me another.

"No, no, it's okay." I stop her. "I'm good."

She sits back down and flicks the thin fringe on her forehead out of her eyes. "But seriously, you're so pretty. You must have guys all over you."

"Hardly." I can't help laughing and wonder what she'd be saying if she'd seen me this morning before my mini makeover.

"I don't believe that. You're, like, one of those girls who doesn't even have to try. Like me. I have to wear make-up and stuff, but you don't. You have the cheekbones where it doesn't matter. And you have, like, the perfect size boobs, not too big, not too small. They're just right, and they're so perky. Mine were destroyed from breast-feeding—totally deflated—so now I have to wear a push-up bra or I don't have nothin' at all." She's looking down at her own chest. "See, feel." She places my hand on her foamy bra. "All padding."

"Well, I'd never know by looking."

"Yup, it's all Victoria's Secret. I wear butt pads too." She snorts again when she laughs. "You'd never have to wear butt pads. You have a killer ass. You probably don't even work out."

"I don't," I admit. "My mother used to call me 'bubble butt' when I was a kid."

She giggles, letting her head fall into my shoulder, her hand grazing my breast. When she sits back up, she's looking at me with pursed lips. "Have you ever been with a girl?"

"No. Never."

"I know, silly," she says, slapping me in the arm so hard it stings a little. "I can tell. I didn't even need to ask, but I thought I would just to be sure." She touches my bottom lip with her pointer finger and moves in for a slow, soft kiss.

I get caught up in her touch, in the physical connection I've been so longing for. I stroke her cheeks lightly and then her neck as she runs her fingertips along my lower back. It tickles and makes me jump. I lose my balance on the stool and fall forward, my head hitting the edge of the bar.

"Are you okay?" she asks, as she tries to help me

up.

"I'm okay. I'm fine," I insist.

But I'm not okay. I touch my forehead, and there's blood on my fingertips. I grab a cocktail napkin off of the bar and put it on the gash.

"Do you want me to call someone?" she asks, horrified. "Wow, that looks really bad."

Seconds later, blood pours into my hands, soaking through the paper.

"No, no, I'm good. Really, it's all good." I start for the door, blood running down my head and into my eyes, obscuring my vision, but I never stop moving. "Let's go," I tell everyone.

Casey and Terry are in a dark corner on a wooden chair practically having sex with their clothes on. "Holy shit. What the hell?" Casey hops off Terry's lap as soon as she sees me and begins shaking Nolan, who's taking a nap in a nearby booth. "Nolan, get up, we're going."

"I'm sorry, I didn't mean to freak you out," the waitress says, coming up behind me.

I open the door. The daylight rushes in, blinding us all.

"You didn't freak me out," I say, as I try to push past her. "I just have to go. We really need to get on the road."

"I shouldn't let you leave." She puts her arm out to block me. "You've been drinking, and you just hit your head."

"I'm fine. I already told you that my friend is driving. He'll take me to a hospital if I need to go, okay?"

I wiggle out of her grasp, and we all run out the door and into the car. She's standing in the doorway of the bar, watching us.

"I'm calling the cops! You're gonna kill yourself

or somebody else!"

The tires burn as we screech out of the parking lot. I'm in the driver's seat, blood pouring all over the steering wheel and all over my hands. Casey has jumped into the front passenger's seat. The boys are in the back.

"Don't you think one of us should drive?" Casey asks, watching me trying to stop the blood with the sleeve of my jacket.

"You said you didn't want to drive," I snap. "No one else wanted to drive, so I am, remember?"

"That was before," she says. "Then, this happened."

"Sosie, Casey's right," Nolan chimes in. "You should let one of us drive. Pull off the shoulder and get out. I'll drive."

"No. I'm fine. We just need to get a little farther down the road, and then we can switch."

"You're getting blood all over Sven's car," Terry interjects. "Give her something to stop the blood. That's gonna be a bitch to clean up later."

"Terry, shut the fuck up!" I scream, all my anger from the day coming to head at once. "All of you, just shut the fuck up, and let me gather my thoughts." I merge onto the highway, but am peering behind me as I berate them. "I've been listening to all your bullshit for two days, and I've had it! Just give me one goddamn second to gather my thoughts, for fuck's sake!"

"Watch the road," Casey says, grabbing the steering wheel and trying to steady it. "You're scaring me, Sosie."

"Stop it, stop it, stop it!" I shout.

Casey backs away, her body pressed up against the passenger side door. She glances to the back at the boys, eyes wide.

"Can't you see how much pressure I'm under

right now? It's like you're all fucking blind and deaf or something. I'm trying to get us out of here, but none of you are letting me do that. You're all running your fucking mouths."

"Why are you under pressure?" Casey asks. "None of us know what's going on!"

"Because we have to get out of here! Because that fucking waitress is probably calling the cops on us! Didn't you just hear her say that? We have to get out of here. We have to get the fuck out of Ohio!"

The speedometer registers close to 80. The wheels rattle like they're about to fly out from underneath us. I weave in and out of traffic, cars beeping at me.

"Tell us what happened back there," Casey demands. "Why are you bleeding?"

I grip the steering wheel and scream as loud as I can, my eyes clenched shut while I shriek until my throat goes hoarse. "Leave me alone, all of you, just leave me alone! Get off my back! Stop asking me questions. I can't take it!"

When I open my eyes, a deer stands in the middle of the highway. I look into her eyes, and she looks into mine, both of us knowing that one or both are going to die if I hit her. I swerve the wheel, and everything goes into slow motion. Casey, Terry, and Nolan scream in terror, their faces frozen with wide, petrified eyes and open mouths, as the car tumbles off of an embankment and rolls four or five times until finally coming to a stop after we hit a tree. I fly out the windshield, glass cutting at my eyes and scattering my hair.

I lay there too weak to call out for help. Debris is all over my face, and I'm wearing it like a mask, the dirt and dust preventing me from seeing anything, including where everyone else ended up. I'm stiff, paralyzed and broken, the cold air rushing over my body and hitting my bare skin. My clothes have been torn off from the impact of the crash, but I'm too weak to be modest or care. My breathing slows down, becoming shallower and shallower, and I drift farther and farther away.

It's then a warm presence—someone's soft fingertips—wipes the dirt and glass from my eyes, gently, lovingly.

"Mom," I croak. "I'm dying."

No response comes, and suddenly everything switches into fast-forward. Voices. Sirens. Rain. People. A stretcher and an oxygen mask. Frantic questions stir around me, and I know the answers but I can't muster a sound. All I can do is close my eyes and drift off into glorious sleep.

Chapter Sixteen

When I finally wake up, it's as if I've been sleeping for days, week's maybe. The soreness lingers in my muscles, every limb on my body, my face, my lips, my scalp, my fingernails, my belly. Everything is bloated, out of proportion, non-functioning. Someone holds my hand, lightly stroking their fingers across the puffy veins that have been stuck with an IV. I groan, tugging at it.

"Sosie," a deep voice buzzes. "Sosie? Sosie, can you … hear me?"

I open my eyes, an instantaneous headache from the bright hospital lights pounding my skull. My lips are dry and crusty as I open my mouth to speak. "I think she's awake," the voice says. "Sosie, can you hear me? I'm here."

When the spots from the lights dissipate, my gaze settles on my father, sitting at my bedside and staring at me. Tears swell his eyes and soon streak his cheeks. Never have I seen him so emotional. "She's awake," he tells a nurse standing nearby. "Tell them she's awake." The nurse leaves the room in a rush, and I'm left alone with him. "Sosie, I'm here. Can you hear me, honey? Can you hear me?"

I try to swallow, but something gags me. Instinctively, I yank at it, and a long tube down my throat comes out like a snake. I hold it up, staring at it in my hand, bewildered. An alarm of sirens begins to roar. My father's mouth is moving, but I can't hear what he's saying.

A nurse bursts through the door and approaches me, taking the tube out of my hands. "Can you breathe?" she asks.

"Yes," I say, my voice coming out like a whisper.

My father strokes my hair, tears still falling down his cheeks. He doesn't bother wiping them away.

A doctor walks in—a young, handsome doctor who looks more like an actor pretending to be a doctor than an actual one. He wears a white coat and badge, and has just enough five o'clock shadow and messy hair to seem approachable.

Another nurse walks in, murmurs something in the doctor's ear, and together they approach me at the foot of the bed. The doctor can't be more than thirty years old, and the nurse, double his age.

"Hi, Sosie, I'm Doctor Felton, and this is your nurse, Sherry. I'm sure you're scared right now. Can you tell me how old you are?" he asks.

"Eighteen," I answer, my voice still soft, low.

"Can you tell me if you know who this man is?" Dr. Felton points to my father.

"My dad."

"Very good." He nods at my father with approval. "So, here's the story. You had a really bad car accident, and you're being treated at the Cleveland Clinic in Cleveland, Ohio. The accident caused some serious injuries. You suffered blunt force trauma to the chest and abdomen, resulting in multiple rib fractures, a punctured lung, several broken ribs, a broken clavicle, and a ruptured spleen. You lost a fair amount of blood and in order to resuscitate you, we needed to keep you on a mechanical ventilator for the last three days to give you blood transfusions, and to allow your body to recover. Can you tell me how you're feeling now?"

"Like crap," I say. "Nauseous."

"Sherry will get you something for that," Dr. Felton says, as Sherry writes something down on a chart. "I know everything must feel pretty grim right now, but the fact that you're awake means you've already overcome a huge hurdle. You probably have a lot of questions, but for right now, I think it's most important to get some rest, and then once you're feeling better, we can get into the nitty gritty of what long-term recovery looks like." He pulls a pen from a pocket in his white coat. "What's your pain level at the moment?"

"I feel numb," I say. "I'm not sure how to answer that."

"Okay, so let's start to lesson the pain meds," he tells Sherry. "And then we'll reevaluate pain management after that. Just make sure to keep the PCA pump going for the next twenty-four hours."

"We're just happy you're awake," my father says.

"I know there's a lot to catch up on," Dr. Felton tells my father. "But let's allow Sosie to get some rest first. Adequate rest can sometimes make or break a patient's recovery."

"Absolutely," my father agrees.

Dr. Felton and Sherry leave the room. At my side, my father clutches my hand in awkward silence. He's too emotional to speak, and I'm too weak. I run my fingertips across my abdomen. A long, rectangular bandage spans the length from my belly button up to my breastbone. I'm frustrated, trapped in my own body.

"Sosie, it's okay." His hand grips mine tighter. "You'll heal. It's going to take a while, but you'll heal."

I roll my eyes. It's just like him to already be lecturing me.

"I'm so glad you're awake. I love you." He kisses my forehead, his chin stubble dragging across my skin. "Please don't ever forget that."

"Where are my friends?" I ask.

"No one has been here to visit you yet. It's just been me. I flew in from London the night I got the call.

Johnny got in touch with me yesterday, though, and he's worried about you. He said that he's going to try and make it out here as soon as he can."

"Are my friends going to make it?" I ask.

"Like I said, Johnny said he's going to try and make it, but it's … tough. You're in Ohio. It's not close."

"I know I'm in Ohio. Stop saying that. Where are my friends, the friends who were in the car with me? Are they going to live? Did I kill them? Tell me." My bottom lip quivers as I speak, my fists clenched as I brace myself for the answer.

He tilts his head, puzzled. "Honey, it was just you in the car when you crashed, no one else."

"No. There were people with me, my friends Nolan, Casey, and Terry. I need to know if they're okay." I'm short of breath as I struggle to sit up.

"Sosie, the doctor said to rest. C'mon, honey, we can figure everything else out later." He fluffs the pillow underneath my head.

"Stop it. I'm not tired. I've been sleeping for three days."

"Let's focus on something else then," he suggests. "What's the first thing you want to do once you get out of here? Do you want to go and get a cherry-dipped cone from Mr. Softee?"

"I don't want to daydream about ice cream," I snap. "Go and get the doctor. I need to talk to him right now."

"The doctor will be back later, and you can ask him whatever you need to ask him then."

"No! Get him now. I need to speak with him this minute."

"Sosie, he's with other patients."

"Where are my friends?" I ask again, through gritted teeth. "There were people in the car with me.

Don't tell me there weren't. What happened to them?"

"Sosie, it was only you."

"If you don't tell me right now where they are, I'm going to scream," I threaten.

"I can't tell you where your friends are, because there wasn't anyone else in the car with you when you crashed."

"Fire!" I scream at the top of my lungs. "Fire! Fire!" Dr. Felton is back in the room within seconds. "My friends who were in the car with me when I got into the accident—two guys and a girl. I need to know what happened to them. I need you to tell me if they're okay." I plead with the doctor.

"I'm at a loss, doc," my father says, trying to commiserate. "I don't know what she's talking about."

Dr. Felton remains calm, unmoved. "It was just you in the car, Sosie. I can promise you that. I was in the ER the night they brought you in. Just you in the car, no one else."

"Maybe they're at a different hospital."

"If there was anyone else in the car, they would've been brought here," Dr. Felton says. "I can assure you that. This is the closest hospital in proximity to where the accident occurred."

"Well, maybe they're still out there then!" I scream. "Maybe they're outside, cold and dying, and no one came for them! Maybe they're all dead by now!"

"Sosie, honey, there wasn't anyone else. It was just you. We wouldn't lie to you," my father says, maintaining his belief.

"You wouldn't? You've been lying to me for my entire life!"

I thrash against the bed sheets, ripping at the IV in my arm, determined to get up.

Doctor Felton steps in, blocking me with one

hand, while he picks up a phone receiver with the other. "Code Gray," Dr. Felton says, simply, and hangs up the phone, turning his eyes back to me. "Relax."

Sherry walks in. He nods at her, and she leaves again as they communicate in an unspoken language. "Sosie, this is a lot to process. I know you're confused about a lot of things, but maybe I can help. Here's what I can tell you for sure. First, we would never do anything to aggravate your recovery, so therefore we wouldn't lie to you. Two, you're going to get better, but only if you rest. And three, I'm one hundred percent sure, without a shadow of a doubt, you were the only one in the car when the crash occurred."

"You're all lying to me!" I shout. "Everyone get the hell away from me. Get away!"

Sherry returns with a large needle drawn up. She walks toward me.

"Get the fuck away from me with that! Don't come near me with that. I know what you're doing. I'll fucking kill you all!" My voice echoes against the stark walls.

Sherry comes toward me anyway, calm, methodical and sticks the needle in my arm, pumping its contents into my bloodstream. I continue screaming, still fighting, as I suddenly fall limp and drift off to sleep again.

When I open my eyes, I'm as angry as I'd been in the moments before Sherry trapped me inside my own body. When I come to, it's dark outside and in my room, and the digital clock on the wall reads 3:30 AM. My father sits in the same position next to my bed but is slumped over in a fidgety sleep.

He opens his eyes, trying to shake the sleep off, once he sees I'm awake.

I turn my head away, staring out the window at

the half crescent moon, incensed and hurt he allowed them to do that to me. It doesn't matter if he's here or not. He brings me no comfort and no protection.

"Sosie … I'm sorry that happened," he finally says.

"You're sorry," I huff.

He sighs as if he expected such a reaction. "Can you look at me, please?"

"No." Instead, I focus my attention on how black and empty the sky looks in Ohio, how the sky muffles the stars.

He drags his chair to the other side of my bed. I turn my head the opposite way, and he drags the chair back to the other side again.

"I can do this all night," he says.

"I can't," I groan, giving up on the game. Our eyes meet. "What? Why are you looking at me like that?"

"Like what?"

"Like that."

"I'm looking at your hair," he observes. "You dyed it. I like it."

I roll my eyes. "Can you just stop, Dad?"

"I can't give you a compliment?"

"You can, but I'm not in the mood right now. You're, like, verbally suffocating me."

"Look, maybe you should give me a list of things I can and can't say to you."

"Here we go."

"No, I mean it. I'm not being facetious," he promises. "Maybe if I can figure out how to stop annoying you, then maybe we can … turn over a new leaf, be … closer. I've been thinking about that a lot over the course of the last few days. I want to spend more time with you, you know, quality time, not just a day or two here or there where I come home and you stare at your phone the whole time and ignore me. Actual time spent together … doing things. Things you like to do. I don't even know what you like to do anymore. There's so much about you I don't know."

"Why's that? Whose fault is that?" I ask.

"Mine," he admits. "But I want to fix it. I want things to change." He's silent for a moment. "I've stayed away for a long time, and I know you're angry about that. All I can tell you is I want the future to be different." His eyes light up. "I've been thinking … we can sell the house after you graduate from high school. Maybe I can get you a little studio in the city somewhere near NYU. You can apply to their film program. I've got lots of connections there, and I can buy a place for myself within a few blocks from you. We can, you know, have dinner together a couple times a week. Sosie, I want to travel less and be in your life more."

This is the most my father has spoken to me in the last five years, and it's in some way, everything I'd been hoping for since my mother died. But for some reason, now that it's here, it's not enough. I resist it all, the moment the ideas and plans come out of his mouth. Even though a part of me wants what he does, I can't allow myself to give in. I've been putting up a wall between us for so long.

"I would never go to NYU," I grumble. "And I don't want to go to film school. The last person on earth I want to be like is you."

The brightness and hopefulness in his eyes disappear, a black curtain coming down over his face. "I'm not the enemy, Sosie."

"Then why does it feel like you're not on my side?" I fire back.

"I don't know. That's for you to answer."

"Okay, well, maybe it's because you're still

197

keeping secrets from me," I offer, sarcastically.

"What secrets, Sosie?" He maintains composure, though I sense he's quickly getting worn out. "What do you want to know?"

"I want to know why no one will tell me about what happened to my friends. Maybe you think you're protecting me from something, but I'm going to find out one way or another, no matter what."

"No one is keeping anything from you, Sosie. We've been telling you the truth. You were the only one in that car. I spoke with the doctor, and he said it's common for people in car accidents to get things mixed up, people, places, things, and timelines. That's all I can tell you right now."

"I'm not mixed up," I counter. "I know what I know."

"Everyone's been telling you the same thing, but you choose to not believe any of us. I don't know how to help you."

"You can help me by leaving," I say, coldly. "Seriously, just go."

"Sosie, I don't want it to be this way."

"It's late, and I need my rest. You remember what the doctor said. Now go." I use my hand to shoo him out, but he lingers, despite my wishes. "Go!"

"Fine," he concedes. "I don't want to aggravate your recovery, but I'll be back first thing in the morning." He starts for the door, his footsteps clicking with each step. Suddenly, he stops, and turns around to face me. "Just so you know, you've got a couple visitors coming to speak with you tomorrow … a couple of police officers. Something about the car you were driving. They have questions. Maybe you can ask them about your friends." He turns again and walks out the door.

Chapter Seventeen

After my father leaves, I toss and turn for the rest of the night. Sven's car. I have no idea how to explain away Sven's car. He must've gotten back from Punta Cana earlier than we thought and reported it missing. The police are going to ask me questions about why I was driving it and how I got it. My worries about what happened to Nolan, Casey, and Terry morph into rage. They must've fled the crash scene for fear of getting caught with Sven's stolen car. I'd expect as much from Terry, but the thought of Nolan and Casey betraying me, letting me take the fall alone, guts me. Where are they all by now? Did they all hitchhike and make it back to New York? Are they holed up in some little motel in Ohio? I don't know, but I'm going to find out.

By the time the sun rises, I'm wired, nervous and sweating through my thin hospital gown as I try to come up with a believable story.

A new nurse named Tara is in charge of me for the morning shift. She comes in around 7:00 AM to give me my pills and check my IV fluids. She tugs on the bags, adjusts the drip, and then hands me a paper cup with three pills. I put them all in my mouth at once, swallowing them with a big gulp of water.

"I need to use the bathroom," I say afterward. She starts unwrapping another plastic bedpan. "No. I'd like to get out of bed and pee like a regular person, if that's okay."

"You feel up to it?" she asks, skeptically.

"I think so."

"Well, I'll need to assist you, and you'll need a walker. Let me run and get you one. Be right back," she says, and leaves the room.

A few minutes later, she returns and sets up the

walker next to my bed. She's not much bigger than me, but she sweeps my frail body out of the bed with ease and props me up on its metal handles so I can hold my weight with little assistance.

"Whoa, I'm really sore." I hunch over in pain, losing my breath.

"Sure you don't just want that bedpan?" she asks, as she helps me shuffle along. "You've got determination. That's a good thing when you're recovering from an accident like the one you had." It takes us several minutes to hobble to the bathroom, and once we get there, she helps me onto the toilet. She stands there and waits, pretending to look at her phone as I sit on the cold seat with no sign of urine coming. I push and push, but nothing. "Pee shy?"

"Guess so."

She places my hand on the safety rail next to the toilet. "I'll be right outside. Shout once you're done, and I'll come get you." I do my business, manage to wipe myself, too, and then call for her. As promised, she's there waiting. She stands me up and helps pull up my disposable hospital underwear. "Now, let's get you back on this thing, and out of here." She places me back on the walker and angles it to get out of the bathroom door.

"Wait," I say, stopping her. "Before I go lie down, I want to see myself."

She nods and guides me to the large mirror over the sink. The walker comes to a scraping halt along the tiled floor, and I look up at my reflection for the first time since the accident.

Purple and yellow bruises cover my cheeks, chin, and forehead. The gash from hitting my head at the bar has been stitched up and is beginning to scab and heal beneath a gauzy bandage. I touch my cheek, my fingers trembling.

"I know, it's always shocking to see yourself for the first time," she says, gently. "But you see how some of these bruises already have this golden color in the center?" She points to one of the marks on my forehead. "That means it's already healing." I smile weakly. "Now come on, let's get you back into bed." She assists me out of the bathroom and then lifts me into bed, getting me situated under some warm blankets. "TV?"

"Why not?" I could use something to take my mind off the police officers I'm anxiously waiting on.

She turns the television on, hands me the remote, and leaves me with the local news. I'm dozing off when the story of a bad car crash on I-280 Southbound plays on the screen. They cut to Sven's overturned car at the bottom of a ravine, every window blown out and the entire hood caved in. The car sits there sad and alone, the rain pounding down on it while a pretty news reporter explains that the driver of the vehicle has gone from critical to stable condition. It's just a news blurb of a report, a follow up to a previously covered story, until the next segment starts.

Tara isn't gone five minutes when she returns, this time with two men. "Sosie, this is Detective Carrington and Detective Matthews. If it's okay, they'd like to speak with you, ask you a few questions."

The officers, dressed in plain clothes, seem friendly enough at first glance. The shorter of the two men wastes no time asserting himself next to where I lay, while the taller officer hangs back.

"Nice to meet you, Sosie," the shorter detective says. "I'm Detective Carrington, and this is Detective Matthews. We work for the Cleveland Police Department, and we want to ask you a few questions about what happened the other day, but first, I'd like to say that we're really glad you're okay, because that crash didn't look good, did it?" he asks, glancing at Detective Matthews who shakes his head no. "You're lucky to be alive, that's for sure."

"I know," I say, speaking softly and trying to come across innocent, meek.

"Well, we know you're busy trying to get better, so we don't want to take up too much of your time, but if it's okay, we'd like to sort through a few things we have some questions about. We'd like to know what you were doing in Cleveland at the time of the crash?"

"My friends and I were on our way to Virginia Beach," I say. "We were just passing through."

"I see, I see," Detective Carrington says. "So, the car you were driving, who's was it? It wasn't registered to you."

"My friend Terry borrowed it from his friend Sven."

"Can you give us Terry's last name?" Detective Carrington asks.

"Mayer," I answer. "I mean, I think his last name is Mayer. Actually, I'm not sure."

"That's okay. We can look into it," Detective Carrington says. "But what about Sven? You said he owns the car? Is he a friend of yours, too?"

"No, just Terry's. He wasn't my friend at all. I've never even met him, actually."

The two detective exchange glances. "So, here's the thing," Detective Carrington says. "When we contacted the owner of the car, Sven Flavia, he said he returned from a trip to find his apartment broken into and his car stolen."

"Terry was taking care of Sven's cat," I explain. "So, he was in and out of his apartment a bunch of times. He did take Sven's car keys, but that was just to borrow it. At least that's what Terry told us. If he stole it, we didn't know anything about that."

"We?" Detective Matthews steps into the conversation.

"My other friends, Casey and Nolan," I say. "Actually, I'm trying to figure out what happened to them, and if they're okay. They were with me when I got into the crash, and no one here can tell me where they are or what happened to them."

"Right, right. Your doctor mentioned you had concerns about them, and we're definitely going to try and help you figure it all out," Detective Carrington says, trying to seem helpful.

"Their names are Nolan Sawyer, Casey O'Conner, and Terry Mayer," I say, speaking slowly. "Well, I think Terry's last name is Mayer, but I'm not positive, like I said before. Maybe you want to write it down? If you guys can help me find them, I'm sure they'll have more information about Sven's car than I do."

"Of course," he agrees. "But before we get to that, you said a minute ago that you and your friends were just passing through Cleveland to get to Virginia Beach? Where were you before that?"

"Michigan," I say. "But just for, like, a night and half a day."

"Why were you in Michigan?" Detective Matthews asks.

"I was visiting someone."

"Do you mind telling us who?" Detective Carrington inquires.

"Does it matter? My mother's boyfriend ... my mother's *former* boyfriend."

"So, you left Michigan and were attempting to drive through Cleveland to get to Virginia Beach at the time of the crash, and then after Virginia Beach, you had plans to make your way back to New York, which was to be your final destination," Detective Carrington says, as if he's thinking out loud.

"Yes," I say. "But before we made it to Virginia Beach, we got into the car accident, and that's where I lost my friends."

"Is it possible that you lost your friends somewhere along the way? Maybe you all parted ways in Michigan before you headed to Virginia Beach?" Detective Matthews asks.

"No, not possible."

"Is it possible that you split up somewhere in Ohio just prior to the crash? Did you all stop anywhere, a restaurant, a gas station, somewhere where you could've broken off into groups, and ended up going your separate ways?" Detective Carrington asks.

"No, I already told you guys that," I say. "They were with me the whole time, from the time I left New York until I crashed in Ohio. We were all in the car together when I…" My voice starts to break as I recall the horrific crash that's led to this mess. Sensations of tumbling inside Sven's car once I lost control flood back. Visions of how the trees, clouds, and sky looked as the car spun in circles, like we were clothes inside a dryer. Casey's scarlet hair fell over her bloodied nose, and Nolan's gold watch floated in front of my eyes once it was ripped off his wrist from impact. Everything is upside down and turning, turning, turning. I try to shake it all away, but I'm dizzied. "It was all my fault," I confess. "I lost control of the car, and I couldn't stop, and then we were flipping over and there was glass everywhere and there was nothing I could do about it. But you guys have to help me," I plead. "I've been asking everyone here what happened to them, and no one will tell me where they are and if they're alive."

"Well, the thing is, at the time of the crash, you were the only one in the car. There wasn't anyone else recovered at the scene of the crash," Detective Matthews discloses.

"That's not possible. Look, you guys have to believe me. My friends and I were all driving together to Virginia Beach. That's why we had the surfboards strapped to the top of the car. We were going to the beach so my friends could surf. I don't even surf," I explain.

"Surf boards? There weren't any surfboards recovered at the crash scene, were there?" Detective Matthews asks Detective Carrington.

"Nope." Detective Carrington shakes his head, not taking his eyes off me.

"Well, they must've flown off the hood when we crashed or something," I say, getting agitated. They exchange glances again. "Would you guys stop looking at each other like that?"

"Like what?" Detective Carrington asks.

"I don't know. Like there's something you know but aren't telling me."

"Sosie, you said the girl you were with was Casey O'Conner, correct? Pretty girl with long red hair, brown eyes?"

"Yes, that's her! You found her? Where is she?" I ask, hopeful.

"We're not sure yet," Detective Matthews says.

"Well, then how do you know all that about her?"

"You had her ID on you at the time of the crash. "In fact, it was hard to identify you at first, because you only had Casey O'Conner's ID on you and not your own. But the good news is, we figured out it was you through the national missing persons database."

"Missing persons database?" I ask. "Why would I

be in the missing persons database?"

"Well, you were unaccounted for after Hurricane Sandy, and your father contacted the local police in New York. He was looking for you but couldn't get in touch with you."

"That's ridiculous. I was never missing. He could've gotten in touch with me if he really wanted to."

"Your father couldn't get in touch with you for days after the storm, and he insisted you weren't a runaway," Detective Carrington refutes. "He filed a missing persons report with the Suffolk County Police. You're actually very lucky we figured this all out so quickly. Some people wake up from a coma with no idea who they are or how they got there, and it takes weeks to sort though it all. It can be a huge mess."

"I was staying with friends."

"Would those friends be Casey O'Conner, Nolan Sawyer, and Terry Mayer?" Detective Carrington asks.

"Yes."

"Your father said you recently dyed your hair red and that it's normally brown?" Detective Carrington continues.

"Yeah, so?"

"Could you have dyed your hair to look like Casey O'Conner, so you could use her ID?" he asks.

"No, no. Oh my God, you guys have it all wrong. Look, if someone can just help me find my friends, then they can help me explain all this." My gut clenches. "They can vouch for me. I think they ran away after the crash, because they didn't want to get in trouble."

"Get in trouble for what exactly?" Detective Matthews asks.

"For stealing Sven's car."

"But you said a minute ago that your friend Terry borrowed it," Detective Matthews points out.

My hands shake beneath the scratchy hospital sheets. "I didn't want to say anything before, because I didn't want to get Terry in trouble, but he's the one who stole Sven's car, and I should've just told you, but I was scared. You see, his dad is a judge in Wisconsin, and a few years back Terry got into some pretty deep crap, and even though his dad got him out of it, he threatened Terry that if he ever caught him breaking the law again then he would throw him in jail himself. Terry was super scared of his dad."

"Are you all right, Sosie?" Detective Matthews asks. "You look a little pale, and you're trembling."

I'm hot, my heart races, and sweat beads drip from my forehead, as everything in the room starts spinning. "Can I get a glass of water?"

"Of course," Detective Carrington says, handing me a cup of water from the side table.

"Thank you." I take gulp after gulp.

"Listen," Detective Carrington says. "It's been a hectic twenty-four hours, and it's obvious this is a lot for you right now. I think it might be best for you to get some rest for now. Tomorrow is a new day, and we can reconvene then. How does that sound?" he asks, but doesn't give me a chance to answer. "We'll come back tomorrow, and we can chat with you then, okay?"

The detectives leave, and as soon as they're gone, I bust into a fit of tears. I can't catch my breath, and I furiously press the emergency button next to my bed for the nurse.

Tara shows up within seconds. "Sosie, what's wrong?" She rushes over to me. "Can you tell me what's wrong?"

"I'm going to throw up."

She hands me a paper bag, but it's too late. I vomit yellow, foamy bile all over the front of my hospital gown and bed sheets. She blots my forehead with a towel and waits for me to calm down.

"I'm going to get you cleaned up now, all right? You need to talk to me. What's going on?"

"I don't know," I say, still shaking. "My heart is beating so hard that it feels as if it's about to come out of my throat."

"It sounds like you just had a panic attack. Your chart didn't say you're diagnosed with anxiety or that you're prescribed any medication for it," she says, sifting through papers from my chart.

"That's because I've never been diagnosed, but don't worry, I handle it. I self-medicate."

"How do you do that?"

"With lots and lots of booze." It's a joke, but she doesn't laugh.

"I'll speak with Dr. Felton when he comes in, and we'll see what we can do for you."

She hands me a clean gown, helps me change into it, and washes my face with a warm, wet rag.

A hospital aid comes in and changes the sheets. He then tosses the dirty linens in a plastic bin he wheels around from room to room.

My father shows up just as all evidence of what happened is wiped away.

He strolls over to my bed and greets me with a limp side hug, his Old Spice after-shave rubbing off on my cheek. "How are you feeling?" he asks, plopping down in a chair. He seems well rested, eager to take on a new day with me.

"Average."

"That's good." We sit in silence, only the sound of the beeping machines resonating in the background, neither of us knowing what to say to one another after our tiff from the night before. "So … did anyone come and see you this morning?"

"Like, the cops? The Po-Po?" I quip. "Yeah, they were here. Left not too long ago, actually."

"How did it go?"

I swallow hard, angry that part of the reason I'm in this mess is because he tipped off the police and alerted them when he couldn't get in touch with me. "Why did you file a missing persons report for me?"

"Because I couldn't find you. You have no idea how worried I was. The last conversation I had with you, you hung up on me and turned your phone off. And then a goddamn hurricane hit New York. I didn't know what happened to you, if you were alive or dead. I was all the way in London, and they weren't letting any planes into New York for days. I even tried to charter a private jet. I had no choice but to call the police. I was worried sick."

"There's a difference between not being able to get in touch with me, and believing I was truly a missing person, as in kidnapped and dead in a ditch somewhere."

"You almost were dead in a ditch somewhere after that accident, so maybe my worries were somewhat valid."

"Oh, God, stop. Don't be so dramatic."

"Sosie, this isn't a joke. It's very serious."

"I'm lying in a hospital bed in the middle of fucking Ohio, and you don't think I realize how serious this is? I hope you know your little overreaction is probably going to get me into a lot of trouble now," I say, bitterly.

"No, Sosie, all of the decisions you made are going to get you into a lot of trouble," he says. "I want to help you, but you need to be honest about where you were and what you were doing for the last couple of weeks."

"I have been honest."

"Sosie, did you steal that girls ID? Did you steal a … car?"

"So, you believe them," I say, not surprised.

"I didn't say that. Did I say that?"

"You didn't have to."

My father chews on his lower lip, thinking. "Sosie, did you go to your grandmother's house in Philadelphia?"

"What?" I ask, truly confused. "No. Why would I go there?"

"I don't know." He sighs, his bright-eyed appearance from minutes earlier already fading into the old, worn out man of last night. "Your grandmother got back from Florida last week and found someone had broken into her house. Money was stolen, some valuables were missing. Remember the mother-of-pearl brooch, the one shaped like a butterfly you used play with when you were a little girl? It's missing."

"Well, don't look at me!"

He walks over to a two-door wardrobe made out of Formica, opens it, and retrieves my messenger bag. Before unzipping it, he takes a deep breath, almost like he's stirring up the courage, and then pulls out the beautiful brooch, showing it to me like he's holding a baby bird in his hand.

"I have no idea how that got there!" I refuse to look at it.

He shakes his head, avoiding my eyes. "I think you need help."

"Are you insane right now?" I ask, outraged and insulted. "Look at what you're accusing me of! You need help if you think I did any of that. I would never steal from my grandmother."

"Sosie, the cops came here to speak with you, and they don't do that unless there's a valid reason. You were using someone else's identity, trying to look like her." He lightly touches my hair. "And you stole a car for Christ sake. Nothing you're saying lately is making any sense, and no one knows where the hell you've been or who these people are that you're claiming to have been with."

"They're my friends! I've already explained that a thousand times. It's all of you who are crazy, not me," I say, contemptuously, arrogant, and ready for a war. "If everyone would just listen to me and help me find my friends, then I can clear all this shit up, but no one will. Everyone just keeps telling me the same thing over and over, and no one wants to actually help me."

"Sosie, that's because there's no record of these people, yet you insist they were in the car with you when you crashed."

"Because they were! Look, whatever you're trying to say, just say it! Spit it out! Stop fucking sugar coating and bullshitting, and just say it like it is." I egg him on. "Go on, call me a liar. Call me a criminal!"

"Fine, Sosie. I'll say it like it is. I think you've made it all up. The friends, all of it, and I think you broke into your grandmother's house, and I think you stole that girl's identity, dyed your hair to look like her, and I think you stole that car. Why? I have no idea. Only you know that."

"You're wrong." I choke back tears. "About all of it. I had Casey's ID on me because I was holding onto her wallet for her. That's what friends do. And I was never in Grandma's house."

He stares at the floor, tears in his eyes. "Were you in Pennsylvania at all?"

"Yes. But it's not what you think. My friend Terry has a buddy who lives there."

"Come on, Sos," he begs. "Just tell the truth. You

can tell me, and I can help you fix it."

"Look, if you don't believe me, then you can just leave. And by leave, I mean, cut me off, take me out of your will, and disown me. Don't talk to me ever again. I don't need you," I seethe. "I haven't needed you for a very long time."

"It's always all or nothing with you." The sadness in his voice reflects in the way his mouth curls down. "Your mother was the same way."

"So, now you think I'm crazy like her? Is that what's been happening here? Everyone thinks that because she was crazy, suddenly I am, too? Is that why no one will help me?"

"No, Sosie." His voice is gentle, easy. He walks toward me, arms extended like he's going to embrace me or hold my arms down to save me from myself.

"Get away! Get the fuck away. Don't come near me. You're like a fucking stranger to me! I hate you! I hate you!" My voice comes out throaty, scary, and possessed.

"I'm going to get the doctor," he mumbles and leaves the room.

I wait for several minutes, on edge, ready for whatever is about to happen, ready for battle. But no one comes. An hour goes by, then two, and still nothing. Not my father. Not Dr. Felton. The morning turns to afternoon, and the afternoon into evening with only Sherry or Tara coming in to check my vitals or bring me shitty hospital food like dried out macaroni and cheese and blue Jell-O, which I refuse to touch.

After hours and hours of adrenaline and anger pumping through my veins, I finally close my eyes to this living hell and float away into a sound sleep.

Chapter Eighteen

The next morning, I awaken to Dr. Felton standing outside my room, the back of his white coat and wavy, dark hair peeking through the cracked open door. He talks in a hushed tone, as do several other voices, but I can't make out what anyone is saying. I sit up in bed, prop myself onto my elbows, and lean forward, as if it might help me hear better, but with all the beeping machines, it's only warbled whispers.

Minutes later, Dr. Felton enters the room with Detective Carrington and Detective Matthews in tow, each man moseying through the door, one after the other.

"Good morning, Sosie, how are you feeling this morning?" Dr. Felton asks.

"Hungry."

"Good! So, maybe you'll finally eat. I heard its pancakes today, and the pancakes are delicious. Buttermilk. You're going to love them, and the best part is, you can always have seconds," he says. "So, how's your pain overall?"

"Maybe a little better," I say, stretching.

"You're making progress, Sosie. We'll start getting you out of bed more and more, maybe start doing some laps down the hall. I think you're ready for it." As he speaks, his eyes scan all over the place, his mouth moving, but his brain disconnected from what he's saying. The detectives stand nearby, to-go coffees in hand, waiting for the doctor to shut up, so they can get down to it. "You know Detective Carrington and Detective Matthews." He extends his hand as if he's presenting them to me.

"Yup. Met them yesterday."

"Wonderful. If it's all right, they'd like to ask you a few more questions?" I nod. "Well, I guess that's my cue. I'll check back in a little bit then," Dr. Felton says and leaves the room.

"You look well rested today," Detective Carrington says, with a phony smile, his weasel face already pissing me off. "So, listen. I won't waste time. I've got some good news I think you'll appreciate hearing. We spoke with Sven Stavia last night, and he's not going to press charges for stealing his car. He said it's a piece of junk anyway."

I perk up a bit. "Yeah, that doesn't surprise me. I told you guys I didn't steal it. My friend Terry borrowed it. I think he'll be more excited to hear that news than me. I'd love to tell him myself. Speaking of my friends, did you guys find them?"

"We did," Detective Carrington says.

"Thank God," I say, relieved. "See, now you all know I'm not crazy. Where are they? Did everybody make it back to New York?"

"Yes, you could say they're in New York," Detective Matthews says, without elaborating.

Detective Carrington takes the last sip from his coffee and tosses the Styrofoam cup into the garbage can, making a basket from an impressive distance.

"So, did they back up my story?"

"Not exactly," Detective Matthews says.

"Not exactly?" I repeat. "What's that supposed to mean?"

"Sosie, all three people you asked us to find—Nolan Sawyer, Casey O'Conner, and Terry Mayer—died on October 29th. They all went surfing in the ocean off Long Beach before the hurricane hit and never came back. Their bodies washed up the day after."

"That's impossible. Whoever told you that is lying."

"The Long Beach Police Department told us, and

I can assure you they're not lying," Detective Carrington says.

"Well, the Long Beach Police Department is grossly misinformed then, because I just saw my friends the other day. They did go surfing before the hurricane hit, that part is true. They were on the news and everything, like, goofing off just before they went into the water. Everyone on the beach that day thought they were crazy for not listening to the warnings, but they did it anyway and rode the best waves of their lives."

"Sosie, is it possible you saw them on the news, and that's how you have that information? You and Nolan Sawyer went to the same high school, right? Maybe you recognized him on TV, and it stuck with you in the back of your mind somehow," Detective Matthew's suggests.

"No," I say. "I did see them on TV, you're right about that, but I also talked to them afterward. When I ran into them at their apartment building. They told me about surfing and how they were all dying to get back in the water. That's why we were all on our way to Virginia Beach."

Detective Matthew's shakes his head. "You couldn't have had that conversation with them, because they didn't survive. They never made it out of the water alive. All of them drowned."

"That's not possible." I refuse to believe it, pushing any notion other than what I know for a fact away. "Look, I don't know what's going on here or why the police in Long Beach would tell you that, but you guys have to believe me. I was just with them a few days ago."

"There's no way you could've been with these people, because they were already dead," Detective Matthews maintains.

"What's going on here?" I become paranoid, looking back and forth between the detectives. "It's you guys," I mutter, the truth hitting me all at once. "It's you guys who are lying to me. I don't understand why everyone is lying to me. Why is everyone lying to me?"

"We're not lying to you," Detective Carrington says, unmoved.

"You are! There's no other explanation."

"Sosie, we have proof you'd been squatting in Casey O'Conner's apartment after the storm hit, and that you stayed there up until you stole Sven Stavia's car. You broke into Terry Mayer's apartment as well," Detective Carrington reveals.

"I wasn't squatting. We're friends, and they said I could hang out, stay over, because my house got hit pretty bad by the hurricane," I insist.

"Sosie, we're not going to play games anymore, okay? We think you were trying to steal Casey O'Conner's identity after you heard she died, and that you got into her apartment, obtained her ID and credit cards, and then broke into Terry Mayer's apartment, stole money from him, and then broke into Sven Stavia's apartment and stole the keys to his car. After that, you took off, dyed your hair, and tried to pass yourself off as Casey O'Conner," Detective Carrington says.

"No, that's ridiculous." I choke back sobs. "I have no idea what you guys are talking about."

"We've spoken with members of Casey O'Conner's family, and they're very upset. Can you imagine how her parents must feel? They just lost their daughter. They're devastated, and then they find out someone broke into her apartment, stole from her, and then tried to become her. The O'Conner's daughter wasn't even buried a week, and they get the call telling them all of this. They weren't happy, Sosie. They're devastated, actually," Detective Carrington says.

Everything crumples around me, coming undone, like I'm a spool of thread unraveling fiber by fiber until nothing's left. My father enters the room, stoic, the worried look on his face telling me he's been informed of what's happening. He comes over and holds my hand.

"What are you doing? Get away from me!" I yell at him. "I told you I never want to see you again. Why are you here?"

"I'm here because I love you," he says.

His words rock me for a moment. But only a moment. He's said I love you less than a handful of times in my life, but it doesn't penetrate. It can't. I'm too unhinged, too distraught.

"If you love me, then you'll tell these people to leave, and that I didn't do any of the crazy things they're saying I did."

"I can't say that," he says.

"Why not?"

"Because I believe you did do what they're saying. But I want to help you. I want to help you in any way I can, Sosie. I believe you're sick, and you did these things out of … desperation."

I pause a moment as I look around the room, surveying, reading expressions. I laser focus, suddenly calm, as the detectives stare at me, eyes wide and eager as if they're anticipating what I might say or do next. Detective Carrington looks like he's about to jump out of his shoes, he's so ready to nail me.

"You guys are right." A collective sigh echoes in the room, as if relief descends on everyone in an instant. "About everything. I made it all up, all of it. I didn't want to get in trouble, and I thought it would all just go away if I blamed other people, but now I realize it was never just going to go away. I'm sick like my mother, and I need help."

My father brushes the hair off my cheek in a loving way. "I'm really proud of you, Sosie, and I'm going to help you through this in every way possible. I'm going to be here for you from now on." His lip trembles, eyes red-rimmed as he holds back tears. "A lot of this is probably my fault. I haven't been around the way I should've been."

"No, don't say that," I say, choosing my words carefully. "Daddy, I love you." He's overjoyed, floored at my declaration. He hugs me, and this time I hug him back, a tight, committed embrace. The detectives stand by and watch, giving us time. "Daddy?"

He pulls away to look at me. "Yes, honey?"

"I'm sorry, but I really need to use the bathroom," I say, with an embarrassed laugh. "I never had a chance to go before Detective Carrington and Detective Matthews came in to speak with me."

"Our apologies," Detective Carrington says. "You should've said something."

"Do you need me to get the nurse?" my father asks, desperate to accommodate.

"Yes, if you don't mind."

My father leaves the room and returns a minute later with Tara. Like the last time, she unhooks the fluid bag, swoops me out of bed and onto the walker, and then helps me along to the bathroom, but this time I'm stronger and moving more independently.

"Well, look at you, Sosie," Tara says. "See, you're getting better already."

When we reach the bathroom, I pause. "Do you mind? I think I can take it from here."

"You sure?" she asks. I glance at the detectives who are still lingering in the room, and she nods, an unspoken understanding between two women. She opens the bathroom door, so I can shuffle my way in. "If you need anything, I'll be right outside the door."

I get inside the bathroom and lock the door behind me. The second I'm alone, I come undone into a silent sob of tears. But the tears quickly turn to blind rage, feelings of disgust covering every inch of me like a hot blanket that I can't get out from underneath of. I open my mouth, a soundless scream coming out, and I shake from head to toe. I abandon the walker and hop over to sink, seething, foaming at the mouth in anger. I look at my reflection in the mirror, my face burgundy with fury, like steam is about to come out of my ears. My father, the detectives—I'd kill them all if I had anything to use as a weapon, and if I had the strength.

It's over. Everything. My life, the future. It's all coming to a crashing halt. Deciding what I must do next has never been clearer. Since I can't kill them, I'll have to kill myself. I'm left without any other option. No one will ever believe me, no one's on my side, and no one understands me. There's no going back now. They all think I'm sick like her, and I've made things up that so obviously happened. It's guaranteed my father will either lock me away in a mental hospital, or the cops will send me to jail. It'll all fit perfectly into his life. There I'll be, imprisoned one way or another like a caged animal, while he won't have to be bothered with me anymore. How convenient. I'll be the perfect sob story for him to tell. Hell, maybe I'll inspire his next movie.

And when I do ever escape captivity, life will be exactly as my father described—a scrubbed clean college student studying film at NYU, the good daughter following in her father's footsteps. The thought of it makes me want to throw up.

The last person on earth I want to be like is him.

I can picture it all so clearly, me having dinner

with my father at his favorite spot in the city, wiped of my afflictions, talking about how much I've overcome with having a crazy mother and being so crazy myself, and all the while my father will be sitting there, proudly nodding that he saved me from myself. I'll know it's all bullshit, but I'll go along with it anyway, because it makes him feel better, because it's easier than fighting it. But I'll hate my life. Oh, how I'll hate my life.

Who can I depend on now to save me from all this? Who can set the story straight? Nolan, Casey, or Terry? Somehow, they got away with it all. Somehow, they evaded the cops, skipped town, and made it look like they all died and it was me who stole Sven's car and Casey's identity. They might all be in Mexico for all I know, or maybe they hitchhiked from Ohio to the airport and just took off and went anywhere. Maybe they're hiding out at Ryan's in Philadelphia. Wherever they are, they betrayed me, especially Nolan.

It's over for me one way or another, whether I continue to live or choose to die. I look around the bathroom for anything I can use as a weapon. I don't have much time now.

"Everything okay?" Tara asks, with a light knock on the door.

"All good," I answer, attempting to sound perky.

Their voices converse in murmured tones, probably discussing me and what the plan is from here, but they have no idea I've got other intentions. I turn the water on and brace myself against the sink, putting all my strength onto my hands, a sharp pain shooting through my clavicle as I pull my stiff body up onto the countertop, legs dangling off the side. My breathing is labored, and I'm sweating from the exertion, an intense pain washing over my chest, arms, and neck. But, somehow, it's like I acquire super human strength. I reach up above the mirror and unscrew a light bulb. It takes everything inside me not to yelp as I hop off the counter. I grab a wad of paper towel and then wrap the light bulb inside it.

"Sosie, are you okay?" my father asks at the door, his voice shaky with worry.

"Fine, just washing my hands!"

I smash the light bulb that's wrapped in the towel against the side of the sink, the breaking of glass muffled and practically silent.

"Sosie, open up," my father commands, knocking louder now.

I unwrap the towel, and lay it out like a display of treasured jewels as I select the perfect piece of glass. The base of the light bulb, with an inch-long shard still attached to it, should get the job done.

I jab the glass into my skin, and drag it across my wrist with all my strength. It takes a minute, but soon blood runs down my hands, and then onto the floor, forming a puddle of bright red gore at my feet. I sit on the ground in the mess, my hospital gown soaking up the crime scene. For good measure, I slash my wrists the other way too, up and down, pushing it in, making sure it busts open my flesh until I demolish my veins. I'm not coming back from this.

I lay my head on the floor, losing consciousness, slipping away, dying. A banging vibrates the bathroom door, voices screaming my name, begging me to open up, but my cheek remains on the cold tile, no intention of moving even if I could. I close my eyes, this time not thinking of my mother, not calling out for her, but instead remembering a conversation I'd had with Nolan while we were in Michigan. His voice sounds in my head. *The problem is some people leave before they figure out what their purpose is.*

I still don't know what mine is, but it's too late anyway. I'm going, going, gone.

Chapter Nineteen

I sink into the leather chair, the wooden legs wobbling on the uneven floor beneath my weight. The seat is big enough to sit pretzel style but too unsteady to get comfortable.

"Is it too cold in here for you, Sosie?" Dr. Lyette asks.

"A little," I answer, trying to wrap my bare feet beneath me.

"I'll adjust the temperature."

"Thanks."

Dr. Lyette gets up from her seat and fiddles with the buttons on the thermostat.

"There," she says, walking back over to her desk, and sitting down. "It should warm up in a minute."

I'm not in much of a mood to talk today, and Dr. Lyette doesn't push. Instead, she cleans the crystal figurines that adorn her desk with a soft, white cloth. Lately, in my sessions, I'm either unable to stop talking, blurting out every mundane thought that occurs to me, or I don't speak at all, spending most of the hour staring out the window, watching the trees not move in the summer sun. However I choose to spend our time, Dr. Lyette is kind enough and intuitive enough to roll along with it, letting me dictate how things go.

"I've missed the entire summer," I say, after a few minutes of silence.

"You've enjoyed the gardens outside, though. The tulips you planted are coming up. That should please you," she says.

"It does, but they're not in full bloom yet."

"They will be soon enough." She flashes me a warm smile. "How do you normally spend your summers in New York?"

I think for a moment. "Well, when my mother was alive, we'd go to the beach, get ice cream cones, and walk along the boardwalk, but we never stayed long. New York summers are so hot and humid, there's no breeze at all."

"So are Ohio summers," Dr. Lyette says with a laugh.

"I wonder if they've rebuilt the boardwalk yet?"

"In Long Beach?" she asks.

"Yeah. Last time I was there, it didn't even look the same. It was all torn up. You couldn't walk on it. It's been months, though. I bet they've rebuilt it by now. New Yorkers work fast." Dr. Lyette puts the last crystal figurine down, a hummingbird with a long, thin beak, and tucks the cloth into a drawer. "What do you do in the summer when you're not at work?" I ask, turning the focus to her. "Do you hang out with your husband and kids, have barbeques, make smores by a bonfire at night?"

She smiles. "Everything you said, minus the husband, and insert a wife."

"Oh, I'm so sorry," I say, my cheeks turning pink in embarrassment. "That was super rude of me to assume."

"No, it's fine, Sosie. Really. But no more questions about me, okay?"

I nod, knowing the limits.

Dr. Lyette is young, beautiful, and simple with her straight brown hair that she parts neatly on the side, and her round, blue eyes, which she accentuates with smoky eyeliner and black mascara. She wears her make-up and hair the same every day and dresses in a steady rotation of a white, navy, or charcoal colored tops with slick, black dress pants. I'm fascinated with her, always wanting to know more about who she is when she's not trying to save my life, but I never get much more than vague little tidbits. She's careful about that, and careful to not put up any pictures. Her walls are bare, except for a framed diploma from University of Michigan's medical school, which tells me she graduated in 2002.

I watch the clock on the wall, another ten minutes going by in silence.

"You're not in much of a mood to talk today," she finally says.

"Sorry. I'm not."

"It's okay. Just making an observation is all. We can wrap up early if you'd like, and you can take the last half an hour and spend it in the library."

"Really?" I ask, surprised. "You've never let me do that before."

"Well, you've done a lot of hard work lately, you've been great about taking your medicine, and you've really been forthcoming in our talks. Personally, I believe when people make progress, they should be rewarded, and I'd like to reward you. Plus, you seem to be in a bit of a rut today. Maybe you need a change of scenery to get back some inspiration?"

"I agree," I say, beaming from ear to ear. "That'd be awesome."

"Great, then I'll see you back tomorrow." She gathers up her things, stashing everything in a navy briefcase. "Just make sure you make it to your group session tonight, okay? That's very important, and you shouldn't miss it."

I have a feeling Dr. Lyette wants to get out and enjoy the beautiful day, maybe get home early, see her wife and kids for once, instead of being cooped up in a depressing mental hospital.

I leave the corridor where Dr. Lyette sees her patients at Morning Star, where creamy, white painted walls line every hallway and fluffy carpet sinks beneath your feet while you walk. I arrive at a set of glass doors that lead into the main part of the treatment center and wait for Kia, a front desk attendant who sits on the other side of the glass, to notice me. She glances up after a few seconds and buzzes me through.

"Thanks, Kia," I say, as I enter the sterile part of the building, the part where everyone wears muted colored scrubs and name tags and carries walky-talkies. Everything reeks of rubbing alcohol, and it isn't uncommon to go hours without hearing anything but the sound of the faint television in the background, only to be startled by the outburst of a patient threatening to blow the whole place up.

I pass by a girl, a new girl about my age, walking with a nurse who leads her around like a dog on an imaginary leash. The girl smirks, one side of her mouth turned up in a sneaky grin. We make eye contact, and she rolls her eyes. I can guess what she's thinking. She hasn't accepted her circumstances yet.

I hadn't either, eleven months back.

She thinks she's getting out and that she can break free if she has to. She thinks there's nothing wrong with her and that she'll be in a cheap motel humping her boyfriend by the weekend. Her shifty eyes say, *"I won't be here long, assholes. I'm not one of you. Don't even think about trying to be my friend."* Gauzy bandages circle her wrists, and scratches crisscross her neck. I quickly look away and continue my walk to the library.

I round a corner and forget about the girl, instead relishing my newfound freedom. It's only been a few weeks since I was granted permission to walk the halls alone. Previously, I was always chaperoned by a nurse. And now to be allowed extra recreational time at the library? It's a luxury saved for patients who are about to leave the center for good. Everybody knows that.

The library is a small space, not much of a library at all, with just a few shelves of books, mostly cheesy paperbacks likely donated after some bored staff member finished reading it on their lunch break. I've read almost every book in the place, which isn't surprising considering I'm a ferocious reader, known to breeze through three hundred pages in a day and a half. A few flimsy, plastic chairs, meant for the patients to sit on while they read, accumulate at the center of the room. An attendant occasionally scans the room to make sure no one's up to anything they shouldn't be.

I finish the last of a collection of short stories by Agatha Christy and go back to my room for a nap before dinner and group meeting later in the evening. My roommate, Anna, lies on her twin bed, staring at the ceiling. Anna has been at Morning Star for five months and has been my roommate for three.

I meander through the door, and don't say anything, not wanting to disturb her.

"Are you mad at me or something?" she asks accusingly after a couple of minutes.

"Why would I be mad at you?"

"You walked in and didn't say anything."

"I didn't want to disturb you. You looked absorbed in whatever it was that you're doing over there. I wasn't purposefully ignoring you."

"Well, actually, I was meditating, so thank you for being so considerate," she says, and closes her eyes again, her lips moving but no sound coming out.

I lie down and close my eyes, too, drifting off into a sound nap. The medication I receive here makes me tired and perpetually groggy. When I wake up, its 4:45 PM and Anna is gone, her bed left in disarray as usual. She's incapable of being neat and keeping her side of the room picked up and in order. Personally, I always make sure my space is immaculate. The doctors and nurses pay extra attention to things like that.

I change my clothes three times before dinner. Not because I'm vain but because everything is uncomfortable and too tight. That's a side effect of the medication, too; muffin tops bellies and flubby butts. The food at the treatment center doesn't help, either. They serve us mostly carbohydrate-heavy meals with fruit cups in thick, syrupy liquid and vegetables smothered in cheese or butter. I've never had a weight problem in my life. Secretly, I've always prided myself on my slim physique that requires little to no effort to maintain. I take after my mother in that way, a naturally flat stomach and a small, round butt, and decent sized breasts. But those days are gone. My new body, the one carrying an extra twenty pounds or so, has taken some getting used to, and so has my double chin that I can't help obsessing over each time I glance at my reflection in the mirror.

I arrive at the cafeteria, wait in the line for food between two girls I don't know, and slog along the buffet while a lady wearing a hair net slops food onto my tray. Off in a corner sits my usual crew: Jess the sexy histrionic, Maude the anorexic waif, and Anna the depressive. I wander over to them and sit down. While we eat, we speculate about which doctors and nurses are secretly bedding each other and gossip back and forth about any new arriving patients. None of us really care about anything we're saying. We mostly do it to pass the time and to give ourselves a laugh.

After dinner, we go our separate ways to our meetings. Anna goes to the group for depression, Maude attends a meeting for eating disorders, and Jess meets with a group for personality disorders. Tonight, I'll attend the schizophrenic group, and tomorrow night, the suicide prevention group.

The longer I'm at Morning Star, the more I look forward to group meetings. In the beginning I kept to myself, only opening up and sharing if I absolutely had to or was forced to by the group leader or doctor. But over time, a significant amount of time, I found myself actually enjoying it, letting people into my life, not scoffing at showing my more vulnerable side.

My group has become a source of comfort. We've all been together since I arrived at Morning Star last November. I spent Thanksgiving with these women, Hanukah, and my nineteenth birthday. Some women had been at Morning Star for only a few weeks or months when I arrived, while others are lifers. Lifers are the patients who aren't getting out anytime soon, some of them wanting to, but never getting well enough to leave, while others want to stay so badly that they purposely don't take their medication and sabotage treatment. In the real world, I'd never be friends with any of them, but at Morning Star the familiarity of their faces is enough to consider them a friend, and in some cases, family.

The group meeting is already getting started when I arrive. We convene in a small room that reminds me of a grade school classroom. It's complete with a chalkboard and the same undersized plastic chairs they have in the library. Four women sit in a semi-circle, including Dr. Melbourne who seams into the group with ease. She could be mistaken for one of us in her crew-neck sweatshirt and turtleneck and with her wiry hair she wears in a bushy ponytail.

"Well, that's everyone," Dr. Melbourne says, as I settle into the last unoccupied seat next to her. "How's everyone doing tonight?"

We all answer with a collective and unenthused, "Fine."

"Lively group tonight," Dr. Melbourne quips. "So, as always, before we get started, just a reminder that all things talked about in this group are confidential. Everyone is to be respectful of each other, no labels, no interrupting. Each person will have the opportunity to have the floor and the undivided attention of her peers if she so chooses. Oh, and I almost forgot, we have a guest speaker who will be joining us in about twenty minutes. Her name is Kimberley Crane and I think you'll all really enjoy her story. I don't want to give too much away, so I'll let her tell you about herself." She waits for a reaction, perhaps some excitement, but everyone is either staring at the floor or lost in their own worlds. "Okay, so let's go around and do our check in. On a scale of one to ten, how are you feeling today? Just a reminder, the range is ten being that you're feeling excellent, grand, wonderful, and one being that you're maybe not doing so great, not your best day. Sosie, let's start with you."

"Ten," I say, without hesitation.

Dr. Melbourne's face lights up, pleased. "Ten?" she remarks. "That might be a first for you. Care to share why you're at a ten?"

Dorothy, a woman in her late forties who's considered a lifer, clears her throat, an agitated and aggressive hawk deep in back of her esophagus. She's fickle with me, one day encouraging and cheering me along, and the next, snarling insults through her eyes.

"Well, today Dr. Lyette let me finish up my individual therapy session early and said I could spend the rest of our time in the library," I say, proudly. "I had the chance to read the rest of an Agatha Christy book I started earlier this week, and then I took a nice nap afterward. It was exactly what I needed."

"Very good," Dr. Melbourne says. "It sounds like you were happy Dr. Lyette gave you the freedom to cut your session short and spend the time how you wanted. She trusted you enough to allow that, so that means you're making excellent progress, Sosie. Keep it up."

"Thanks," I say, grinning with all my teeth. "I will."

"Dorothy?" Dr. Melbourne asks, moving along. "What's your number today?"

"Four," she says, without expanding.

"Want to tell us why?" Dr. Melbourne asks.

"Nope," Dorothy huffs, and then turns to me. "But I'd like to say, if Sosie thinks she's going to be the next one getting out of here, then she has a rude awakening. I've been here longer than everyone put together in this room. I'm next." Her lips are tight and clenched as she speaks.

Dr. Melbourne allows her to finish and express herself how she needs to. "I know everyone's on edge a bit since last week when Asha went home. It can be disappointing to watch others have what you want, but that's why it's important to put the work in at group, take your meds, and be committed to getting better. There's no reason why each of you can't have the same opportunity as Asha when the time is right."

Dorothy shakes her head, not satisfied. "Well, it's not going to be Sosie. I've been here longer," she continues. "That would be complete garbage."

"Okay, Dorothy, and everyone else for that matter," Dr. Melbourne says, snapping her fingers to get everyone's attention. "We're all to be respectful of one another. I just got through saying that before group started. There are no personal attacks. This is a safe environment, and I know you don't need to be reminded of this. We go through the same instructions before every meeting. Dorothy, you're allowed to be upset, but you also have to allow Sosie to celebrate her victories. Now, let's move on. Olivia? Where are you at?"

Olivia reminds me a lot of myself. She's twenty-one and showed up at Morning Star a frail little thing but is quickly ballooning up from the meds. She also attempted suicide last year, not by cutting, but by jumping off a bridge.

"Um, seven. No, eight," Olivia corrects herself. "I've been sleeping better, and I started doing some exercises in my room, like jumping jacks and sit-ups, and I think it's helping to release the endophamins," she says, struggling with the pronunciation.

There's something childlike about Olivia, and Dr. Melbourne is always a little easier on her than the rest of us.

"Endorphins," Dr. Melbourne says, gently. "And that's great to hear. Keep it up." Olivia smiles, and Dr. Melbourne turns her attention to the last patient, Allison, a thirty-something-year-old married mother of two who hasn't seen her children or husband in a year. Her family hasn't attended a visitor's day session once, and they happen about once a month. "Allison, what about you?"

Allison giggles. "Zero. Fuck this place," she says.

Dr. Melbourne keeps her cool and doesn't react. "I know you're feeling negative lately, Allison, but let's work on some relaxation techniques this week to relieve some of your stress triggers and anxiety. We've got a lot of negative energy in the air tonight, ladies. Let's get that in check before next Wednesday's group."

We spend the rest of group listening to Kimberley Crane, the guest speaker and a former patient at Morning Star, talk about how she completed a year of treatment a few years back. She's gotten her life together, lives in a studio apartment in Toledo with her boyfriend, and tells us she hasn't heard voices or experienced paranoia or delusions in more than two years. She's attractive and well spoken, fashionably dressed, giving off no clues of ever having suffered from a mental illness. I listen to Kimberley speak, watch her mannerisms and study her, taking it all in, trying to learn what I can about being normal. Dorothy watches me as I observe Kimberley.

After group, I'm too amped up to go to the recreation room and watch *The Bachelor* as I usually do on Monday nights with Anna, Maude, and Jess. Too many thoughts race in my head, too many ideas and plans. Inspired by Kimberley's talk, all I want to do is get to my room and start journaling, get my thoughts out on paper. Maybe I'll even write a few letters I've been meaning to get to.

I reach my room at the end of the quiet hallway. Most of the doors around me are already closed, the patients who still have curfews settled in for the night and shut away until morning. Suddenly, out of nowhere, a firm hand pushes me hard into the wall, my chin hitting the doorframe in a clunk. I see stars, and my fists instinctively go up. This time I'm ready for a fight. It's not going to be like at the warehouse a year ago when that group of girls attacked me and I hesitated to defend myself. Today, I turn around and face my aggressor head on.

"What the hell are you doing?" I shriek, discovering its Dorothy. "What's your problem?"

She's paranoid, looking around every which way. "This is a warning, bitch," she says, pushing me again, her palm hitting my breastbone, taking my breath away. I glance around for a nurse, for anyone, to help. "If you scream, I'll fucking kill you," she warns, reading my mind. "Listen, bitch, we're not friends, okay? I've always thought that you were nothing but an annoying, rich little bitch who thinks she's better than the rest of us. You think you can cut corners and outsmart the doctors.

You're not fooling anyone. You're the exact same person as you were when you got here. The only difference is you're better at hiding it now."

"I'm not trying to fool anyone, and I'm not hiding anything."

"Bullshit!" Her spit sprinkles all over my face. I'm too afraid to wipe it away, too afraid to move. "If you think you're just going to sweep right through and take the next spot to leave, you're wrong. You're dead wrong. It's my turn, bitch. I'm next. I've been here longer, and I've been waiting." She pokes her pointer finger into my collarbone for emphasis as she threatens me. "Your daddy can't save you from everything, so get in line. If I were you, I'd get real comfortable, because you're not going anywhere."

A door down the hall opens and then quickly shuts. We both look in the direction of the sound, but whoever it is, is already gone.

"I'm not the one who decides," I say. "And neither are you. They are."

"I'm next," she says, inches from my face, before tearing off down the hall like a wild beast.

Once she gets to the corner, she begins to walk calmly and slowly, her entire body shape shifting into that of a stable person, a person who hadn't been up to anything, but rather found herself in the wrong quarters by accident. Her nurse appears, and Dorothy starts talking with her hands, explaining. The nurse nods, buying whatever garbage Dorothy is feeding her.

I slip into my room and shut the door. Sweat drips from my armpits, trickling down my sides. I consider calling for help. I think about telling someone, but I don't. I'm scared of Dorothy, of her crazy eyes, and the fact I know she meant every threat. Instead, I lie down with my clothes and shoes still on, afraid to move even in my own room.

Chapter Twenty

The next morning is visitor's day, and since I'm not expecting anyone, I don't bother getting up to shower or dress, and instead decide to get some extra sleep while I have the opportunity. That is, until my door flings open, and Katrina, one of my nurses, barges in.

"Sosie, you've got a visitor," Katrina says, hurriedly moving about the room. "They're waiting for you. Get up, get up."

I pull the blankets over my head, and turn over. "I'm not expecting anyone," I say, my voice muffled beneath my heavy quilt. "It must be for someone else. I'm going to sleep a little more, okay?"

Anna groans from across the room. "Be quiet, Sosie, I'm trying to sleep."

Katrina turns the overhead light on, and Anna grumbles even louder. "Not for anyone else, for you," Katrina says, pulling the blankets off of me. "Half the visit is already over. We've been trying to call you for fifteen minutes. Get up. Now."

When I don't oblige right away, Katrina physically stands me up and all but slaps me across the face to get me going.

"I got it. I got it," I say, shaking her off. "Just give me two seconds."

Katrina waits, hands on her hips, watching me wipe the sleep out of my groggy eyes. I throw a sweater on over my wrinkled t-shirt and skip brushing my teeth. I don't believe I have a visitor, but I also know that challenging a nurse on the matter is a bad idea. The nurses are known to take issue with the patients who dispute them, and they make it hell for those who do. It's the culture of the hospital. It's better to go down to the visitor's room, find that it's all been a misunderstanding, and then go back to bed.

"It's the lady over there at table B," Katrina tells me, once we enter the visitor's area.

At a small table with two chairs at the center of the bustling room sits a woman in her mid-fifties with short strawberry blonde hair. She's calm, wearing a pleasant look on her face as she politely waits.

"I have no idea who that is," I tell Katrina. "Did they give you a name?"

"None of my business," she says, flatly, shooing the matter away with her hand. "That's not my deal. My deal is to retrieve you and bring you here. That's it."

"So, I'm supposed to just go over to that lady and sit down with her, even though I have zero clue who she is?"

"Yup," she says, and pushes me along. "Go on now. You've already wasted enough of her time. Go."

The woman glances up as I pull out a chair and sit down across from her. There isn't any emotion on her face.

"I'm so sorry, but do I know you?" I ask.

She tilts her chin up, eyes narrowing. "You asked me here. Don't you remember?" she says. "Your letter. You asked me here in your letter."

Even though I'm sitting down, my knees ache and then go weak. "Mrs. O'Conner," I say, realizing who she is. I stand up to give her a more formal greeting, a hug, but she doesn't budge, and instead, shakes her head 'no' at the gesture. "I'm sorry, I didn't mean to…"

"I'm here to ask you to leave me and my family alone. No more letters, no more contact." She stares me in the eyes as she speaks, enunciating each word. It's like she's rehearsed this spiel a hundred times, watching herself in a mirror. "We're trying to move on, and what you did to our family was bad enough. We just want you to stop. If forgiveness is what you need, you have it. I'm serious about this. I didn't come all the way from New York to play around. If…" she starts to say, but gets choked up. "If my husband knew I was here, if the lawyers knew, they'd kill me. I'm doing you a favor, trust me."

"You look just like her," I whisper.

"You've never met her, so you couldn't know that," she says, firmly.

"But I have. I know what everyone has probably told you, and I know none of it makes any sense at all, but I know Casey. I knew Casey," I correct myself. "I wrote to you, because I wanted to tell you I'm sorry for using her ID, and all that. I know how it must look, but I cared about her very much."

She swallows hard. "You broke into her home after she died and pretended you were her for a week. You stole from her. You wore her clothes," she winces, as if that's the part that hurts her the most. "Stop writing to us. Just stop it. The reason I'm here is to tell you to stop, to go away. Let us move on, let us heal, and I won't report it to the police. This is your last chance, and then we'll be getting a restraining order."

"Don't you want to know about your daughter's last days on earth? I'll tell you everything I know." My mind scrambles for some evidence that might make her believe me. "She loved Simon and Garfunkel. Did you know that? We both loved the song *America*. It was our song together, and its what we bonded over when I first met her."

Mrs. O'Conner listens for a moment, her head tilted in wonderment, but then quickly comes to.

"That was one of the things you stole from her. The cross-stitch her sister made her for Christmas last year. That's how you know she loved that song. That gift was precious to her, and you took it. You just took it."

"I'm sorry you think I stole from her, but I never took anything. She let me borrow her clothes, and…"

"There it is," she says, stopping me before I can finish. "You sit there and say, 'I'm sorry you think I stole from her.' You take no responsibility. You've been here how long? A year? You're still singing the same tune. You're manipulative and sick. I don't know how you managed to write to me, how you got to our family, but I'm guessing you made it your life's mission to find a way around the system. What are you doing here if you're not getting yourself well? Are you playing, pretending? You're mentally ill." She flings the label around like an insult. "I don't need you to tell me about my daughter's last days on this earth, because I know what happened to my precious baby. She drowned, end of story. When I went to see her body the next day, she was cold and blue."

"I'm sorry," I say, quietly.

"No. No, don't tell me you're sorry. I don't need your apologies. My family and I need you to go away. That's what we need. No more letters, don't email us, don't communicate with us in any capacity, got it? Please, just get yourself better," she begs, before standing up.

"I'm not sick." My words stop her, and she stares at me. "I'm just not."

"You *are* sick. You *are* sick. Got it?" She escalates quickly. Her voice rises with every word as she begins losing it. "Stay away from me! Stay away from us!"

She lunges at me from across the table. I stand up and back away, Katrina suddenly at my side, blocking her from getting to me.

"Please get this woman away from me. She's

239

crazy," I tell Katrina.

"I'm crazy? I'm crazy?" Mrs. O'Conner laughs, still trying to get at me.

I'm scared Mrs. O'Conner might strangle me, so I hide behind Katrina, cowering into her back, crying. Three nurses enter the room to back up Katrina. I don't know what to do, so when I see the door to the visitor's area open, I run.

I book it down the hall, my legs propelling the rest of my body forward like a gazelle. No one is coming after me, not yet anyway. I duck into a bathroom and go all the way to the last stall and lock myself in, curling my knees up onto the seat so no one can see my feet from underneath. Sitting in this position calms me. It feels familiar, like the way I used to camp out in the bathroom at Bolton Academy when I was skipping class.

A minute later, the door swings open, the hinges squeaky and loud. Wasting no time, the feet scuffle over to the stall where I'm hiding. I sit frozen, watching the floor, waiting for the feet to appear, but dreading their arrival. And then there are shoes, clogs with printed socks poking through, and they get closer and closer until they stop in front of the stall and wait.

"Sosie," someone's voice calls out gently. "You need to come out."

I don't say a word, just close my eyes and pray whoever it is will eventually give up and leave. My eyes focus on the lock, a flimsy safeguard from whoever stands on the other side. The clogs don't move. They stay put, the heels of the socks, ripped and dingy.

"Sosie, come on," the voice urges. "Open up."

Fingers fiddle around with the lock.

"Leave me alone," I warn.

A shoulder pushes hard into the stall, then someone's entire weight plows impatiently into it, hurling it open.

"Surprised to see me?" Dorothy reaches in to grab me, but I'm too fast and duck underneath her, scooting past in a fluid movement. She grabs hold of my hair, stopping me before I can fully escape.

"Get away from me, you psycho!" I shout, biting her arm to make her let go.

"I saw what happened just now," she says, with a smile. "You've dug your own grave just like I knew you would. My work here is done."

"Then why are you here?" I shriek.

"To rub it in your face, rich girl."

"Fuck off, Dorothy." I push her as hard as I can, her hip hitting the ceramic sink. She clutches her side in pain, her frizzy, salt and pepper hair falling in front of her eyes. "Don't fuck with someone half your age, bitch."

My words reignite her fury. She flips her hair off of her face and comes at me again, grabbing me by the neck and yanking my head down until my face is inches from the floor.

"This is for Mrs. O'Conner." She shoves my head into the ground repeatedly. "You think you're so goddamn smart. I bet you've gotten your way your whole life."

She doesn't let go, and I can't breathe. With the little strength I have left, I reach up from underneath her and gouge at her eyeballs. She screams in pain, writhing, and then finally lets go. We both stand up and tussle back and forth, each of us spent like a couple of boxers in the last round, but we still go at it, taking turns pushing, punching, and scratching each other in any way we can. I hit her in the face several more times, but she doesn't go down. One of us probably would've killed the other if Katrina didn't burst through the door.

When we see Katrina, we throw our hands up like nothing is going on, even though clumps of hair litter the floor, and we both sport bloody scratches all over our faces.

"She attacked me," Dorothy says, instantly turning on the tears. "I came into the bathroom to see if she was okay, and she snuck up from behind me and starting wailing on me. Please get me some help, I'm hurt horribly."

"She's lying," I explain, calmly. "She followed me in here and attacked me first. I was just defending myself."

Katrina listens, but keeps a tight grip on my arm. Dorothy's nurse comes in moments later. Dorothy cries to her, tells her the same story. Her mouth moves and moves, but after a while, I don't hear any more words. All the sounds jumble together as the nurse runs water in the sink and soaks a paper towel for Dorothy to put on her face. Katrina talks to me sternly, the voices outside of the room growing louder and louder until it feels like everyone in the entire building is speaking into a megaphone. My hands cup my ears in an attempt to block it all out, but there's shrieking and the screeching sounds of interference, and I swear I can hear the local television station practicing a disaster alarm test.

Doctors and other nurses enter the room, ushering Dorothy out and speaking to me. They inundate me with questions, so many questions, but I just stand here, shivering with no answers. Eventually they lead me out, too, and take me to the crazy people's ward, a separate wing where only the craziest of the crazies are shunned. The same place I spent my first few months at Morning Star. It's less like a dormitory and more like a hospital, with around-the-clock supervision. You can't even use the bathroom alone.

As I walk there with Katrina, we pass the new girl from a day earlier. She's made a friend, another pretty girl close to her age. They lean their heads together and begin talking to each other as I go by. They're talking about me. I know they are. Their expressions drip with judgment. And they're laughing at me. One of them smirks. I swear I see one of them smirk. They think they're getting out of here before me. I know that's what they're telling each other while they watch me being escorted by Katrina.

"Stop looking at me. Stop talking about me," I whisper.

"What did you say?" Katrina asks.

I look behind me at the girls. I look them both in the eyes. "I said, stop fucking talking about me," I scream. "Make them stop talking about me!"

"No one is talking about you." Katrina grips my arm tighter. "Keep moving, Sosie."

We pass by the standard hospital rooms, the rooms with gurneys and restraints if it should come to that. When I realize Katrina is taking me to "silent room" I wail, begging not to go. "Silent room" is the lowest of lows, saved for the most out of control patients. The most violent. Everyone speaks of "silent room," but nobody has actually seen it.

"No!" I cry, as she pushes me along. "No, no, no, no, no, please, no! I swear I'll be good. No, Katrina, please. Please, don't take me there. Don't take me there. Please!"

Another nurse appears at my other side, a man at least six foot five and close to three hundred pounds. They practically carry me into the room even as I plead with them not to.

The floor and walls are padded with thick white foam, and there's only one tiny window, which is on the door. Katrina draws up her syringe as the male nurse holds my arms still, restraining me like a human straight jacket.

"No!" I beg Katrina. "Please, don't do this."

She plunges the needle in my arm anyway, and I'm out within seconds. Everything goes black. Everything fades away.

Chapter Twenty-One

"The only reason you're not restrained right now and sitting in my office is because I vouched for you, Sosie," Dr. Lyette tells me. I stare out the window, eyes heavy. Barely alive and heavily medicated, my spirit is broken. I sit like a vegetable, a shell of my former self. My eyes shift to where she sits, slowly making the trek and using up all my energy. I blink, saying nothing, and instead stare straight through her. "I told them I wasn't in danger," she continues. "Because I don't believe I am in danger."

"Dorothy started it," I finally say, my words coming out slow, dead.

"What exactly happened with Dorothy the other day? Are you ready to talk about it?"

"She attacked me."

"I thought you two were friends?"

I shake my head. "No. Never friends. But I never thought we were enemies until she almost choked me unconscious."

"I'm sorry that happened," she says, sympathetically. "What made her do that?"

"I don't know." My eyes flicker, dry and burning from forgetting to blink.

"You have no idea?" she probes.

"I guess she was afraid I was going to get out of here before her. Or something like that."

"Where would Dorothy get such an idea?"

"In group the other day, I told everyone that you let me leave our session early and go to the library. She knew I was starting to get more freedom, not having to be escorted by a nurse all the time. She flipped out. She followed me back to my room after group on Tuesday night, and threatened to kill me."

"Did you tell anyone?"

"No."

Dr. Lyette is more stoic than usual. She sits in her chair, straight backed, with no expression. I can almost see her brain filing away the information, sorting through it, trying to make sense of everything, trying to make sense of me. She wants to help me. She's trying to understand.

"Why did she think you being released from Morning Star would have any bearing on when she's released?"

"I don't know. She's crazy. We're all crazy here."

"Sosie, no derogatory labels," she reminds me.

I nod. "But was she right? Was I about to get out?"

Dr. Lyette begins to twist back and forth in her swivel chair. She opens her mouth to speak and then stops herself, obviously choosing her words carefully since she thinks I'm so fragile. "No," she finally says, honestly.

"Why?" I instantly snap out of the dead zone.

"Because I, along with the other doctors and nurses and staff here, don't feel you're quite there yet. There's still much work to be done."

"What more do I have to do? I've done everything you've asked of me. I go to all the meetings, take the pills, talk about my fucking feelings until I want to…" My voice trails off. I almost say, *kill myself*, but I stop short. Saying something like that can be held against mc at a later date.

"You have done much work, yes," she agrees. "You've come a long way, I'm not saying you haven't, but working through mental illness, getting the medication right, the dosage, coping mechanisms, working through stress relief tactics—it all takes time. It doesn't just happen overnight."

"I've been here almost a year."

"It can take *years*," she counters, emphasizing the last part.

Dr. Lyette's poker face pisses me off. And her hair, how it never changes, and how she always looks exactly the same whenever I see her, all makes me feel like I'm reliving the same screwed up day over and over again.

"I hate how you wear your hair the same every day," I blurt out, angrily.

Her head juts back, away. "I'm sorry you feel that way."

"Oh, give it a rest. Why are you sorry? That doesn't even make sense. Tell me it's a rude thing to say. Tell me to fuck off, or something. I'd respect you more if you did."

"I won't tell you to fuck off," she says, clearing her throat. "But I think we can both agree that what you said was rude."

"Of course you won't tell me to fuck off. You're so professional. Break the fucking fourth wall once in a while. Tell me I'm a crazy bitch, and that when you go home at night, you make fun of me to your wife and kids. Sosie, that crazy little psycho bitch." I laugh.

"I'm not going to tell you that, because I don't do that, not about you or any of my patients. Maybe you have a hard time believing it, but it's the truth."

"Whatever. You're impossible to have a real conversation with."

"Is this your tactic when something doesn't go the way you'd like it to? You get angry and lash out? I'm guessing it usually works for you. The other person backs down, etcetera, etcetera, you control how the situation is going to go, and you in turn have the power again. You like to have the power. You're uncomfortable when you don't have control," she says.

"Don't most people like to be in control? Who doesn't like to be in control of their own life? That's just stupid and a moot point."

"There you go with the insults," she says. "Look, no one is forcing you to go against the grain of who you naturally are. So, you like things to go your way? Fine. I'm not asking you to change that about yourself. What I am asking you to do is to have more self-awareness. Recognize your triggers, your coping mechanisms. Because you've functioned most of your life resisting opposition with anger, why not try a different approach? Do the opposite. Try listening more. It'll help in your treatment here. It'll help in life once you get out."

"I've listened plenty since I've been here," I say, bored.

"You haven't listened enough."

I roll my eyes. "You're so annoying."

"I'm sorry you feel that way about me."

"Oh my God. Just stop," I say, getting up. "You're like a robot. This is insane and so infuriating. If you can't be real with me, I'm done. I'm not doing this."

"Where do you think you're going?" she asks, just as I make it to the door, my hand about to turn the knob. "You won't get very far. Trust me."

"I'm leaving. What does it look like?"

"Sosie, you know you can't just leave, especially now. There are two security guards right outside my office just waiting for me to give the go ahead to restrain you. I know you don't want to go down that road again," she warns me. "I've done you a favor by letting you in here. You could be in a 'safe room' or restrained, but you're here instead. Don't screw it up."

Even though I don't want to, I slog back over to

her and sit down. She's leveled me. "I hate this fucking place."

"I know you do."

"Well, then let's not play games. I hate games. Just give me the verdict. When am I getting out of this dump for good? When can I leave? Tell me, so I can start counting down the days."

"This isn't jail, Sosie, and I can't answer that. It's not how it works. You know that's not how it works," she reminds me.

"Why not?" I scream, savagely, hoping to frighten her.

She barely blinks. "You're not ready, Sosie. I just got through telling you that."

"You suck!" I scream.

"I'm sorry you feel that way."

"Stop saying that!" I hit my fists into my thighs as hard as I can over and over.

"You're frustrated," she says, gently. "Try a different tactic. Remember."

"I don't want to try a different fucking tactic. I'm mad! You say this isn't jail, so why do I feel like a fucking prisoner? Sometimes I wish they had just sent me to jail! At least in jail, you know when you're getting out."

"You're lucky to be here and not jail, trust me."

"Whatever. I'd probably get a year."

"Identity theft, burglary, grand theft auto, harassment. I'm not so sure about that," she says. "You're lucky someone recognized you'd be better off getting the mental health intervention you so badly needed instead of jail time."

"Yeah, I'm so lucky." The sarcasm drips from my voice.

"You are." She pauses, watching me, thinking.

"You asked me to be real with you, right? Okay, here's real. I don't think you've been serious at all about getting better since you've gotten here. I think you've been going through the motions, doing what we've asked of you, doing your time, but I don't think you ever truly believed your diagnosis. I believe you think you're fine, misunderstood, a victim. You think everything you've done has been justified, and you think everyone you've encountered wants to destroy you."

"Wrong!"

"Am I? You wrote letters to Casey O'Conner's family. You've been writing her family for months. And I now know you've also been trying to contact Nolan Sawyer's family."

"Who told you that?"

"I can't disclose that. The point is, you knew you shouldn't contact them, so you paid a nurse to mail the letters for you. That nurse got fired yesterday, Sosie."

"So, I sent them letters. There were things I needed to say to them. I don't get what's the big deal."

"Sosie, it shows me you still believe everything you believed the day you got here. You don't believe you saw delusions or were in the middle of a schizophrenic episode when you tracked down Nolan Sawyer, using that opportunity to break into Casey O'Conner's apartment and steal her identity, or when you stole that car and went on a road trip. You've been nodding your head at the doctors this whole time, feigning self-awareness and recognition for your illness, but you didn't believe any of it."

"I did it for their families. There are things that only I can tell them. That's how selfless I am. I risked everything to help them, and now look at me. I'm the one suffering."

"Sosie, it was all a delusion, so there's essentially

nothing you can tell the families. You never spent any real time with Casey or Terry, and the only contact you had with Nolan Sawyer was in passing at school. They weren't real. You said you went to Philadelphia? You did go, but you went there alone. You drove all the way to Michigan? Yes, that happened, but you did it by yourself."

"It was real. They were real," I say, through gritted teeth. "Don't tell me they weren't."

"I know it seems very real, but it wasn't," she says, unapologetically.

"They were my friends. I know things about them, about their families, personal things I couldn't know if it wasn't real."

"But there are other ways, Sosie. The mind is very complex. Mental illness is very complex."

"Enlighten me."

"While staying in Casey O'Conner's apartment, you could've learned things about her through photographs, journals."

"What about Nolan and Terry?"

"Nolan was in your English class at school, so I'm sure there were things about him—snap shots into his life—you gathered through being in a class with him. Take his poem, for example. You know, the poem you've recited to me several times in this very room. It might've been one of the catalysts for your delusions. It touched you profoundly, maybe even more than you realized at the time. Through that poem you discovered his love for surfing, for the water. It could've been the reason you were so sure there were surfboards attached to the top of the car and that you were all headed to Virginia Beach."

"There were surfboards."

"There weren't."

"What if I told you that the police lied? Would you believe me?"

"Sosie, you have told me that, many times, but the police have no reason to lie," she reminds me.

"Because there aren't any corrupt cops out there," I say, throwing my head back and staring at the ceiling.

"If you don't start letting go of these ideas, then it's going to be extremely difficult to get you better so you *can* leave as I know you so badly want to. Are you hanging onto the idea of Casey, Nolan, and Terry because you feel like admitting it wasn't real would be accepting defeat—letting us win, letting your father win?"

"That's ridiculous. They were my friends. I miss them. I'm fighting for them."

"It's okay to miss them, but you have to let them go if you want to get better."

"But they told me things. I told them things I've never told anyone. If it wasn't real, then I don't know anything," I say. "He told me … Nolan told me he tried to kill himself. He tried to hang himself after he first moved to New York. He said he was glad he didn't die, because if he had, then he never would've figured out what his purpose here on earth is."

"That's profound," she agrees.

"I couldn't know that story, know his pain, if it wasn't real," I point out.

"You could," she says. "That could be *you*, Sosie. It could be your own pain. Nolan's words could've been a projection of something inside of you, unfinished business and ambivalence about your own suicide attempts. It could be your subconscious steering you away from hurting yourself. A religious person might say it was God speaking to them." She pauses. "There are things only you can examine about yourself. But first, you have to let go of them. You have to stop believing they are still somewhere living and breathing. You have to say goodbye."

"I don't want to say goodbye."

"I know. But if you want to get better, really get better, you must."

"Her favorite song was *America* by Simon and Garfunkel. Casey's. I tried to tell her mom when I saw her, but she didn't care. She wouldn't even listen to me."

"Sosie, didn't you once tell me it was your favorite song? I remember you saying it moved you deeply, that you listened to it on repeat after your mother died."

"I do love that song, but it doesn't mean she couldn't have loved it, too."

"Sosie, Casey wasn't real," she says. "Not to you anyway. She was real, a living and breathing person at some point, but you never knew her that way. What you knew was a delusion. You have to let her go."

"She was real. They were all real." I grasp for air, the tears running down my cheeks. "They were real. They left me, because they were angry with me for crashing the car and ruining their trip to Virginia Beach. They hated me for it. That's why they ran away and left me when the ambulance came. If they were here right now then I would tell them I was sorry. I'd tell them I didn't mean to lose my temper and crash the car. I didn't mean to put their lives at risk."

"Sosie, listen to your words. You're describing your mother's crash. You're taking on her mistakes and making them your own."

Dr. Lyette's words halt my emotion, and I start shaking. "No, no, no, no, no, no. You don't know what you're talking about. I don't know what to do. Nothing makes sense anymore." I bury my face in my hands while I sob. "I'm just so confused. It's like I don't even know what's real and what isn't."

Dr. Lyette gets up from behind her desk and pushes her chair next to where I'm sitting. I hear and feel her presence, but I can't bear to look at her.

"I'm sorry you're hurting," says.

"I'm sick of it. I'm sick of hurting so much. I don't want to feel like this anymore. I want to get better, but I don't know how."

"It's going to take work, Sosie, but I believe what you're experiencing right now is a breakthrough. As painful as this is, you're taking the necessary steps to heal yourself. I'm proud of you."

Her hand rubs my shoulder. "If I'm having a breakthrough, then why do I still feel so terrible? I don't feel any different than before."

"One step at a time," she reminds me. "It doesn't happen overnight, but you just took the first step, I don't even want to call it a step. It was a leap. You took your first leap. That's not easy." We're both quiet for a moment as I follow her gaze into the gardens. "What do you think of doing a field trip for our next session?"

"To where?"

"Outside in the gardens. I know how much you love it there, and you haven't been outside in days."

"I'd love that, but somehow I think you'll have a hard time convincing everyone else to go for it. They're keeping pretty strong tabs on me lately. I can't even pee by myself."

"Don't worry about that," she assures me. "I'll take care of everyone else. Would you like to do that?"

"I'd love to," I say, quietly. "I feel like my skin is turning grey from being cooped up in this place."

"Gotta get that Vitamin D," she says with a soft smile. "So, I have an idea." She talks to me like we're old friends, and slowly my guard comes down. "I want you to collect four items, one item that symbolizes your mother and a little something that symbolizes Casey, Nolan, and Terry. It can be anything at all, but nothing too big. You can write something like a letter, or draw a picture, or pick a flower. Whatever you'd like. Just make sure it represents each person to you."

"Okay." It's obvious where this is leading. "I'm going to say goodbye to them, aren't I?"

"Yes, Sosie, you're going to say goodbye."

Chapter Twenty-Two

It's a poem for Nolan, his poem of course, which I've scribbled dozens of times in my journal since I'd seen him last. I'm terrified of forgetting it, more terrified of forgetting him. Anytime my memories begin to fade, I write it down, and he comes back to me all over again. His voice. His face with those gentle expressions. I rip out every entry and fold each one neatly with care. There must be twenty or more.

In one of the bathroom stalls, a heart sticker decorates the beige metal. It's been stuck to the door since my first day at Morning Star and has probably been there for years. Old, peeling and faded, for some reason, it always makes me smile, brings me comfort. It reminds me of my mother. She used to put heart-shaped stickers on my lunch bags for school with a little love note, even when I was much too old for such a thing. I carefully remove it from the wall and stick it to the back of one of Nolan's poems.

Terry never was much of a friend to me, and I never really minded leaving him behind. Still, I need to bid him farewell, too, and I will. I scribble the words, *Goodbye, Dude* on a scrap piece of paper while Katrina watches from over my shoulder as I wield a ballpoint pen.

It's hardest to come up with something for Casey, and by the morning of the mock funeral, I still haven't thought of anything satisfying. I decide to let the moment take me wherever it will. Maybe I'll sing a line or two from our song, or maybe I'll just talk a little bit about her. I'll know what the right thing is when the time comes.

I wear all black for the occasion, head to toe. It's a funeral after all. Katrina even lets me borrow a little shimmery pink eye shadow and allows me to blow dry my hair, though she uses her body as a human shield, and stands in front of the outlet while I do so. Electrocuting myself is not the way I'd like to go, but still, she doesn't budge.

When I finish getting ready, I examine myself in the mirror. My hair is long and back to mousy brown with only bits of red hair dye tingeing the ends. I'm thinner from the few days I spent in protest starvation during my stint in 'silent room,' and as a result, I look more like my old self than I have in a while.

Katrina escorts me through the halls. She's entrusted to take me outside to the gardens where Dr. Lyette will be waiting for our special session. Nolan's poems are in my back pocket, the thick paper rubbing against my skin as I walk.

On the way to the gardens, a nurse stops Katrina to ask about the dosage on some medication for another patient. The nurse shows Katrina charts, and she's thorough with her instructions. They go back and forth for several minutes, and I begin to shift on my feet the longer they speak.

"I'm going to be late," I mutter under my breath.

"Don't push it," Katrina warns me, continuing with her directions.

After a couple more minutes, they finish their talk, and we make our way outside to the gardens. The warm sun beats down on my face. It feels wonderful. It feels like freedom. I stop for a moment to take it in, a wide smile sweeping across my face.

"C'mon, you're going to be late, remember?" Katrina reminds me.

We meet Dr. Lyette near the tulips, beautiful and yellow in full bloom, sitting on a bench with a small brass plaque honoring some millionaire who had donated a hefty amount of money to Morning Star. Dr. Lyette is sitting on it while she waits for me to arrive. She looks warm and relaxed, yet uptight all at the same time, in her measured hairstyle and typical uniform in the summer heat. She smiles when she sees me. Katrina hands me over like I'm a child being dropped off at daycare, not bothering to say goodbye.

"I dressed for the festivities. All black," I say, unsure of how to greet her in this unusual setting.

Dr. Lyette remains professional, in control. "It's important to dress in whatever way that makes you feel most comfortable. How are you feeling today?"

"Honestly, I have a lot of emotions," I admit. "I'm sad, obviously, a little scared, but deep down I just feel really excited. I think I'm ready for what's to come, you know? I'm ready to leave this all behind and start over. I don't want to be the person I've been lately."

"Well, you certainly look better," she remarks. "You seem more relaxed, and I'm really pleased with your ability to articulate what you're feeling so concisely. It's okay to feel a whole host of different emotions at once, you know. Just because you feel excited for what's to come, doesn't mean you can't also be scared. Just because you feel a readiness to say goodbye doesn't mean you're not going to feel sad. It's called being human."

I smile. "The tulips are in full bloom."

"Yes, they sure are. They're gorgeous, aren't they?"

"My mother would've loved them. She loved tulips. She loved lilac trees too, like the ones over there. They smell wonderful and…"

A blood-curdling screech for help rings out through the nearby trees, desperate, demanding, urgent. The outline of a woman's silhouette flails repeatedly against the trunk of a tree.

"Help me! I'm bleeding!" the woman cries. "I'm going to die! I'm going to die right now! Help me, help me!"

Dr. Lyette jumps up, her hand to her chest. She peers in the direction of the woman, and then looks at me, unsure of what to do. The woman screams some more, pleading for help, but Dr. Lyette freezes. It's as if she's waiting for someone else to come and save the woman, but no one comes. She waits some more, and still no one else shows up.

Through the brush, the woman throws herself headfirst into the tree again. Blood drips from the woman's chin onto the ground.

"I want to fucking die!" the woman wails.

Dr. Lyette knows she needs to act. "Sosie, I need you to stay right here, okay? It's imperative you do not move. Do you understand?"

"Yes, I understand. I promise I won't move."

"I'll be back in less than five minutes, as soon as I can get someone to help me with that patient." Her voice trails off as she leaves me alone in the garden.

Fear swims in her eyes before she leaves. Fear for whatever she's about to walk into, and fear for leaving me alone. Neither is a good choice, but a choice has to be made nonetheless.

Dr. Lyette runs through the brush toward the woman. When she reaches her, she places her hands on the woman's shoulders and talks to her patiently, softly, trying to calm her.

I look around as they converse. Then, I pull the hoodie of my sweatshirt up, and I take off, disappearing in the opposite direction, through the thick trees.

I run, army crawl, and hop fences. No one's around. No one can stop me. A pick-up truck waits where I know it'll be, and I sprint toward it, the passenger door swinging open. I hop in, the car already in motion, the speed almost taking the door off before I get it closed.

"What took you so long?" she asks.

Her face is red and full of worry, and though she's driving fast, it's not fast enough. We're barely down the road from Morning Star when the alarms blare in the distance.

Alarms for me.

"Drive faster," I yell, glancing over my shoulder.

"If I go any faster, we'll get pulled over, Sosie."

"Faster. You have to go much faster."

"What took you so long? I was out here waiting for fifteen minutes. You said 2:15 on the dot. Those were your words. That could've been bad, Sosie. Really bad." She stomps on the accelerator, flooding the engine with gas. We lurch forward, going faster.

"Katrina stopped to blab with a nurse," I tell her through ragged breaths. "And by the time I got outside, Christina started doing her thing, and I got here as fast as I could."

"How did she do?"

"Amazing. There was blood and everything. It was actually pretty crazy and super believable."

"Fake blood?"

"Don't think so."

"Shit. What did you pay her for that?"

"I paid her plenty, trust me. Enough for a mild head injury," I say, glancing out the back window to see if anyone is coming. They aren't. I lean back into the headrest and let the summer wind from the open windows hit my face.

We drive for four hours before making it to the abandoned farmhouse, which can only be found by removing a chain-link barrier and taking an isolated mining road. The sky is pitch black as we pull up in front of the house.

"Well, here we are," she says, as we sit in the cab of the truck, the engine idling. "There isn't any electricity, so you'll have to light a candle, but I wouldn't light too many. You don't want to draw any attention if they come looking for you."

"Don't think anyone is going to come looking for me out here," I say. "It's even more secluded than you described."

She pulls out an envelope and hands it to me. I slide my finger beneath the flap, lifting it, and pull out an ID and a social security card.

"Angela Lieberman, age twenty-two, one hundred and five pounds, brown hair, brown eyes. Hi, I'm Angela Lieberman," I say.

"Maybe you should go by Angie. You look more like an Angie."

"Where did you get this?" I ask, examining the plastic.

"Does it matter? The point is, it's legit. You can trust it's one hundred percent real."

The girl on the ID looks strikingly like me. "You went above and beyond." I reach into my underwear and pull out several twenty-dollar bills.

She counts it, and then looks at me incredulously. "Sosie, this is it? C'mon, I got fired for you. I got you a new identity for Christ sake. That wasn't easy, by the way. I had to deal with some really shady people."

Tamron, always eager to please me, sounds as if her patience is wearing thin. I can see that. From the time I arrived at Morning Star, she treated me like some sort of local celebrity, idolizing me simply because I'm from New York and because my father works in the movie business. Though she's a nurse, she has dreams of being a fashion designer and living a fancy life in the city someday. I promised her I knew people. She's nearly ten years older than me, but she's Ohio young, incredibly naïve for a thirty-one-year-old, and easily manipulated. Even if I had the connections she thinks I do, she'd never stay afloat in a place like New York City.

"Look, I promise I'll send you more as soon as I can, but that's all I have. It won't be long, I swear. I just need to keep a little cash with me to get a train ticket once I leave here, I promise. You know I'm good for it, and once I get on my feet, you can come and stay with me in the city for as long as you'd like. Maybe we can even be roomies."

"Promise?"

"Of course."

She reaches into the cubby behind her seat and hands me my duffle bag. "Stay here for as long as you can stand it. It might get lonely, but you're safe here. You won't see a soul. My parents have been saying for years they're going to come out and do work on the house, but they never do. When you're ready to leave, walk as far as you can, and see if a truck driver might pick you up or something. But don't get into the car with anyone who seems like a weirdo. Girls have gone missing around here."

"That's comforting."

She hands me a couple of candles that are stowed in the center console and gives me her cigarette lighter. "That's my lucky lighter."

"Thank you. For everything." We hug. "I'll get in touch as soon as I can."

"Hey, do you promise to take me to Junior's for that cheesecake when I come visit you?"

"Without a doubt."

I get out of the truck and walk toward the rickety, dark house.

"There should be some cans of baked beans and a can opener in the kitchen cupboard," she calls out the rolled down window before driving away. The dirt sprays beneath her tires as she speeds off into the summer night.

Later that night, I sit in the middle of the living room floor, a single candle lit, the shades drawn, Nolan's poems unfolded, and his words displayed softly in the flickering candlelight. I unzip my duffle bag and remove every item: a couple of t-shirts, a pair of jeans, some underwear, socks, and place them in front of me. At the very bottom of the bag, something remains. I know what it is—Casey's cross-stitch. I reach my hand in and run my dirty fingers along its side.

Purpose.

I know what my purpose is.

My purpose is to be free. My purpose has always been to be free.

The End

www.sarahbarkoff.com

ACKNOWLEDGEMENTS

First and foremost, all the glory to God for helping me find my true, artistic destiny and for putting the dream in my heart to write a book. Though the path was often complicated and the waiting was brutal, I can see now that your timing was perfect. Thank you for bringing this dream to pass and for your undeniable presence in my life always.

To my husband, Matt: Since the day I met you, just being around you has inspired me to do more and achieve more. I truly believe if we'd never met, I wouldn't have ever actually written a book even though it's something I'd often thought of pursuing. If I'd never gone to Grenada with you for those two years, if you hadn't encouraged me to finish my degree, this would still be something I held in the back of my mind but never got around to doing. You're the reason I can do what I do, and the reason I've done any of this at all. So, thank you.

For my children, Matthew and Mia: I wrote so much of this book while you were teeny tiny. There were so many times I was exhausted but I kept writing while you napped. So many times the rejections were rolling in and I thought I should just give up, because what was the point? But I didn't give up. Because of you both. I wanted to show you that you should always fight for your dreams. If God puts a promise in your heart, don't let anyone tell you no. Never ever, ever stop listening to the voice in your heart telling you who you are and who you're meant to be. Be relentless with anything you want in life.

For my parents: Thank you for allowing me to have a colorful childhood surrounded by the arts and for making the sacrifices you did so I could chase my dreams. Now that I'm a parent I understand that it mustn't have been easy, but you did it anyway, because you could see my passion. Thank you for that. And thank you for always encouraging my artistic endeavors and making me feel like I'm the best at absolutely everything I've ever pursued in life (even when I wasn't. Ha!)

For my mentor, Brandy: I don't even know where to begin. When you chose me for #WriteMentor, you changed the course of everything with my writing. I was ready to give up for good, but you saw something in me and you took a chance. Thank you for picking me, being my friend, and all the hard work you put into helping me make this book happen. It wouldn't have happened without you. Fact.

For Stuart White and all my #WriteMentor friends: Thank you, Stuart, for creating #WriteMentor and for being an advocate to all involved. Thank you to the friends I've made through #WriteMentor. When I met you all, I met the best cheerleaders ever and friends for life! I'm so happy I found you guys.

Special thanks to Bonnie (Melissa): You were the first person to ever read anything I wrote, and you always kept it real! Thank you for taking the time to read this book and indulging me in long discussions afterward!

To Stacey Adderley, Melissa Hosack, and everyone at Evernight Teen: Thank you so much for seeing something special in this book. Getting the email with your publication offer was one of the most exciting things to ever happen to me. I'm so thankful you took a chance on this book and me.

Lastly, thank you to anyone who reads my book. Whatever the reason you choose to read, whether we're old friends, family, you're someone who's drawn to the cover or premise, you're a follower of my blog, whatever the reason and whoever you are, thank you, thank you, thank you. There have been so many moments I never thought anyone would ever read a word I wrote, so the fact that my book is out there and you're choosing to read it is more awesome than I can even explain. If you end up enjoying the time you spend reading, please tell me so. It would mean so much.

Evernight Teen ®

www.evernightteen.com